Rebel

THE BOYS OF WELLES BOOK TWO

by USA TODAY bestselling author

GINGER SCOTT

REBEL

The Boys of Welles Book 2

Ginger Scott

WELLES

For David.

Chapter 1

Brooklyn Bennett

I should have worn my brace. I've been standing in the same place, by the headmaster's two-story bookcase and a grand piano I doubt is ever played, for nearly forty minutes, and my leg is shaking from the unbearable pain and strain I'm forcing my remaining muscles to endure.

My leg will never be as strong as it was. That's what the doctors said after I woke up from surgery. Two pins and some stem cell therapy got me on my feet faster than expected, but the rest of my healing is going to be up to me.

"Unusual tear and damage." That's what they said before giving Mom and me the slim menu of options for recovery after the accident. I was lucky to have my leg at all. Lucky to have my life, really. My best friend in the entire world, Anika, wasn't so lucky. She had a seizure and drove the car carrying us and two of our closest friends hood-first into the Solemn River. My friend Lily pulled me to shore. She saved me only months after Anika invited her into our friend group. Sometimes I wonder if my best friend knew that one day I would need an angel and that's why she brought Lily to me.

1

"It's a lovely get-together, don't you think? I love that he hosts this for you all every year." If Caroline Powell weren't standing next to me, I'd collapse right now. But I can't do that in front of the headmaster's wife. *Oh God, the scene that would make!*

"*Mmm,* it is," I agree, sipping the next inch from my sparkling water.

A perk of being a sixth form at Welles Academy is being invited to a handful of special *soirees* at the headmaster's home. The parties are hosted a block away from campus, in a home that has been lived in by only five men and their families over the history of the academy. Headmaster Powell has been in the position for nineteen years, and I have waited for five of them to be in this position. These parties with New England's elite are a privilege, and I should be roaming from room to room, shaking hands with every single guest. I can't seem to find the motivation, though. And my legs are so tired.

"How is your father these days? I haven't seen him since the inauguration." My father, Walden Bennett, is Welles Academy royalty. He's chief energy advisor for the White House, at least for the next year, until he formally enters the senate race. And there's no questioning a win to serve the people of Massachusetts. Walden Bennett is loved by the public. He has meticulously sculpted his image for this moment, and one day I want to be just like him. Of course, that would require me to get off my ass and start mingling.

"Oh, you know, busy *busy,*" I say with a flash of a smirk.

Part of being a politician's daughter is navigating the strange world of leverage and influence. People always need things, and my dad has a unique position that can sometimes get those things. Caroline runs the Welles endowment. She needs money, yes, but more than that, she wants a seat on a commerce board. I've been briefed about this by my dad at least a dozen times, and I've become adept at dodging the asks. If I weren't worried about my leg buckling from strain, I'd make an excuse to move to a different room. But I'm trapped. *Out maneuvered.*

"Yes, he must be. I left a few messages with his office and have yet to get a call back." She eyes me over the rim of her wine glass as she brings it to her lips and sips. Her burgundy lipstick leaves a Cheshire cat smile stain behind. "When you talk to him again, maybe you could . . ."

I pull my lips into a tight smile and nod.

"Of course."

My turn to sip from my glass. I wish it were wine instead of water. *I wish it was vodka.*

"You know, there are a few people here who would love to meet Walden Bennett's daughter. If you don't mind joining me on the terrace." She steps toward the open double doors. I move to follow, but my leg gives way and I stumble. Despite my inner prayers to be strong, my damn leg lets me down. Caroline's arm is under mine in seconds and before I can stop her, she's already shouting for help.

"I'm fine, really," I plead.

I don't need a scene. I don't want an audience while I sit and work blood through my limb. Someone will want to run and fetch my brace and my crutches, and I'll have to explain that they're buried under my bed behind boxes of shoes— shoes I shouldn't wear in my condition. Then will come the questions about the injury, shared versions of the accident everyone knows about, feigned shock and empathy. Someone will call me brave, and others will chime in with my favorite phrase, "poor thing."

Headmaster Powell is the first to rush to his wife's call for help, and he swoops in at my other side despite my insistence that I don't need help to the piano bench that has a film of dust on it.

"Poor girl," Caroline mutters. I cringe at the words, squeezing my eyes shut and reminding myself that telling people to fuck off and leave me alone isn't part of my brand.

"What's going on?"

My eyes open at the sound of a familiar voice. Cameron Hass can be a lot to handle, but he's also an excellent distraction, causing a scene just by being in a room.

Thank God he's in this one right now!

"Mr. Hass, good timing. Can you support Miss Bennett while I call on some help—" Caroline is insistent. I'm precious to these people, mostly because of my connections. *Only because of my connections.*

"Really, my muscle just spasms sometimes. I stood too long. Please . . ." My voice cracks pathetically, but I cover it by clearing my throat. My mind is racing through the possibilities, knowing there is probably a doctor in this house right now that she would no doubt drag over to look me over just to say she's done something to help me. What she doesn't realize is telling my father she helped me out when I was weak won't impress a soul. Walden Bennett believes in powering through and never letting people see the cracks.

"We worked out too hard, didn't we? I'm sorry, Brooky." Cameron winks at me when he utters that appalling nickname he's thrown my way since first form. I bunch my lips into a silent, sour response, but only because nobody is looking at my face. And really, if he saves me from this scenario, he can call me whatever the hell he wants.

"Probably, Cameron. He's been helping me with my physical therapy exercise, and *oof!* He's a stickler for not cutting corners." I lay it on thick. He's lucky I didn't call him

Cammy. If I weren't so focused on selling this lie, I might have.

Caroline snickers.

"Sorry, just . . . I thought cutting corners was basically your career choice, Mr. Hass." she utters.

"Only for the shit I don't like, *ma'am*," Cameron responds without missing a beat. I shake with a single, silent laugh.

"Language!" Headmaster Powell points a spindly finger in Cameron's face, which gets zero reaction from my friend. I suppose years of being seen as the class clown and the one constantly being barked at for talking out of turn, acting out of turn, or just plain turning the wrong way has hardened Cameron while also sharpening his come-back game. If the headmaster pointed at me that way, I would probably have to fight hard not to cry. Cameron doesn't flinch.

"Well . . . I'm glad you're able to exercise. But really, it would make me feel better if you at least let us get a walker or a wheelchair or something, just for tonight." Caroline gestures to her husband and he races off to no doubt dig up some piece of equipment they've probably kept in their basement for just such an occasion.

I stand quickly, masking the wince my face wants to make with an exuberant smile.

"No! Really, see? Better now." My leg is trembling, so I sway a little on my feet to disguise the motion.

Headmaster Powell ducks back into the room and before his wife has a chance to insist again, I pull out a few steps from my youth tapdancing classes. *Kick, ball, change.* "I promise. All I needed was a bit of a stretch."

The blood moving through my legs is helping, but the nerve zaps around my knee are intense, and I'm seconds away from buckling again.

"I'll make sure she gets back safely. We both walked here, so we can leave together. I'll take her the fast route, cutting corners left and right, you know . . . through lawns and such." Cameron's mouth ticks up on one side, dimpling his cheek in the perfect passive aggressive *F-U.*

Caroline's eyes narrow, but the growing chatter down the hall draws her attention away from us and she seems to let Cameron's comment slide. This is her party as much as it's supposed to be for us. This is her way of wooing donors, and the more time she spends with me, the less time she's spending urging checkbooks out of purses and collecting business cards for follow-up.

"I'll make sure my dad knows you're looking after me. He'll be grateful," I lie. He won't give two shits, but those are the magic words she needs to hear.

Her blood-red lips pucker into a pleased smile.

"All right, then. But if you change your mind—"

"I won't." I shake my head in confirmation, and it's hard to read her expression. She's either impressed with my stubborn determination or suspicious. Rightfully, she should be both.

She hits Cameron with a warning glare before leaving the room with her husband. I stumble toward the piano bench the moment the coast is clear, falling on my ass with a whimper.

"If I have to give you a piggyback ride to avoid more of *that,* I will," Cameron says, sliding onto the other side of the bench. Leaning forward, I rub my knee and calf with my palms.

"Thanks, but I remember your last piggyback ride. I ended up in the lake." We were twelve and partners for the Spring Fling obstacle course. When it became clear we

6

weren't going to win the race, Cameron turned the activity into an opportunity to get me soaked.

"To be fair, it was pretty hot out. I don't think you minded." He presses his fingers down on the piano keys, playing a soft chord. A concert for one.

"Uhm, to be fair, you dumped me in the lake when I was wearing Givenchy sneakers, so yeah. I minded." I sit up straight but continue to rub my knee.

"Who wears Givenchy sneakers to field day? *Pfft.*" He rolls his eyes then lays his other hand on the keyboard, playing a soft chord an octave lower than the last one. My gaze focuses on his fingers, the delicate way they press the keys with familiarity. I didn't know he played the piano. It's clear that he knows his way around the ivories, though.

"Says the guy who wears the same blue and white Adidas Gazelles for everything," I retort, leaning into him and dipping my chin to catch a glimpse of his feet, which are in fact in the blue and white shoes. The contrast with his dark gray suit is comical.

He taps his toe on the piano's pedals.

"Comfort over both form and fashion." His hands inch along the keyboard toward me, tapping out a faint melody that's muted by the pedal he presses to the floor. I catch myself smiling at the deftness of his hands as much as the melody.

"Man of many talents." I smirk at him.

His fingers curl against the keys, his heavy monogram ring scraping the surface. He shrugs. I think maybe I've embarrassed him by calling out his musical ability.

"Many, *many* years of forced piano lessons." He leans into me, his bicep touching mine, and for a blip, I have this urge to lay my head against it. Instead, I clear my throat and swing my legs around the bench to turn my focus on the shelves of books. Cameron does the same then stands, moving forward and pulling out a copy of Gulliver's Travels.

"I hated this book," he says, flipping quickly through the pages before sliding the heavy novel back into its place.

"It's satire," I respond.

He glances over his shoulder to meet my gaze.

"It's boring." Cameron drags a heavy hand against the spines of the books that line the shelves on his way to the rolling ladder parked on the far end. He flashes a grin only a second before pushing off from the ground and hopping on the ladder to ride it halfway across the room. He holds an arm out exaggeratedly, as if he's truly flying, and when the ladder abruptly stops, he leaps off and stumbles back to his spot on the bench.

I can't help but giggle.

"Why are you so good at making me laugh?" I ask as he blows upward at the loose locks of brown hair that have fallen over his chocolate-colored eyes.

"Oh, that's because I am very funny," he answers with a wink.

I nod with a closed-lip smile and for a moment, the room feels smaller. I've hung out with Cameron here and there, and we've always gotten along. But I don't know that we've ever spent a lot of time alone. When did he get so big? I swear, a year ago he wore that same suit and it draped on him. Now . . . Cameron has muscles?

We break eye contact at the same time, almost as if we both got caught doing something we shouldn't. Cameron plays another chord on the piano, as soft as the last two. This time, the sound is rather melancholy.

"I should go before Caroline Powell tries to force me into a mobility scooter," I say as I stand. My leg is tired, but I've worked the muscles out enough to make it home.

"I'll walk you," Cameron says, quick to stand at the other side of the piano. We both walk around it to meet at the point where a gold-plated rod props up the lid.

"You don't have to." I swallow because I'm looking at him differently again—as though he's attractive. Because . . . *shit. He is.*

He leans into me and cups my ear.

"I welcome the excuse to get out of this place—every chance I get. Please, I insist," he whispers, his lips, *I swear,* brushing my ear with his light laughter. A thousand watts of electricity channel down my spine, and suddenly every muscle in my body feels primed and ready to sprint.

"All right," I croak.

Cameron leads the way through the vast room built for nothing but show, and he holds up a hand at the open double doors as he looks to the left then right.

"Coast is clear," he whispers, waving me to follow.

He grabs a long wool coat from the mudroom near the front door and I spot my red pea coat hanging across the room. Before I can slip my arms through on my own, the fabric slackens as Cameron holds my coat open for me to put on.

"Thank you," I say, blushing. *I'm blushing!*

The mudroom is dark, *thank God!* I pull the knit hat from my coat pocket and stuff it on my head as Cameron holds the door open for me. The breeze outside is strong enough to carry dry leaves across our path, and we spend most of the walk with our hands crammed in our pockets and our chins tucked into the collars of our coats.

"For someone who was about to fall over, you're moving at a pretty solid clip," Cameron teases. I slow a beat in response, realizing I am close to a walking jog, if there is such a thing.

"I really wanted to get out of there," I laugh out, meeting his gaze. He smiles with full lips that push dimples into his cheeks, and I'm not as cold as I was a minute ago just from seeing it. My pulse is also racing, which has nothing to do with the pace of our walk.

We reach the corner of campus in minutes, and when we reach the spot where the pathway divides—one route heading to my hall, the other to his—we pause.

"You think you got it from here? I mean, I could still run back and get you that walker," Cameron teases.

I push him gently and he grabs my hands awkwardly before we both recoil, hiding our hands in our pockets again.

"Don't you dare," I say, not thinking about his joke at all now, instead thinking about his hands, the ones that made the piano sound so lovely, how warm they felt in those brief seconds just now, how big they are—strong. His monogramed ring. His tanned skin. The soft lines on his knuckles.

"Well, you take care, Brooky." He stirs me out of my head, and I laugh nervously as I back away toward my dorm. "I've got a date with a few buddies." He nods over his shoulder, toward the riverwalk, and I get without him saying that he's going to smoke. For someone so fit and healthy, the guy sure likes his weed.

"Yeah, I'm going to find out why my roommates skipped out on tonight's party." Lily and Morgan were on the fence about coming, and I am pretty sure they both ditched me for boys, though Morgan's situation with her quarterback crush is . . . complicated.

"You do that." He's several steps away now, still walking backward, still looking at me and smiling. I wonder how long he can walk like that.

"You're going to trip," I shout.

He shakes his head.

"I never fall. Besides, I promised I would make sure you made it to your dorm, and you haven't climbed those steps yet." He's adamant, which is clear by the way he manages without even looking to weave around a stone bench that divides the pathway behind him.

"Fine, but only because I'm afraid you'll fall in the river if I make you keep this up." I chuckle, then turn to scale the steps, careful not to put too much weight on my right leg.

"I told you; I don't ever fall. I know right where that river is. Now, get inside!" His playful scolding has me grinning.

"I'm getting! I'm getting!" I tug the door open and step inside, turning to stare through the glass when it shuts. Cameron salutes me and promptly spins on one foot to continue his journey.

I remain at the door until he's completely out of view, and I linger for a few extra seconds knowing he's only on the other side of sculpted hedges that lead to the walking path. Catching myself, I shake my head and laugh at my silly insta-crush.

"It's Cameron Hass, Brooklyn. Get a grip," I mutter to myself.

By the time I make it to my room, I've pretty much banished the flirtatious thoughts about Cameron from my mind. As expected, Morgan and Lily are nowhere to be found, so I treat myself to a rare night snuggled in my jammies with a good romance. And despite my iron-clad will, I somehow mentally morph the hero into Cameron, and that vision follows me all the way into my dreams.

Chapter 2

Cameron Hass

I dressed nice today. Seemed I should since it's my dad's birthday.

It took a little longer to get here than most Saturdays because of the extra stop at Clifford's Bakery in the city. I was looking forward to seeing my dad's face light up when he spotted the bright green box. I probably should have known better—no food allowed. I took the T here and walked from the station, so unless my box of cupcakes survives the shit hiding job I did by the front gates, I'm out twenty-seven bucks and I won't get a bite of the best chocolate cupcakes in New England.

Wouldn't want me smuggling in a key under all that frosting.

I roll my eyes for the hundredth time since the guard tapped the box with his baton and told me to "throw that fancy-ass shit away."

I've been coming here for years, but it's only been a few months since I turned eighteen and could come alone. The guards treated me a lot differently when I was here with my

13

mom. Now they treat me like I'm the one serving twenty-five years for armed robbery.

I'm up for a lot of dumb shit, but I won't do something that lands my ass in prison like my dad did. He may be a criminal, but he's taught me a hell of a lot about actions and consequences.

"There he is!"

Michael Hass's growly voice fills my chest, and I swear I'm still that little kid inside who wants to rush him and wrap my arms around him. I don't, opting instead to stand and hold out my hand. We hug, briefly, under constant supervision. This is how I have been raised—in pieces, under guard, by a lot of rather rotten people. Of them all, this man is my favorite. I see the glimmer of good that's grown in him. I've watched it, visit by visit.

"I tried to bring you cupcakes, but—"

"Ah, don't sweat it. It's the thought that counts and all that." He waves a hand before snaking his long legs under the table and taking a seat at our usual spot. His hair is neatly trimmed, probably a birthday visit to the prison barber. His square chin is never closely shaved, and it makes the scar that slices from his right cheek bone down to his chin more prominent. He got that scar flipping his motorcycle after sneaking my mom home after their first date, but he tells everyone around here that it was from a fight. Street cred has kept him out of trouble here, mostly.

I slide into the side opposite him, and we mirror each other, both rubbing our chins at the same time and laughing at the simple similarity.

"It was Clifford's." I shrug with a sheepish half smile.

"Aw, damn!" His fist lands on the table but he follows it up with a grumbling belly laugh. I smell the smoke on his breath. Birthday cigarettes in the yard. "Next time there are

Clifford's cupcakes involved, I'll make sure you fill out the form."

I nod.

"I didn't think about it," I say.

He waves me off again, but I think he's genuinely a little disappointed.

Pulling my hands together on the tabletop, I bob my leg under the table as I scan the room out of habit. Years of visits like this, but I still haven't gotten used to the guards and other duos just like ours sprinkled around the stark, gray room.

"Season going all right?" My dad played football in high school, probably at a much higher level than Welles. He went to a big public school on the southside, and I have a feeling in a match up, his team would destroy ours. The common thread between us is nice, though, all the same. He would have been a good coach growing up. Who knows, maybe I'd be a quarterback.

"We're decent. I went for eighty yards last week. James was dropping them right in my hands," I say, half acting out my diving stretch. My dad's grin stretches. I wish he could see me play, just once.

"You play last night?"

"Off week," I answer.

I shift in my seat and glance to my side out of habit. Nobody cares about the things I have to say to my dad, but still, it feels weird to have every conversation so public. I've always suspected this place was rigged with hidden mics capturing every word. It's not that kind of place, I guess. Not like the prison he was in for his first two years. Good behavior earned him more time in the yard, computer privileges and an education. Hell, man probably never would have earned his GED if it weren't for prison.

Silver linings and all that.

"Spill it, Cam. I smell the smoke from your brain working so hard."

I draw in a deep breath and flatten my hands on the rubberized metal tabletop while leaning back and staring at the water-stained ceiling tiles.

"Spent some time with the girl last night." I sit back up straight and meet his curious expression. "You know—*the* girl."

My dad's mouth curves up on one side. He fucking loves dissecting my love life. I think half the reason I tell him about my unrequited crush on a girl who's way too good for me is because it seems to make him so damn happy to hear.

"You finally take her out?"

I punch out a quick laugh.

"No. School function for seniors. One of those hoity-toity parties for networking or some shit," I say through pursed lips.

"Your girl is kinda hoity-toity, ain't that right?"

I chuckle silently at my dad's use of my words.

"Sure," I agree.

My neck feels warm, and I know my dad is anxious for more details. As embarrassed as I am talking about Brooklyn with him, he's also the only person I can talk about her with. Mostly because she's this anonymous being with him; he lacks any kind of connection with my life at Welles. My life, period. Except for the bits I choose to share.

"Remember I told you about that big accident last spring?"

He nods.

"Right, well, this girl—"

"*The girl.*" He points with his interjection. My dad is an incarcerated romantic. I'm pretty sure he still thinks he can win my mom back.

"Okay, well . . . *the* girl was one of the ones in that crash. She got hurt pretty bad."

My dad's mouth twists with sympathy and his brow draws in.

"You never told me." He sighs, crossing his arms over his broad chest.

I think maybe he's hurt that I didn't share.

"I wasn't sure how to talk about it, and it was such a major event everywhere else in my life—school, home, with my friends. I didn't want to live it during my visits here more than I had to, I guess." I shrug and shift, suddenly uncomfortable in my skin. "My best friend's sister died in that crash, Dad. I guess I've felt that should be the focus anytime I talk about it with anyone."

"Not with me. We don't got rules around us. No judgement and zero rules when it comes to me and you, okay?" he growls.

The guard behind him takes a step toward us, probably assuming my dad is getting worked up and angry. It's hard to read his emotions because they all come through his tough exterior, but that was him being passionate and empathetic. I've learned the signs over the years. When I was a kid, I used to get scared.

I hold up a palm to the guard and he steps back.

"Sorry, I'm loud," my dad apologizes.

"It's all good."

"Go on, tell me about the girl," he prompts, leaning forward and folding his hands together.

"Not much to tell, really. She just got a little fatigued at the party and was having a hard time standing, so I sat with her until she felt better and walked her home to make sure she was okay. It was . . . *nice*." A bashful laugh slips out and I roll my eyes and grab the back of my neck as I look away.

"Look at you, knight in shining armor. Well done, boy!" He reaches across the table and punches my arm.

"Yeah, yeah." I glance up at him with a tight smile then look down at my lap where I'm peeling my fingernails into shape, a nervous habit I must have inherited from him. An enigma for nature versus nurture.

"I played the piano for her. A little," I say, holding up one hand to show a pinch.

"Oh, that's the move! What did she think?"

I don't have the heart to tell him it was nothing more than a chord or two, so I lean my head to the side and shrug.

"She called me talented." That was one hell of a paraphrase.

Our time is almost up. Others in the room are hugging and saying farewells, and I know I should too, but I want to linger here like this for a little while longer. A dad coaching his son on how to talk to a girl, as if we're normal.

Nothing about us is normal.

"Internship is going well. I've got people at the firm who I think might write me recommendations," I say.

My dad is less interested in this stuff, but he pretends, nodding and patting the table. He's never said it out loud, but I think he feels guilty, like he hijacked my life's goals by fucking his up. And maybe he altered my direction, but I'm happy with it. I want to go to law school. I want to help guys like him who made shitty choices but have truly reformed. Our prison system is so fucked; our mission got lost in the politics.

The buzz of the security door draws our attention to the emptying room behind us. I got here late. Our time was short.

"Damn," my dad grumbles. He turns back to face me, and our eyes meet briefly, reflections of one another at two different stages of life.

"I'll get one of those forms next time," I say.

My dad cackles as he stands.

"You do that," he says.

I round the table and take his hand. He pulls me in for a short hug, nothing to draw suspicion, but long enough that I feel his heart pounding behind his tatted chest. My dad tried really hard to be a longshoreman. A Southie who practically raised himself, he got caught up with the wrong crowd in the neighborhood. He saw dollar signs and a way to win my mom over completely. She saw a guy cutting corners.

Guess that's another trait I inherited from my old man.

I wait until my dad winks in my direction before ducking through the security door, then file out with the other day-pass visitors. The cold is settling in, the wind blowing my hair over my eyes on my way out to the main gates. I do manage to clear it enough to glance inside the security booth as I sign the clipboard chained to the counter and turn in my pass. Taunting me like a first grader slobbering out a solid raspberry, the green Clifford's box sits open and eaten from on the guard's desk. I make sure to give the box a long, hard stare until the guard takes notice and barks for me to move on out.

I breathe out a laugh then tighten my coat around my body.

Fucking asshole. I hope he got a bad batch and spends the rest of the day in the shitter.

Chapter 3

Brooklyn

I wonder if my roommate Lily realizes how much I look up to her. I mean, yeah, it's hard not to hero-worship your real-life hero, and Lily saved my leg, probably my life. But that's not what has me in awe of her.

She battled some pretty aggressive demons after the accident. She's got a long way to go—we all do—but she's come so far.

"You should really try swimming laps with me sometime. It's the best exercise!" She twists to hold the fieldhouse door open for me and Morgan, our other roommate, to step through. Lily is a competitive swimmer, and she fought like hell to get back in the water after our trauma.

"You're probably right, but I'm not really down for swimming with the team and letting you guys lap me while I pathetically dog paddle my way across the pool." My description is not far from accurate. I have a decent stroke actually, but nothing compared to the rest of the girls who work out with Lily.

"You wouldn't be in our lanes. You'd have your own

21

space." She's persistent. It's been the same lecture and plea for the last three weeks, trying to get me to swim to build up my leg strength.

"Gee, you mean I'd be able to hide in the transparent water behind that floating rope that separates me from you all by a mere seven feet? Hmmm, let me think. *No, thank you!*" I hug my gym bag to my chest and push with my back through the women's locker room door as Morgan and Lily follow.

"Nobody would pay attention to you. I promise," she continues.

My shoulders crawl up to my ears before I let them drop with a heavy sigh.

"Lily—"

I feel a palm on my back before Morgan steps in front of me.

"What she's doing is working for her, Lil. Let her be." Morgan is more forceful than me, and maybe that's what we need right now. Still, I don't want to hurt Lily's feelings.

"You're right." Lily nods, but I see the flicker of guilt and hurt in her eyes.

"Maybe down the road," I add. Morgan shoots me a glare over her shoulder then rolls her eyes. She knows I'm only trying to keep Lily happy. I'm always playing politics.

Lily dresses out quickly and jets through the door to the pool area, leaving Morgan and me alone in the locker room. I feel it coming before she speaks, but it doesn't make the tight squeeze in my chest ease at all.

"Why do you do that?" Morgan flings the door to her locker shut with an extra zing that makes me flinch at the clanging sound.

I sigh and pull my legs up to the bench so I can tie my shoes.

"I don't know. I just don't want her to feel bad. She's trying to help."

"You want her to like you. That's what it is. You think letting people down will translate to turning them away." Her mouth lands in a straight line and she juts her hip out as she leans against the lockers and stares me down.

"I mean, it seems to work that way with you," I half joke. I'm not laughing. Morgan rolls her eyes.

Again.

"All I mean is maybe being honest would relieve some of that pressure. Lily would understand. Hell, she'd probably get it more than anyone here after all she's been through." Morgan's face softens as she exhales and studies me. I can't hold her gaze more than a second before blinking my focus down to my lap.

"You're probably right," I admit.

Morgan's fingertips tickle my shoulder and I glance up, relieved to see her smiling, even if it's forced and slight.

"We're both here for you, is all. Same way you're here for us. We all get to play Anika now," she says, squeezing my shoulder once before leaving me alone with my thoughts.

We all get to play Anika.

I run my palms down my leggings, applying compression to my thighs, knees, and calves. I miss Anika. I was a better version of myself when she was here. I still don't think I'd be slipping into a swimsuit that shows every divot and scar that mars my right leg, but I might be more open about talking about my body issues.

I form my regular clothes into a tight roll and tuck them in my gym bag then toss it into my locker, shutting the door gently, as if I'm somehow balancing out the emotional universe in contrast to Morgan's slam.

I pull my phone from my hip pocket and push my

earbuds in my ears before scrolling to the workout listed on my physical therapy app. This is what I'm able to handle. And it has been helping. Though I cheat my way through some of the exercises.

A little Halsey and Grimes pumping in my ears, I feel stronger by the time my feet hit the mat flooring in the weight room. It's crowded today, which I oddly prefer. I'm anonymous this way, just another co-ed working out after classes, trying to stay fit. I take my seat on the leg press machine and prop my phone in the cupholder so I can keep track of the various exercises I need to knock out today. I've learned that the hard stuff comes at the end, so I start there while my strength is up.

Shaking my head to the thumping bass in my ears, I center my right foot on the platform and push—ten pounds less than my workout tells me to, but I can handle this. I'm counting in my head, excited to be close to ten, when my final push and release reveals a shirtless Cameron Hass straddling the bench across from me. He shoots me a crooked smile and I let the platform fall toward me, my leg suddenly Jell-O. *My body suddenly Jell-O.*

He chuckles before bending down, grabbing his towel from the floor near his left foot, then shooting me that damn crooked smile before heading my direction.

So much for being anonymous. And so much for banning fantasies about Cameron from my brain. The slow stroll toward me, sans shirt, shorts hugging hips, muscles moving around his midriff like hypnotic, unfair warfare—this is all going to haunt me at bedtime.

I pull my right earbud free, leaving the music on in the left as if drowning it out will somehow make my heart stop the rapid-action fluttering business going on.

"Hi, stranger." *Really? Those are the words that come out of my mouth.*

He nods, like a dude, and sits on a nearby bench.

"Looks like you're having some trouble there?"

My mouth opens, and I continue to stare at him, straddling the bench with his shirt off until he dips his chin and lowers his head enough to catch my attention and bring it back up to his face. *OMG!*

"Oh, that. The slip, you mean? Or rather, I didn't slip. I should be doing more weight, and I was admonishing myself for it and about to up the amount." *Lie, lie, lie!*

"Lemme see," he says, swinging a leg over the bench to stand and walk over to me. I swallow hard, wishing I wasn't trapped in this contraption and able to run away.

I hand over my phone because the other option—hugging it to my chest and saying nuh-uh like a toddler—is absurd.

Cameron palms my phone, flipping through today's workout list with his thumb while he runs his other hand through his hair. I lean back and scan the weight room while he reads the list of exercises I'm knowingly not doing correctly. Most of the football team is in here for optional lifting before their practice. Morgan is running on one of the treadmills near James, our new quarterback. And Theo, Lily's boyfriend and Anika's brother, is staring at his own muscles in the mirror with intense scrutiny.

Okay, all right. Nobody is seeing me fall apart in front of Cameron Hass. Because of Cameron Hass.

I swallow again and bring my attention back to Cameron's eyes. They're scanning my phone screen and he's nodding.

"So according to this, you're about fifteen pounds too light for this exercise," he says, moving toward the pin and adjusting the weight.

"Oh, yeah. I mean, I realized . . ." My fake laugh trails off as Cameron cranes his neck and squints one eye at me.

"Brooky."

That tone was clearly scolding. And *Brooky*—clearly meant to annoy me.

I let my head fall back on the headrest and drop my arms at my sides with a huff.

"Fine. I'm not really working out at one hundred percent. I've maybe been going a little easy, but it's hard. And truthfully, I don't know if I would be able to lift this kind of weight without an injury." My head rolls to the side and my gaze lands on his judgement-free eyes.

"You know, that BS we both rolled out at the party this weekend about motivating each other during workouts wasn't completely without merit. And you would be surprised how much stronger you would feel with someone rooting you on." His brow ticks up.

"You? And me? Workout buddies?"

Oh God.

"Not all the time, but maybe in the afternoons. And if I could motivate you on a weekend here and there. Hell, we don't have to do just gym stuff, either. I mean, I could show you things . . ."

His mouth abruptly stops, the words hanging between us unfinished. A few seconds pass and he breathes out a short laugh, lip curling on the left side just before his eyes flutter closed.

"I didn't mean it like that," he adds.

"Of course not," I add, burying the brief awkward moment under our words.

We both grin, the embarrassed kind, and I'm pretty sure my cheeks are as flushed as his. I'm relieved when he turns to his side and looks down, unable to handle the pressure of a shared moment. It makes me feel less ridiculous for squeezing my eyes closed tightly and giggling like a pre-teen.

"I meant there are ways to work out that make it feel less like, I don't know, work I guess. I can show you if you want," he offers.

I shake off the butterflies and open my eyes, glancing at him sideways. Morgan is standing in line with him several feet away, and she's done running. She's leaning on the treadmill instead . . . *watching*. She waves, and it isn't that kind meant to signal that she's doing good or ready for a break. She means to let me know she sees everything and is reading all kinds of good gossip between the lines.

"Sure," I say, agreeing before I fully realize what I've done.

"Great. So, tomorrow, same time. I'll see what you should *really* be doing in this app thing. And then we'll take it from there."

He hands my phone back to me and my palm covers his on the exchange. His ring is missing, probably off for practice, but there's a slight divot on his finger where it belongs. I was so tuned in to our touch that I noticed. My insides tighten, my stomach dropping like a roller coaster. This is bad.

Cameron runs his towel over his face and winks before heading back to his original side of the gym. A few girls laying on a mat near me whisper, and I don't have to exert myself by eavesdropping. I know they're trading opinions about Cameron talking to me. We don't match, and I get it. He's . . . well, a bit of a campus hottie. Girls fall for him on the daily, and he's had his fair share of girlfriends at Welles. And at other nearby private schools. And there was that one girl from Vermont. Or was it New Hampshire?

I don't date. Ever. Or at least rarely. And my relationships have all been strategic and parent approved. The guys

I've gone out with have all been from the same circle I spin around in, usually sons of lobbyists, people from The Hill, or well on their way there.

Boring.

Like Gulliver's Travels, according to Cameron.

I'm thinking about Cameron.

"What was that?"

I knew it was only a matter of time before Morgan zeroed in on me with her special laser-precision brand of questioning.

"Apparently, I'm not exercising right or something." I grimace and turn my attention to the leg press platform to re-center my foot, knowing full well that Morgan is not going to take that answer without follow-up.

"Uh huh," she says, leaning against the weight rack part of the neighboring machine, barely in my periphery. I glance at her, but give nothing away, instead putting every ounce of my attention on pushing my new weight amount with one leg. I move the sled about six inches before grunting and letting it slide back to the starting position.

"Ugh!" I grit my teeth and press a fist to my forehead.

"Don't try to redirect me by playing it up," Morgan nudges.

I exhale, suddenly defeated for real. My vision rolls toward my friend as I sink lower into the press seat.

"Sadly, I'm not playing anything up. And Cameron is right. I'm not where I should be, and I should probably be wearing that fucking brace, but I hate it, Morgan. It doesn't go with anything I wear, and it's bulky, and people just ask about it. I don't want to be at the mayor's office for my internship clanking around the desk with my bionic brace."

I breathe out, blowing up at the stray hairs that have slipped loose in my face as my friend moves to stand in front of me. Suspicion still hazes her eyes, but she's put it on the back burner.

"You're doing the best you can, Brook. Maybe your way doesn't check the boxes on some prescription form for healing, but look at you—you're in a gym trying to gain strength. And yeah, you are walking around the mayor's office . . . like a fucking boss!" Morgan wiggles her head with pride, and it eases the shot my self-esteem took with my lifting fail.

"Thanks, and you're right. But I am putting the hard things off. Physically, at least."

"Just physically?" she adds.

I hold my friend's gaze for a several seconds, a little offended, but I remind myself through a long, deep breath that she's coming from a good place. Morgan lacks tact, but her candor comes in handy.

"I've got to get my work in. No half-assing this time," I say, avoiding her secondary question completely. For once, I don't feel like making her feel better. And she's lingering, I think maybe waiting for me to apologize or tell her she's right. When I don't and instead give my all to completing one rep on the leg press, she walks away. Not before giving me a little parting shot, though. At Cameron's expense.

"Then maybe you shouldn't be spending so much time with distractions that won't get you *anywhere*."

It's the way she says that last word. Like it's a stain. Like Cameron is worthless.

We're all friends in our tight group, but other than Theo, I'm probably the next closest to Cameron. Maybe what I feel has nothing to do with physical attraction. Maybe I'm finally coming around to the fact he and I are friends and should be better ones.

I force my way through five more reps, my leg trembling and muscles spent. Cameron has moved on to the free weights area, right next to the barre where Morgan is stretching—*showing off for James.* After a minute's rest, I decide to commit fully to my self-realization, carefully treading my way over to Cameron.

His head lifts and he meets my gaze as I step up, his face full of focus as his lips move to silently count his reps.

"You were right. And I'd like to learn some of those other things you mentioned. Maybe getting out of the gym will motivate me more."

His lips curve on the side closest to me as he sets his dumbbells down. His gray T-shirt is back on, which makes his body slightly less distracting, but all it takes is one lift of the bottom front up to wipe away the sweat on his face to tear my eyes from his face, lower.

"That's the spirit!" He stands and holds an open palm out for me to slap. I feel silly, but I do, laughing nervously and worrying what the hell I've gotten myself into.

"I've got practice, so let's meet out front at six tomorrow night. I've got an idea." His hands rest on his hips, and he stands in front of me like some superhero. I swear he's casting a shadow.

"Got it. See you then," I say, fishing my earbuds from my side pocket and tucking them back in my ears as I walk away to drown out the gossip whispers. Too bad it won't silence the ones in my own damn head.

Chapter 4

Cameron

I've been avoiding my mom's phone calls for days. I know she won't show up here, so I can get away with it up to a point—until I start to feel guilty. My mom avoids Welles like it's a black hole ready to swallow up the universe. I don't think she even drives within the town limits, instead spending most of her time in the city where she teaches a course on religion and war at the university.

My phone buzzes with her latest attempt while I lay on my twin mattress in the room I share with Theo. This is what I get for dragging my ass in the morning. If I were on my way to class, I wouldn't hear the phone. My friend leans over after slipping his arms into a clean shirt and glances at my screen.

"You should answer that, bro." His lips twist, and even though I don't talk about my family with anyone, Theo's gathered enough to know my situation is kinda fucked up.

I sigh exaggeratingly and flatten my palm over my phone, pressing answer then slapping it against my right cheek.

"Hi," I groan.

My eyes shift to Theo, narrowed to let him know this

conversation I'm about to have is all his fault. He chuckles as he slips his Welles tie around his collar then snags his shoes from the floor, slipping them on a step at a time before leaving me alone in this room with my enigma of a mother.

"I've been trying to get hold of you. Is everything all right?" I can hear the city traffic through the phone.

"I'm fine. Why wouldn't I be? Are you walking somewhere?" It's seven in the morning. I hate when she calls me between more important things. It makes me feel like an appointment to her, a line on her planner that's scheduled somewhere between lunch date and office hours.

"I'm having breakfast with the provost. I'm getting another class, and we're talking about tenure," she says, lowering the phone to whistle for a cab. I smirk because it's an impressive skill. My mom is one of those people who can jam two fingers in her mouth and shrill loud enough to turn heads a block away. When I was a little kid, that's how she called me in from playing basketball with the boys down at the park. It's a sharp contrast to everything else about her—a put-together, overly-educated young professor bursting at the seams with ambition and zero real connections. A tad selfish. A lot like my grandparents. Nothing like my dad.

"Tenure. *Wooo whoo.*" My sarcasm is obvious as I wiggle my finger for my own amusement.

"Well, it's important to me. I've worked hard for this, Cameron . . ." She says a few more things in that same lecture-like tone that I don't hear because I pull my phone away from my ear and lay it back on my mattress. When it quiets, I pick it back up to continue our riveting conversation.

"I got an email notice that you visited Michael," she says.

That's what her calls are about. My mom has always been supportive of me having a relationship with my dad. I think partly to piss off her parents who would rather he remain a story they could make up and shift into whatever they want. Anything but a convict who tried to lure their baby girl to the dark side.

"I'm eighteen now. You shouldn't be getting those notices," I grumble.

"Well, I'm still in the system as guardian, I guess. I'll call later this week to see if they can remove that function." *She won't call. If it's not penciled in after lunch, it isn't happening.*

Several seconds pass without conversation, and I listen to my mom get into a cab and give the name of some restaurant I'd probably hate to the driver.

"Sorry, you still there?"

I sigh.

"I'm still here."

Quieter, minus the regular thrum of cab tires rolling over spacers in the road. She must be going over the bridge.

"How was he? Your dad?" And this is where things always get weird. Her tone changes, and I've decided that it's because she's ashamed for caring about him so much. She does care about him, though. Otherwise, she wouldn't ask about my visits. And she wouldn't have made sure we had a connection.

"He's good. I tried to bring him cupcakes for his birthday, but—"

"*Shit.*" She forgot.

"Yeah, it was Saturday. Don't worry, he didn't have a party or anything." We both laugh faintly at my bad joke.

"But he's good? How . . . how does he look?" My mom saw him six months ago when she went with me on my last underage visit. She's seen him age over the years from across the room. All those visits, and she never once sat with us and talked to him. My dad never pushed, either.

"He had a fresh haircut. I mean, he still looks like he could lift a truck, and he seemed in good spirits. So yeah, he looks good."

When I was younger, my dad put on a good face for me. I never questioned it until I was maybe sixteen, and that's when we started to talk for real. I would ask him the hard questions and he would slice through the bullshit and give me real answers. He's the only one who ever does. He told me he got his ass kicked at least twice a week for the first few years, but the older he got, the less people bothered him. Maybe he matured, or maybe the system did around him, but he's been resolved to his situation and focused on the good parts for most of my teenage years.

"He's thirty-six," she says, her voice quiet now. She's talking to herself.

I chew at the inside of my cheek and do the math on my own, my chest weighed down with the realization that I'm the same age he was when he fucked up his life. Doesn't feel right. I don't feel like my decisions right now are those of a well-formed adult. My friends would agree. Just last week I made a bet with two of the linemen on our football team that if I lay on the train tracks they would break first and tell me to move before I would. It was kind of a cheat, though, because I've lain on those tracks before and let the train roar over me. There's a lot more clearance in that spot than people realize.

Dumb decisions are part of the Hass DNA when we're young. I guess when the group you hang with fires a rifle inside a bank and kills someone, it doesn't matter how newly minted your adulthood is. Unlike me, my dad picked the wrong friends. And he's been paying for it for my entire life.

"I've got class soon. I still need to get dressed," I say, sitting up and swinging my feet to the floor.

"Right, well, wish me luck. Love you, Cam." She ends the call before I say 'bye.'

I drop my phone to the bed and rub the sleep from my eyes. The only time my mom utters those words, *love you,* is at the abrupt end of a phone call. I can't remember the last time she said them to me in person. It's fine. I know she loves me, in her own way. She gives affection the same way it was shown to her as a kid.

Deciding I don't have time to rush through a shower, I throw a white T-shirt over my head and grab the button-down I wore yesterday from the back of my desk chair. I never undo my ties if I can help it, so I'm able to tighten the knot against my throat and slip into my jacket in under a minute. I'm not as graceful as Theo at slipping shoes on without untying them, so I let the laces dangle around my ankles while I grab my backpack and rush out the door.

I slide around the corner—literally—a second before the first bell sounds. My economics teacher, Mr. Philips, eyes me over the black rims of his glasses and says my name the same way the agents talk to Keanu Reeves in *The Matrix.*

"Present," I say, assuming he's taking roll.

I dip into my seat and drop my backpack between my feet, kicking it back so the straps don't trip anyone. After a few seconds, I realize he's not calling out any other names, and a quick glance around the room reveals everyone's eyes on me.

"Mr. Hass, might you look down at your lap and tell me what you see?" He pulls his glasses a fraction lower on his nose, and at about that time I hear a muffled laugh break free behind me.

Yeah . . . my thighs are cold.

My chin drops and my eyes take in my hairy, pale thighs peeking out from my Grinch boxer shorts. *How the fuck did I get out of my room without my pants? I put my shoes on for Christ's sake! I guess I didn't linger to tie them, so poof—no pants.*

"Weirdest thing . . ." I start my mental rolodex of excuses and land on making this one of those epic stories that will live on in Welles infamy for years. "It's why I was late, actually. See, I was taking the long route to class, by the main road—the public one, outside the gates."

Mr. Philips holds his attendance book against his chest and crosses his arms over it as he leans his weight into his desk.

"Right, because you went the long way. Go on," he indulges. This isn't my first go around with him. He moved into economics fulltime after spending a decade teaching third form students. He had to deal with me in eighth grade, and I was an ADHD handful. I get the distinct sense he wants to see where I take this.

"Exactly," I say, pointing to him and buying myself time to work out a great story. I slide back in my seat and man spread, which gets a few groans and even more muffled laughter. Physical comedy is where I excel.

"And let me guess, Mr. Hass. A tornado whisked by and ripped your pants from your body." His mouth rests in a straight, tired line.

"*Pfft*, that's ridiculous," I say, pulling myself back upright to sit tall. My knee bobs with my nervous energy. "I ran into a mysterious man walking the opposite direction. He needed pants, which . . . *I know, weird, right?* He stopped me and asked if I had any to spare, which technically, I did. I would survive without pants for the day, and this man was carrying a very expensive brief case and looked like he was going somewhere incredibly important. The pants were far more valuable to him. But you'd be proud of me, Mr. Philips."

He sighs, pulling his glasses from his face to rub the bridge of his nose. He puts them back on and shifts his weight to the opposite leg.

"And why is that?" He's such a good sport. Always has been.

"Ah, see . . . because I used what I've learned in economics to barter with him. I knew the pants were of greater value to him than me, so I refused his first offer of fifty dollars."

Mr. Philips holds his palm to his cheek and blinks slowly.

"I see," he says.

"And I know what you're thinking—"

"You couldn't possibly," he responds.

The entire class laughs.

"You're thinking maybe I got lucky and bargained him up ten more bucks. And he tried that. Believe me. We went through several rounds, and each time he raised his offer by ten dollars. Finally, when I refused a hundred, he turned the tables and asked me what it would take. I nodded toward his briefcase."

"Of course you did," Mr. Philips says through a forced smile. He glances at his watch, probably to check how much time I'm sucking up with this. Instead of kicking me out straight away, though, he twirls his finger in the air, urging me to speed this story up.

"I told him the pants were his for the contents of his brief-case. The man was no dummy, though. He insisted on getting the pants first. I had no choice. My gut told me that whatever was in that briefcase was far more valuable. I stepped out of my slacks in seconds and tossed them to him. He put them on, to ensure a good fit."

"Sure, yeah. Of course." A faint smile sneaks through his practiced stern face.

"Satisfied, the man bent down and opened up his brief-case. I waited patiently, my mind racing through the possibilities. What could it be? Millions? Diamonds? The deed to a mansion?" I glance around the room to find everyone rapt by my story.

"Well?" Brooklyn's voice draws my eyes to the back of the room. Her red lips showing off the perfect smirk, she clicks the pen in her hand as I twist in my desk enough to stare at her easily.

"He handed me five magic beans. He told me to plant them, which I did on my way into this room. That's why I was late. I had to cover them with dirt and somehow get enough water to their spot to help them grow." I sell the childhood fable like I'm Denzel delivering Shakespeare.

Brooklyn's smirk curves deeper and she leans forward, setting her pen on her notebook and clasping her hands in front of her, just like the courtroom lawyers do at my internship.

"Let me guess. They will grow into a beanstalk that reaches the sky, where a giant is hoarding gold," she says.

I hold her stare for a few solid seconds, mentally debating which way to go with the end of my tale. Crinkling up my face, I wave my hand at her, spit out a laugh, and spin around to return my focus to Mr. Philips, who is already holding out the pink slip—my ticket to one visit with the headmaster.

"Just another Starbucks, I'm afraid. The beans should make a lovely Italian roast."

"Mr. Hass." This time my teacher's calling of my name comes with the clearing of his throat.

"That's my cue," I say with a grin as I stand. Slinging my backpack over my shoulder, I pluck the slip from Mr. Philips's hand and exit to a round of applause. The regret doesn't sink in until I'm halfway to the headmaster's office, catching glares from prospective students and their parents.

I shift my backpack and clutch it to my waist when I enter the office, as if that will somehow mask the bright red and green boxers catching everyone's eyes. I slide my pink slip across the desk to Karen, the school admin, who pulls it toward her with a drag of her index finger while tilting her head to the side in that perfectly disappointed way.

"Hey, it's been a while." I shrug.

"Has it?" She purses her lips then scans the note from Mr. Philips, lifting up in her seat after reading it to take in the evidence standing on the other side of her credenza. I flash a smile, which earns me a quiet chuckle as she shakes her head.

"Wait here. I don't want you mingling with anyone like that," she says, taking the pink slip to the office door behind her where she knocks gently.

I glance over my shoulder and am met with the hard glare of two parents here with what looks like a future first form. Their son seems to think my situation is funny, which only pisses his parents off more.

"I'm incontinent," I say. Their eyes flit to mine, their mouths still straight, unamused lines. "Been wetting my pants since the toddler years. Can't seem to outgrow it."

"Mr. Hass!"

I squint at the sound of Headmaster Powell's voice. My last name has been said a lot today and I've only been awake for maybe thirty minutes.

"Yes, sir," I respond, rounding Karen's desk while keeping my bag in place to hide, well, my goods.

The door closes behind me with a snap, not quite a slam, but jerked closed with enough oomph to foreshadow how this conversation is about to go.

"Cameron, what in the ever-loving hell?"

I collapse into the soft leather cushion of one of the head-master's chairs while he takes his seat in the red leather throne behind his desk. Okay, maybe not a throne, but really . . . for an office chair, it's ridiculously ornate. I have the same thought every time I'm in here.

"It was a rough morning," I start.

"Clearly!" He rubs his temples while resting his elbows on his desk.

I've learned the best way to survive these meetings is to wait for him to gather his thoughts. This visit requires nearly a full minute of temple rubbing, nose-bridge pinching, and not one, but two slow spins in the throne.

"How am I supposed to explain . . . well . . . *you* to that family out there?" He holds out open palms then flips them and slaps them down on his desktop, defeated.

"There were a few families out on tours too," I throw in.

"Oh, good lord," he grumbles.

I'm still hugging my backpack, and I fidget with one of the zippers, which ups his ire after a few seconds, so I stop.

"I talked to my mom this morning," I say. He knows the complexity of that relationship, and that seems to buy me a shred of sympathy.

"Did you have a fight?"

I shake my head then shrug.

"It wasn't much of a conversation at all, really." Replaying it in my head, the only highlights I can remember are the sounds of traffic and the bit at the end, when I talked about Dad.

He leans back in his chair and twines his fingers together, resting his hands on his protruding belly that he tries hard to mask with the flashiest of ties. How he doesn't realize that only draws the eyes to his midsection baffles me. His gaze settles on mine, and we sit in silence for a few long seconds.

"I'm sorry," I finally break. I actually am this time. I didn't mean to make a scene this morning. That's not really my style. I'm more late-night party trickster or fireworks from the roof guy. Half-ass streaking in holiday underwear wouldn't even make my top-ten list.

"Cameron, families are . . . complicated," he says.

I shake with a silent laugh.

"Yeah, I know. You've told me." I stand, hoping I can speed this punishment session up. I don't need yet another lecture from him about the value of family and connections out in the world. I swear, he makes family seem like a business opportunity. And his lectures always morph into his trademarked speech on the right way to behave, how to be a Welles man, blah blah blah. He's been trying to force those lessons on me for years.

"So, should I tell Coach I'm suspended for the next two games? Or do I need to check in with maintenance on Saturday morning for my cleaning shift?" He won't suspend me from football, so I'm guessing the second option is what I'll be getting. I don't mind scraping gum from table undersides and walkways so much anymore. I practically have my own technique.

"No, no . . . the next two games are too important. We have the rivalry and all, and I know you're a valuable member of the team. I wouldn't want to let our coach down or let the team down."

I knew it. He doesn't want to disappoint alumni with fat checkbooks.

"Okay, well I'll let Vic know to expect me on Saturday," I say, nodding with a tight smile before making my way for the door. He stops me when my hand touches the knob.

"Actually—"

Shit.

41

I turn slowly. Punishments at Welles rarely differ. The guys lose privileges and extra curriculars or get maintenance. The girls lose the extras or get stuck licking envelopes and answering phones. There have been a few times demerits were given out ceremoniously, which wouldn't faze me, frankly. I'd probably garner applause, though I don't imagine this school wants to celebrate my boxer-short situation.

My brows raise in anticipation as I rest my back against the door.

"You were with Miss Bennett the other night. You two are friends, yes?" The temple tip of his glasses rests between his teeth as he studies me.

"We're friends," I say, my chest cavity emptying of all feeling—no heartbeat, no breath.

His mouth ticks up on one side and he slides his glasses back on his face.

"You know her father is announcing his campaign very soon." He smirks.

I breathe in deeply and blow out a heavy exhale that drops my shoulders several inches.

"I do," I respond.

"Perhaps you might be able to work with Miss Bennett and convince him to host his announcement here, at Welles." His eyebrows lift over the rims of his glasses to accent his greedy ask.

"I'm sure he has plans for that already, and I don't know that she would be the one to—"

"It would really help out the school," he interrupts. What he means is they want the cachet of a future congressman on campus—*on television.* The board would be pleased, and the happier the board, the bigger his bonus. That house he lives in, the perks of his position, the pseudo-power; it's all so tenuous. Headmasters stay at Welles for decades, but they sell their souls for the gig. I've grown to realize the position has very little to do with educating young minds. It's really about influence and pushing the right people in high places to do the bidding of a few.

A breathy laugh slips out as I smile in response, glancing to the floor to keep myself from spilling out the unkind words sitting at the tip of my tongue. Sauntering toward his desk, I lift my chin to meet his expectant stare.

"I would rather scrape gum from the inside of toilets for the rest of the year. I'll tell Vic he's got me every Saturday morning until he hears otherwise. And don't worry, next time I'll tell my mom you said hi."

He doesn't even wince at my words. My mom isn't as important as Brooklyn's dad. And he doesn't care about my mental wellbeing or how my family relationships might impact my mood—my everything.

I pull the signed pink slip from his desk and shove it into the side pocket of my backpack, which I swing around to carry the right way as I march proudly through the main lobby and hall before crossing the quad and heading to my room for my goddamn pants.

Chapter 5

Brooklyn

Cameron's performance in our econ class was the talk of campus by the time lunch rolled around. Morgan couldn't get enough of it, and she kept grilling him at lunch about why he decided that, of all things, would be funny, or why not go full monty and sprint through the next pep rally.

Cameron kept insisting it wasn't some idea he cooked up for attention, which is what Morgan thinks *everything* he does is about—attention. I get that it's not; it never has been. I've never dug deeper to find out why, though. None of us have. Even Theo, who is closer to Cameron than any of us.

I decided to keep my plans with Cameron this evening off my roommates' radar. Partly because I didn't want them to tag along to see what *crazy thing* Cameron might do next. But if I'm being honest, it's mostly because I didn't want to face Morgan's scrutiny anymore. Her inquisition at the gym yesterday was enough to already make me feel uncomfortable around a guy I've known for almost six years as a friend. If she dug in with teasing or shot me suspicious glances on my way out tonight, I don't know if I would have come. And I want to be here. I want his help, and I want to spend time with him. It doesn't have to mean anything more than that, but if Morgan were involved, it would mean everything but the simple stuff.

Of course, that also meant telling a lie, which is not in my skillset. I went with dinner plans with my father because those are always last-minute affairs that none of my friends have any interest in mooching off of. My dad is very serious, something not everyone appreciates. And when my mom isn't around to soften his edges, he can be rather sharp. Not everyone can take that.

The walkways are empty, and through the large panoramic window on the second floor of the fieldhouse, I see a few girls running on the treadmills. They're two years younger, and they don't seem to be scanning the grounds while they run, so I take a seat on the brick bench that wraps around the front of the gym.

The football team spills out of the side door a few minutes after I settle in and start scrolling through my social media, so I slip my phone in my side pocket and stand, pulling my legs up one at a time to stretch my quads. Cameron is laughing alongside Theo as they walk toward me, and my chest tightens in sudden fear that Lily is going to show up nearby to meet Theo for something. I don't know why I feel like I'm supposed to be hiding, but I do.

"That's what you're wearing?" Cameron scans my body which is cloaked in a tight-fitting long-sleeved running shirt and my trademark black leggings. I guess I do look like a burglar.

"It's a little cold, so I thought I should dress warm?" I smile awkwardly, patting my palms against my hips while I bounce on my feet.

"You're dressed fine, Brooklyn. Don't let this asshole judge you because he thinks everyone should suck it up and wear shorts in forty or below." Theo slaps Cameron with an open palm to the chest then reaches down, pinching a sizeable patch of hair on Cameron's calf then yanking it hard.

"Oww, fucker!" Cameron shouts, hopping around while pulling his knee to his chest and rubbing his leg.

Theo nods to me with a smug grin then glances to his friend.

"Don't let him bully you, Brook. He's got weaknesses," he teases before reaching a fist toward me to pound. I do before he begins to walk backward toward the dorms. That's when it hits me—he's probably going to see Lily.

This is why I can't lie. Too many loose ends to consider.

"Oh, hey . . . Theo!" I hold up a palm to Cameron and jog over to where Theo has now stopped.

"What's up?" His breath fogs in the outdoor air, which sort of proves both of our points—it's cold out and Cameron is insane.

"I maybe didn't mention this workout to Morgan or Lily," I say, my face twisting to match the burn attacking my cheeks. Theo's mouth ticks up in a knowing grin and I open my mouth to explain more. *To lie more.*

"Brook, it's fine. I don't like people in my business either. I didn't even see you," he says, flattening his palm over his eyes. "See? Can't see a thing."

"Thank you," I sigh.

He chuckles and spreads his fingers just enough to peek at me before spinning around and letting his hand fall into the front pocket of his hoodie.

"You were never here," he says into the breeze.

The squeeze in my chest eases but flares up again when I turn back to face Cameron, who probably heard most of that.

His brow furrowed in what I assume is confusion, I brace myself for him to ask me what that was all about. I'm relieved when he doesn't.

"Come on, we have a bit of a hike in store for us," he says, tilting his head toward the pathway that leads down to the riverwalk.

"I'm not smoking pot with you, Cameron," I say, instantly digging in my heels. Of course, that's his grand idea. I'm so stupid for thinking he'd have actual physical therapy plans.

I fold my arms around my chest, clutching my sides to lock myself into my stubborn stance as Cameron laughs under his breath, dropping his gym bag at his feet before closing the few feet of space between us. His stare meets mine, both of our mouths pulled into tight lines, and when his head leans to one side, mine leans to the other, like some childish body language battle of wills. He's the first to break with a real laugh.

"I do not have some grand plan to get you high, Brooky. We're just taking the trail to a spot where I can show you some things—things you can do on your own without me if you decide my moral compass is not worthy of your presence."

His words are soaked in sarcasm and my eyes narrow a little with suspicion, but mostly I feel guilty for jumping to that conclusion. Cameron tugs my wrists until my grip loosens and my arm lock on my body breaks. He leans his head to the right and lifts a brow, sliding his hands down my wrists until our fingers are hooked. My pulse increasing, I breathe in deeply and look over his shoulder, mostly scanning to see if his usual crew of burnouts is anywhere around the water's edge.

"Fine, but you can't blame me for freaking out. You are known to—" I stop myself. Cameron lets go of one of my hands but holds on to the other, turning to lead me toward the path.

"I'm known for a lot of things. I get it. But I'm not a drug dealer, Brooky. I wouldn't push my bad habits on you." His hand keeps mine, his grip just strong enough to signal that he'd prefer not to let go, so I don't try.

He bends over to snag his bag as we pass it before leading me around the back of the fieldhouse to the mulch pathway. The trail is narrow, forcing me to walk behind him, which is good because I don't think I can look him in the eyes. Cameron's never been anything but sweet to me. I think I simply feel the effects of lying to my friends.

We trek about two hundred yards, stopping where the pathway lights end and the walkway dips, wrapping around a wooded cliff maybe thirty feet high. Cameron lets go of my hand and I instantly hide it under my arm, hugging myself again. His gym bag falls to the ground, making a clanking noise. My mental wheels turn as he kneels and unzips his duffel, pulling out some bright yellow ropes and what I'm pretty sure are climbing harnesses.

"Ha," I punch out, stepping back slowly and waving my hands in front of my body. "Oh, hell no!"

Cameron's head falls forward as his shoulders shake with quiet laughter.

"Bet you wish we were getting high now," he jokes, standing with the tangled rope system in his hands, metal clamps dangling every few linear feet.

"I wish I were in bed watching K-dramas on my phone if we're being honest. Cameron! I'm not . . . whatever that contraption is meant to have me do. I'm not doing it." I plant my feet in the brush and fold my arms over my chest tighter than before.

He sorts out the places where the rope has knotted, then

unbuckles the first of two harnesses, approaching me with the caution of a dog catcher about to hook something that might be rabid. I lick my lips nervously and stare at the mesh apparatus with a million buckles.

"Do you trust me?"

My eyes flit to his at that question. Brow denting with enough force that I feel it on my skin, I suck in a breath. It's strange that I know this in my gut, but yeah . . . I trust him.

I nod once, a tiny movement that makes him laugh.

"Would it help if I told you that doing this is worth about two days' worth of that workout app list you were half-assing your way through yesterday?" He holds the harness in front of my waist and nods toward his right shoulder, urging me to use him for balance. I squeeze his shoulders with my palms, unable to ignore their size. How are they so round? So . . . hard? How is he wearing a T-shirt out here?

"I wasn't half-assing. I was drag-assing. There's a difference."

Cameron's head falls back with laughter. I playfully smack his right shoulder in response but tangle my foot in the harness as I do and end up gripping him harder. His hands move to my waist, squeezing to hold me steady, and his nose grazes my cheek in the exchange. The harness slides down my hips and we both freeze in place for a beat before Cameron steps back and scratches at the side of his head.

"Uh, sorry. I ran out of hands, I guess." We make brief eye contact, his lips sucked in just like mine.

"If putting me in a harness is any indication of how successful rock climbing with me is going to be, we're in trouble," I say, working the harness back up the hips on my own.

"Nah, this is the hardest part," he says, stepping back into our tiny bubble to take over tightening the straps around my waist. He kneels in front of me to fasten the ones around my thighs, this time obviously careful with his touch. His hands somehow never brush my leg, despite having to wrap them in nylon belts. My skin tingles despite the lack of his touch, almost as if the cells of my body are jumping out to be graced by him next.

"Besides, I fall all the time," he says, standing up and squaring my shoulders with his and hitting me with a wide-eyed, grinning exclamation point.

"You fall. That's super reassuring, Cameron. Thanks," I say, while he slips into his gear in a matter of seconds. "What happened to *I never fall?*"

He winds rope through hooks on his belt then through mine before urging me closer to the cliff's face. The surface is speckled with various metal eyehooks, which I know is supposed to set me at ease, but all I can do is mentally calculate how deeply they are embedded in the rock, how many rain and snowstorms have worn at them, how many bodies they have lifted already, and how absolutely unprepared I am to do what Cameron is about to make me do.

"Quit thinking," he says, somehow knowing. "And I only fall when I want to, so it doesn't count."

He turns me to face the wall, nudging my shoulder blades with his warm palms until I stand directly at the cliff's face. The rock is dark, the only light from the moon. It's enough to reflect on the hooks that scale all the way up above me.

"How far do I have to go?" I see three hooks that don't seem too disarming, so I hope maybe we call it a beginner's session.

"As far as you can," he says, all vague and shit. Dammit.

I swallow hard and Cameron reaches around my body, taking my carabiner in his hand and linking it to the first hook.

"May I?" His chin is inches from my shoulder, his breath

hitting my neck. My body rushes with the sensation of having someone that looks like him this close to me. *This is why I lied to Morgan and Lily.*

"Uh huh," I nod.

He slides his hands along my forearms until his fingers layer over the backs of my hands. He guides my reach up to deep crevices and nooks, teaching me what to feel for, then showing me the best ones to start my climb with. I grip as he says then wait as he kneels behind me, his hand wrapping around the ankle of my bad leg. He glances up as I look down and our eyes meet.

"Start with this one?" His brow raises to confirm that this is my injured leg. I nod, suddenly finding it hard to breathe. I can't tell if it's Cameron's touch or fear that I'm going to fail, that I'm going to get hurt.

My leg is trembling. I feel it, and I'm sure he does too. His grip tightens around my ankle, steadying me in place as he slides his other palm up my calf for support.

"I'm going to show you where to step, okay?"

I nod.

I focus on the top of his head, his messy hair that corkscrews in all directions, and then on his hands as he lifts my foot and guides me to a ridge about a foot and a half up the wall face.

"Now, you're going to step and lift here," he says, rubbing along my calf then sliding his hand up the side of my leg to my thigh. "And you're going to feel it here."

I give him the same quick nod as before when he looks up at me, swallowing hard the second he looks down because . . . *his hand is on my thigh!*

"It's going to be hard. Even though this isn't that high of a lift, it's going to be harder than you think it will be. So that's where those hands come in. Share the burden with your legs, okay?"

I nod again, blinking my attention to the rock in front of me. Maybe it's good it's completely dark out here. Nobody can accidentally see me fall to my death. Or crush Cameron on my way down.

"On three," he says.

I prime my muscles and breathe out, trying to think more about the climb than the boy touching me.

"One," he begins.

I bounce on my leg with his count.

"Two," he continues.

On three, I step up and pull with my arms, my chest and biceps flexing more than I think maybe they ever have. The burn is instant, and it travels from my armpits down my core and all the way to my calf, which is still being guarded by Cameron's warm palm. I grunt with my exertion, a little embarrassed by the noise I made.

"That's it, you're there," he says, lying because I can tell I'm not.

"Keep standing tall," he encourages.

He wasn't kidding when he said this would be harder than I imagined. It's about a thousand times harder. The rock leaves little room for error, and even less room for taking a step. My margin for bending my knees, for pulling my body up toward the tree lines above my head, is less than one percent. But I feel it, the moment when I pass that halfway point and the work slips from impossible to probable. I flatten against the rock, letting my cheek rest on the cold, dirty surface while I huff in and out.

"Woo whoo!" Cameron shouts, his celebration echoing around us.

"Shhhh!" I chastise. People have to be able to hear that.

"Nobody cares, Brooklyn. They probably think it's a wolf or something."

"There are wolves out here?" I crane my neck as much as my clinging body will allow only to find Cameron's amused smirk.

"Bears too." He shrugs.

"Cameron Hass, I swear to God if you get me eaten by a bear—"

"I'd go in after you, Brooky. Don't worry." He pats my back, his touch friendlier now. I miss the concerned, intimate version from a second ago.

"And don't call me Brooky, dammit!" I'd swat at him if I weren't afraid to let go.

He simply laughs and goes to work hooking the next rung of hooks together and adding his own into the mix.

"You know you're only about a couch height from the ground right now, right?" he teases.

"Cameron, I don't even climb stairs right now, I'm so afraid of falling."

His hand finds my spine again, this time soft against my body, reassuring and calm.

"I'm sorry," he says, and I can sense he's genuine.

I'm freezing, but I think it's because I'm so afraid. Cameron may as well be enjoying a summer day. He doesn't even have goose bumps. If his breath weren't foggy, I'd swear he was living in an entirely different climate than I am.

"I'm going to be right behind you. You literally won't be able to fall because any slip will send you into me, and I'm not falling," he says.

"You said you fall all the time!"

His body rumbles at my back, his chest touching me, making me instantly warm.

"I meant other times. Right now? I won't fall." He leans

in close enough for our lips to touch, our gazes mingling with his promise.

I give a single nod and whimper a timid okay.

"Your next move is right here," he says, lifting himself up easily, his feet on either side of mine, legs stretched wide so his entire body cages me. He glides his palm up the rock from where my fingertips end to the next ridge.

"This one is bigger, so the grip will be easier," he says.

I nod again.

"Your foot is aiming for this step, right here," he says, dropping his hand to a rock shelf that cuts just below my waist.

"That's bigger than before," I protest.

"Yep."

I blink through my stare at what feels impossible. He doesn't offer anything more than affirmation, and I appreciate it. He's not going to give me outs or help me make excuses. He's going to push me. Like I should be pushing myself.

"All right. On three again?" I ask.

"That's my girl."

His girl.

Cameron counts again, and I ready my muscles. His body shifts as I work my body up the cliff, his hands and feet somehow sticking to the sides as if he were a magnet, or some comic book hero. My face warms with the blood rushing to my skin as I grit my teeth and growl my way up the side of the rock.

"You can do this, Brooky . . . Brooklyn," he corrects, and I'd laugh at his charm if I didn't want to pass out from exertion.

I don't feel like I've moved at all, but I must be close. Cameron pulls one hand away from the wall and is somehow able to grab the back of my thigh, lifting me as I work to stand on my own. His boost is just enough to help me clear the final distance, and in a second, both of my feet are resting on the wider ridge, allowing my hands to rest and recover.

"Yeah!" he shouts, his voice echoing again.

"Woo whoo!" I repeat his celebration from before, and his warm laughter hugs me from behind. I'm a little delirious from this effort, and maybe a bit drunk off of his nearness, so I scream out again, this time startling a few bats that better not be living in a cave a foot away from me.

"Oh, my God!" I flatten to the wall as Cameron laughs hard, covering my body with his.

"They're more afraid of you. I promise. You just scared them out of their home," he says at my ear.

My heart is racing, and even though I'm tired, that's not what has my pulse beating so wildly. And I swear I feel Cameron's heart beating too, his chest flat against my back, his fingers woven through mine where they grip the ridges in the rock.

His nose tickles my jawline and I swallow as his lips part.

"What do you say. One more step?"

He's too close to be able to focus on his face as a whole. All I see is the lines of his features, the slope of his nose, plump curl of his lip, rough skin along his jaw. His breath is warm, and he smells like honey and fire. Maybe it's the woods around us. Maybe it's my imagination. I know if I quit, this closeness goes away, though, so I nod slowly.

"One more," I whisper. I'm able to catch his eyes dart to my lips when I speak, and my body thrums with renewed energy.

"Okay, I need to hook us up to the next peg. Hold on," he says, practically jumping on one leg from our comfortable shelf up to a jutting rock that he grabs with his hand. He pulls himself up with one arm, bracing his weight against the wall with his foot as he reaches down for the rope, sliding it through his palm until he finds the next carabiner to hook in place. He makes it happen then palms the wall to steady himself on his way down. His feet bracket mine again in a second.

"Where do you want to step?" he asks.

I jerk my head in his direction with wide eyes.

"Part of the process," he says.

I return my focus to the wall and lift my chin, looking for signs of a good place to land. Everything looks the same to me, as if I'm scaling a blank canvas or a smooth wall covered in faux rock that barely boasts texture.

"Feel it," he breathes.

My chest quakes at his suggestion. He's talking about the rock, but is he maybe also talking about the intangible? His heavy breath moves slowly through his chest, pushing his body into mine more before releasing. I dare say he meant that both ways.

Feel it.

My hand ventures away from his without me giving it much thought. I turn my head so the bottom of my chin is flush with stone as I look to follow my own hand's path. Every lip feels too small, every crack too tight. My fingertips run along old holes left behind by climbers before us, or hooks that have given way.

"I can't," I say, starting to panic. We're still not so high that I would get hurt on a fall, but we're up a lot more than a couch height now.

"Try your other hand," he says, leaning into me for support.

I rest my right hand back in its original spot then palm my left one along the rock's face until I feel a good-sized ridge that seems to fit my palm almost perfectly.

"Here!" My body jolts with excitement.

Cameron reaches up and clings to the rock next to me.

"That's perfect," he says. "Where will you step?"

I glance down, using the distance of my last step as my guide. Nothing pops out, so I let go with my right hand and feel along the wall as I did before. There's one spot, and the standing room is mere inches from what I can tell, but I think if I can hold on with my hands, I can do it.

"Here," I say, patting the wall.

Cameron's right hand lets go of its hold, and he has to grip at my side to keep himself in place before centering his balance again. My stomach tightens under his touch, instant visuals of his hand continuing to move along my body, caress . . . touch.

"Oh, shit!" I blurt out, my balance lost in an instant. I slide several inches down the face of the wall even though Cameron's grasp is fast around my waist. The ropes tethering us are taut as he basically smashes me against the rock to keep me from falling further.

"I got you," he says.

His lips touch my ear. I'm panting.

"I lost it. I can't find my footing." My voice is panicked; my heart is beating wildly. His mouth is still right there, at my ear.

"It's okay. You did good. That's part of it, recovering from a slip. You did good," he says, his voice steady. Reassuring. Kind.

Sexy.

Fuck.

His hands guide mine to new holds before he slides along my back until his feet are on the ground. His hands wrapped around my ankles, Cameron holds up most of my weight, my arms shaking and numb from the adrenaline coursing through them, doses that came partly from the fall but also from all this damn touching.

"Let go and fall back. I got you," he says.

I shake my head, which pulls a deep laugh out of him.

"Brooky!" he scolds.

"Do not call me Brooky!"

His laughter grows, but his hands remain firm on my legs.

"Look, I didn't let you fall then, and I won't now. I will catch you."

I turn to face the wall, which is pretty much an inch away from my nose. My only other options are to die here or to climb down on my own. Neither of those are great choices. No, those are truly stupid thoughts.

"Okay, but no count on three. I'm going to tell you when I'm ready and your ass better catch me."

He laughs but cuts it off when I glare down at him. It may be dark out, but he can still see my laser beams.

"Okay, I'm ready. Whenever you say," he says. His voice is so calm, not a hint of worry. I know anyone looking on would find this whole thing comical. I'm maybe five feet up. It's probably an easy jump for almost anyone else at Welles. A third grader could probably do this with no problem at all. Heck, our headmaster and his wife could probably jump in tandem. But I'm terrified. What if I land wrong? What if my leg pops, or something tears? What if Cameron drops me?

"Just say when," Cameron says, basically reminding me that I need to get moving along.

I nod, mostly for myself, mentally psyching myself up.

"Okay, ready . . . right . . ." The word *now* gets swallowed up by my loss of breath as I let go, expecting to free fall. My descent, however, is very anticlimactic. More of a slow float, like when a figure skater is lifted by her partner for a tour around the ice and she gets to spread her glittered arms out for the judges to see.

Cameron's arms circle my legs, and he backs away from the wall, letting me slide through his grasp in slow motion until my feet make the sweet crunching sound on the ground. Dramatically, I bend down and flatten my palms in the dirt, smacking my lips loudly as if I kissed it too.

"You're ridiculous." Cameron laughs.

"Come here." He motions for me to stand tall so he can unwrap, unbuckle, and unhook the sling he put me in, and I hold my breath every time his hand accidentally grazes my leg.

"That was amazing," I finally let out. Cameron slips the remaining belts away from my body before darting his eyes up to meet mine.

"Oh, yeah? I was pretty sure you were going to murder me for a minute there." He unsnaps his gear in one quick motion, stepping out of it like it's a pair of boxers he puts on every day. I smirk at the thought, considering how his morning started.

"Do you come out here a lot?" I stretch my back and peer up at the wall I scaled. Our hooks and ropes are still linked to the anchors, which Cameron unfastens next. From this view, I realize how dramatic I was being. Maybe it will make me braver for my next climb.

"Here? Not so much anymore. I started climbing this in first form." He wraps everything up into a tangled mess and stuffs it into the bag he pulled it from.

"And you wonder why it was so knotted," I mock.

He shrugs then tosses the bag to the ground. The wind kicks up, and I shiver in response. Cameron is completely unfazed.

"So that climb . . . it's kind of nothing for you now, huh?"

I imagine his lanky junior high body scaling up to the top. He's always been a climber, so I can see how he would take to something like this so young.

Cameron glances over his shoulder at the wall then looks back at me with a crooked smirk. My mouth barely opens to tell him *no* before he's already scaling the rock without any assistance. At one point, about twenty feet up, he hangs with one hand, swinging his body the way those people do on that *Ninja Warrior* show, catching his heel on some crevice I can't see from where I'm at. Making the seemingly impossible happen with ease, he shuffles his hands along a ridge until he's standing tall again, less than five feet between his reach and the top of the cliff.

"Meet me up there? Grab my bag." He points as if I need direction on where his stuff is simply to show off that he can dangle with one hand.

"It's going to take me a minute," I shout, snagging his bag from the ground. By the time I glance back up, he's standing at the top with his hands on his hips.

Well, shit. Now I definitely have to make it higher than five feet.

I follow the path back to the main sidewalk then cut through the trees and drying grass that wrap around the field-house. I use Cameron's gym bag as a machete, swinging it wildly in front of me to clear away the tall weeds and stalks of lord knows what. I stop when I see Cameron's bare back, his shirt tucked in his waistband and his muscles showing off.

"Impressed?" he fishes before I have a chance to compliment him on his climb. Of course, his question stumps me briefly because I am impressed, but not with what he's insinuating. I clear my throat and turn my attention to his bag in my hand, swinging it toward him. He catches it in the air.

"You were all right," I joke.

"Ha! Way to keep me grounded, Brooky," he responds.

I wiggle my head side to side but eventually give in and gush a little for his benefit.

"I think maybe that was under a minute," I say.

"It was."

My mouth snaps shut, and he gives me a smug grin.

"Wow, humble much?" I shoot back.

He winks at me and chuckles before pulling his shirt free and wiping sweat from his face. He unfurls the shirt in his hands and slips it over his head in one smooth movement.

"Okay, but you *have* to be cold now," I accuse. I'm warmer, but that's because of my view.

He glances to the side, feigning consideration.

"Nah," he finally says.

I shake my head at him then turn to head back to the campus sidewalk. Cameron follows as we tread through the path I cleared, and we make plans to try climbing again in two days. Cameron swears I will be sore, but I'm not so sure that was actually harder than the routines I've been prescribed. The fall definitely banged me up a little.

We reach the side door to Cameron's dorm, and I use the glow of the walkway lights to inspect my arms and legs a little closer, brushing away some dirt and twigs.

"That one's gonna need a Band-Aid," Cameron says, pointing to a fresh tear in my leggings at my knee. I bend at the waist to take in the bloody gash.

"Dammit!" I grit out, pulling on the material near the wound to see how bad it is.

"I'm sorry, Brooky." His voice is soft, and for a second he's the awkward pre-teen boy who kicked a soccer ball at my face in physical education five years ago.

"It's not that bad. These are ruined, though," I say, peeling the frayed material away from the dried blood.

"You know, if you wore shorts like I did . . ."

I lift my head and shoot him a glare, but it's hard not to laugh at his dumb joke.

"Yeah, then I'd only be bleeding," I say, squatting slowly to test the sting. It's mostly surface scratches from the rock. The leggings got the worst of it.

"Does this mean climbing is out?"

I stand up in protest with a quick, "Absolutely not!"

"Thata girl. Get back on that horse!" He play-slaps at my arm. The seconds that follow, though, are quiet and rather awkward as we stand two feet apart, swaying our arms, smiling like fools. Eventually, my gaze drifts off to the side, in search of the right way to end our evening.

"We can try again Wednesday. I have a thing tomorrow," he says.

"Great." My answer comes out excited and fast, and my enthusiasm draws a breathy laugh out of him.

"Okay then, Brooky. We'll make you a climbing beast in no time," he says, his mouth landing in a closed-lip smile as he backs away.

I should hold up a hand now and say thanks. I should nod in agreement and be on my way, tell him it sounds like a good plan. And I should probably throw something at him to make him stop calling me Brooky. I'm not doing any of those things, though. Instead, I rush forward, almost in a panic, grab his bicep, and smash my lips to the side of his face.

Mortified in an instant, I blurt out, "Thanks," and rush off to my dorm.

I'm talking to myself by the time I get to my door, my confidence bounding around internally like a racquetball. I'm so proud of what I did tonight, right up until the end when I turned into a Jane Austen heroine who hasn't yet hit her stride. My pulse is racing, and while I'd like a redo on ending my night with Cameron, I can't say I regret it completely. Maybe I don't regret it at all.

All of those giddy feelings puddle at my feet the moment I am lit up by my father's severe glare and the wide eyes of both of my roommates, who now know I lied to them, and have probably done a piss poor job of trying to pacify the man who never waits long for anyone.

"Brooklyn, what in God's name are you wearing?"

"Oh, my God, you're bleeding!"

My father and Lily overlap one another with their initial reactions. The difference in tone matching their words.

"I f—" I stop myself from using the word *fell*. "I tripped."

I've learned a fall makes everyone worry, makes me sound unstable—at risk. Tripping is just me being clumsy.

"Were you out practicing walking?" That's my dad's attempt at humor. It's dry, which I guess is perfect for a politician until it's misread by the press. Basically, everything about my father is politics perfect—six-foot frame, dark hair that sits in a perfect wave atop his head, brown eyes framed in black-rimmed glasses, and a chiseled chin. He's Clark Kent with a touch of gray, an engineering degree, and a captain's rank.

"No," I huff, moving toward our sink to clean up my knee. "I was trying to get a workout in, like I'm supposed to."

I say that last part with some zip, as if I'll get credit somehow for doing something I'm constantly putting off and should be doing anyhow. My dad doesn't care where I've been, just that I wasn't instantly accessible. I slip my phone from my pocket and set it on the counter by the sink and note the four missed calls and sixteen text messages.

"Why are you here?" I ask, keeping my back to the three people no doubt staring at me with their own individual suspicions. I pat my knee clean with a wet towel and pull a bandage out of my small First-Aid kit, sneaking a peek at my phone again to sort out who left me messages. As I predicted, one call from my dad. Every other notification from my friends.

"I'm on my way to a summit, in Canada. I knew I wouldn't see you for a couple weeks and wanted to make sure you had the gala tickets. Remember, it's formal." He pulls a yellow envelope from inside his gray suit jacket and drops it on Morgan's bed.

"I'm over there," I say, nodding toward my bed, which is made perfectly as if I were in the military. Crisp sheets tucked in all the way around, comforter folded over right at the golden stripe in the pattern, pillows straight out of a Ritz Carlton photoshoot. He should recognize it. The Bennett house has always been in extreme order. My older brother, Sam, followed my dad's military footsteps, and now runs his house the same way—Navy, tight ship. Morgan and Lily's messy beds have to be driving my father crazy.

"Right," he says, reading something on his phone as he picks up the envelope and moves it to my bed.

"I have to go, sweetheart. But you will be at the gala, right? It's very important." He doesn't look away from the message he's reading, but he moves toward me and bends down to plant a kiss on top of my head. He may be an unfeeling person in many ways, but these little things remind me I'm special. I'm his little girl.

"I promise, Daddy." I smile up at him from the place where I've propped myself against the sink. His dark eyes meet mine briefly and I get a flash of his smile before he turns to my friends.

"Ladies. It's been . . . interesting," he says, surveying the clothes strewn around Morgan's bed and the papers scattered around Lily's.

"Nice to see you again, Mr. Bennett," Lily says, awkwardly shaking his hand. Morgan and I cringe behind her back, and when my father leaves, letting the door close behind him, she falls on her back and slaps her palm over her face.

"Why do I act like such an idiot around your dad?" she exasperates.

"Because he's fucking hot, that's why," Morgan adds.

I pick up a nearby towel and toss it at her. She promptly snaps it at me.

"Don't you try and change the subject, miss 'I'm having dinner with my dad.'" Morgan levels me with her tight-lipped smirk while Lily plops down on the bed behind her, both of them staring at me armed with enough suspicion to put Sherlock and Watson on edge.

"I was really working out. Like I said," I say with a shrug. I roll down my leggings and survey the tear in the knee. Meanwhile, Morgan picks the towel up again and snaps me with it. *Again.*

"Dammit, that hurts!" I swat at her.

"Brooklyn Marie Bennett, don't you dare be evasive with us. Now spill it," Morgan demands. Lily nods over her shoulder.

I rub my eyes with the butts of my palms and remember how I felt when I made it through that second step. How I felt when Cameron caught me. The lame way I ran away from him after planting a kiss on his cheek.

"I was doing a workout with Cameron, okay?" The minute his name leaves my mouth, Morgan's eyes light up. Lily actually claps.

"Oh, my God, you were right," Lily says.

"See? I told you!" Morgan says.

I move from the sink's edge and head into our shared

closet to change out of my clothes and slip into my oversized sweatpants and Bruins jersey.

"Great. You two were speculating about me. That feels awesome," I deadpan.

"Only because you have been keeping secrets," Morgan fires back.

I turn to face her, hands on my hips.

"I haven't been hiding anything. Cameron and I are friends. He's helping me out. I don't want to be lazy anymore with my leg, and—"

"And you like spending time with him," Morgan cuts in.

My mouth hangs open, but I don't really have a retort for that, so I promptly snap it shut and move to my bed. I leap into the center, drawing my legs in and pulling one of my pillows into my lap. I pick at the seam on the pillowcase, a lose string begging to be tugged and unraveled.

"I do," I mutter.

I'm hit with one of Morgan's pillows and I promptly shove it away, refusing to look up and meet their eyes. Lily throws one at me next, and I discard it in the same way. Pretty soon, we are all throwing pillows at one another, my corner of the room quickly becoming as messy as theirs as we overturn hampers and slingshot stuffed animals at each other. The laughter feels good. And when it ends, we clean up our mess—mostly—and finish up our studies for the next day.

Once our lights are out, I wrap myself tightly in my blanket and stare at Morgan's silhouette across the room. There are a lot of unsaid things in the atmosphere. We both know that if Anika were still alive, I would have told her the truth about tonight. And I know that stings. I wish it weren't the case.

Lily is the first to fall asleep, her breathing a soft wisp of air that has been putting me to sleep since we moved in together. I'm too wired to sleep anytime soon, though. My mind won't quit racing from worry to worry. I don't know how I'm supposed to behave tomorrow with Cameron. More than that, however, I'm anxious about Morgan's thoughts about him.

"Hey, Brook?" she whispers. I wonder if she senses the tension.

"Yeah," I respond, shoving my palm under my cheek.

She doesn't speak for several seconds, and the more time that passes, the tighter the vice gets around my stomach.

"You deserve someone better, is all."

My eyes close slowly, and the tear I've been anticipating slides down my cheek, hitting the back of my hand. I don't know how to respond to her backhanded compliment. I don't want to say *thank you* because I'm not grateful for it at all. Maybe a month ago I would have agreed. What does that say about me?

Cameron Hass is a lot more than some class clown who smokes a little pot. *A lot of pot.* He's got depth. I've glimpsed it. It makes me curious. *What if it turns out I don't deserve him?*

"Good night, Morgan," I finally say. When she doesn't answer back, I assume she's either asleep or understood my curt response. We're done talking about Cameron in this room.

Chapter 6

Cameron

For the first time in, well . . . actually, for the first time ever, I woke with the sun and went for a run. I didn't roll out of bed with minutes to spare, squeak in a hit off my joint, and race to first hour. I woke up alive, ready to go. Ready to see what this day had in store for me because yesterday was one for the record books.

I don't realize I'm whistling until Theo points it out.

"Damn, you're jolly," he says, working his tie through his button collar, redoing his first failed attempt.

"Huh. I guess I slept well for once. Kinda felt like maybe I should start some better habits," I say, slipping into my shirt with my tie still intact.

"Ha, ya think?" Theo jokes. I straighten my tie in place and laugh when he has to start his over a third time.

"Karma," I say, pointing at his neck.

He scowls.

It's internship day, which for me means swapping out the Welles jacket for the more formal gray one to match my suit pants. I've been helping to pull files together for a big financial case the firm is handling. My work is mundane, but I feel important. I only hope I can parlay it into law school. And maybe one day, far down the road, helping my dad earn back his right to vote.

"Hey, bro. This mood shift wouldn't have anything to do with you spending time with Brooklyn lately, would it?"

I shrug.

"Maybe."

It does.

I flatten myself on our floor to scan for my missing shoe, finding it halfway under my bed. I use my belt to loop it and drag it toward me then stand to dust off my pants. When I take a seat on my bed to finish getting ready, I'm hit with Theo's mashed up lips and generally miserable expression. It's hard to tell whether that's meant for me or if he's just moody. He's like that.

"You all right, man?" I toss one of my shoes from one hand to the other then slip it my foot.

"You know she doesn't date, right? I mean, anyone." Yeah, that grimace was meant for me.

"Okay," I say. This conversation is pointless. I'm not naïve. I know that whatever is happening with Brooky and me is transitory. It's flirting, and it feels nice. And maybe it's all I get, and that's fine. I like how being around her makes me feel. I always have. Now, I just get that time one-on-one. I like to make her laugh.

I glance up to see Theo has moved closer, his hands dropped in his pants pockets and his head tilted like he's my boss. I lean back on my palms and mimic his stare.

"Fuck, man. What's your deal?" I sigh out.

"Cam, you date everybody. Sometimes twice. You have relationships that last days, sometimes hours, and leave girls so pissed at you because you like to fall in love and leave," he accuses.

I sit up tall and point at him.

"That is a falsehood. I do not fall in love. Never have. Nobody can accuse me of that."

Do I like affection? Uh, yeah. I love attention. It's a greedy, selfish trait I have, but I'm fully aware of it. I've never made promises to any girl that I would be more than a good time. I've never been cruel. And I have learned something from every relationship, however brief they may have been.

"Fine, but Brooklyn is different. You know it, and I know it. You mess something up there and you'll find yourself shipped off to be homeschooled or to one of those online high schools or some shit. And forget about getting into a good college. You'll be blacklisted by her father so fast."

I wave my hand and stand, turning my back to him while I tuck in my shirt and thread my belt. My gaze narrows on my twisted blanket, blurring while I soak in his words. He's leaping to a lot of conclusions, improbable ones. Of course Brooky's different. Of any person on this planet, she's the only one I *would* fall for. But the odds of it being mutual are the kind that blow statisticians' minds. I know what our relationship is. We're friends. Good friends. Maybe a little attracted to each other. That's not an epic romantic tragedy in the making. It's an afterschool special.

Rolling my shoulders, I turn to face him, putting my hands on his cheeks, because I know it pisses him off. His brow furrows.

"I hear you, friend. And I promise, we're just two friends getting along. I showed her some climbing exercises. She did well. We made plans to climb again. That's it." I pat his right cheek and he shirks me off, rolling his eyes.

"Fine, but remember that I warned you. If you get

burned—"

"You won't be there to eat gallons of ice cream and watch chick flicks with me. Got it," I say, ticking my finger in the air to show his point is made. He smacks the back of my head as we head out our door.

"Dipshit."

"Wow, hitting me with an old man insult. You learn that from your grandpa?" I tease back.

We both laugh and by the time we leave McKinley Hall, the subject feels closed. My phone buzzes in my back pocket and I stop to read the message while Theo continues on.

"See you at practice, man," he says, walking backward to where Lily is waiting for him to head to the train.

I mumble out a *bye* while I read my summons to the headmaster's office. This is becoming a daily thing, and I'm not keen on it. Especially because I'm going to miss my van ride to my internship if this takes too long.

I jog up the steps and pull on the main hall's door just as it flies toward me. It catches me off guard and I stumble down a step or two, only to look up and see Brooklyn standing behind her father in the doorway. My stomach clenches at the coincidence, considering the offer I got yesterday to try and persuade political favor out of this man.

"Cameron, uh . . . hi!" Brooklyn's eyes dart from me to her dad as her words stumble out.

"Good morning. Hello, sir," I say, clearing my throat and reaching out my hand. Walden Bennett has one hell of a smile, and when he hits me with it, I feel at ease.

"Cameron, is . . . is that what you said?" He glances over his shoulder to Brooklyn, who nods.

"Yes, uh. He's in my class. I've known him since first term." Her voice quavers, and it's nice to know she's weird in front of her dad, too.

"Yes, I was at her thirteenth birthday party, the one you all held at that ice cream parlor on Cherry Street." I loved that party. All you can eat ice cream and the place all to ourselves. Plus, the man hired a band who covered anything we requested.

"Cameron, right," he says, his eyes crinkling at the sides as we continue to shake. I let go when he initiates it, and while I'm pretty sure he doesn't really remember me, I admire his effort to make me feel important. Damn, he's suave.

"I guess you could say we're workout partners too. Right, climbing partner?" I wink at Brooklyn who suddenly looks ghost white and mortified, despite her efforts to hide it with a smile. I grit my teeth and put on a forced smile of my own, realizing that my rambling probably was over the top and unnecessary. That was an overshare.

"Is this where you tripped?" He lifts a sharp brow and stares at his daughter. I open my mouth to try to explain it away, figuring she doesn't want him worrying about her banged up knee. I'm surprised she mentioned it to him.

"Aren't you going downtown today?" Brooklyn asks before I have a chance to speak, making a quick change of subject and looking to me.

Her father pulls out his phone, looking at a message.

"I have to run. Rescheduled my flight . . . *finally*. Glad we got to have breakfast this morning, though," he says. Her dad kisses the top of her head and nods to me before taking big strides toward the main parking lot. He does that cool thing where he jerks his arm to expose his fancy watch so he can check the time while he walks away. I try the move while I look on, and it works. Only, I don't have a fancy watch.

"Cameron?" Brooklyn brings my attention back to earth. Away from the sexiest man alive.

"Oh, yeah. Uh, I am. But . . ." I hold up my phone to show the message. "I have been summoned. I'm gonna have to take an Uber."

"I'll wait for you. I can drop you off." She pulls her coat tight and sits on the planter wall right by the door.

"You sure?"

Theo's voice slips into my mind. *Brooklyn's different.*

"Absolutely," she says, her smile taking up her entire face, red lips that part to hit me with one of those magical sparkles from her teeth. *What is it with that family and dental hygiene? Damn!*

"Okay, I'll try to hurry this along," I say, bouncing on my feet.

I rush toward the office, stopping to show Karen my text message. She's on the phone, so she nods me toward the head-master's door. It's clear he's waiting for me as he stands from his chair with an envelope in his hand that's probably meant for me.

"Let me guess, you changed your mind and those are my expulsion papers," I say, only half joking. We both know that walking around campus in boxers is mild for me.

"I'm afraid you're stuck here, but . . . I have had a change of heart." He taps the envelope against his open palm as I look on suspiciously.

"I'm guessing you aren't changing the dress code to incorporate an underwear day." I chuckle. He does not.

"You're off the hook for maintenance work. In exchange, I am going to need you to help out as a server for a very important gala Walden Bennett is hosting for his campaign. There will be a few Welles students helping out. In a way, you could say this is a privilege." He hands the envelope to me, and I peek inside to see a formal letter with instructions on parking at the hotel, arrival times, and a badge for workers.

"What's the catch?" I glance up and lift a brow.

"No catch. We need volunteers, and I'm aware I may need to *persuade* a few of them to work. This event is a way for Welles to be involved, and it is vital that our institution be mentioned in rooms like this."

No catch, huh? There's always a catch, but he may be showing his cards with this one. The catch is that he has leverage against me—I can either scrape gum and clean toilets or spend one night holding a tray of hors d'oeuvres in a room of Boston's elite. Brooklyn will be there, too.

"All right. I'll do it," I say, tucking the contents of the envelope back inside then slipping it into my suit pocket.

"Wonderful. And maybe you can see if there are any members of the football team who would, perhaps . . ."

I nod. This is also part of the catch—asking my friends so he doesn't have to. I don't think Theo or James will mind, and maybe a few other guys I know.

"They'll want compensation of some sort. Community service hours, maybe?" I add, knowing that I'm excluded from any extra perks.

"Done," he agrees.

I leave him with a tight smile, still not sure whether I gave the devil a part of my soul just now.

Brooklyn stands the second I exit, and I can tell by the way she takes the stairs slowly that she's sore from our climb.

"You feel it, don't you?" I say, glancing to her legs. She's not in her normal high heels, but flat black shoes that look like ballet slippers.

"I'm dying," she laughs out, clutching her thighs and bending slightly. "You win. Climbing is a million times harder than pushing a machine with my feet."

"Ha ha, yeah. I mean, what you were doing—*or supposed to be doing*—isn't bad. But weight machines sure are boring compared to climbing with me, right?" I sling my arm over her shoulder as we walk, and everything feels natural. Theo's being crazy. There's nothing wrong with what we're doing, and I'm not going to start trouble with one of our best friends. Because that's what we are . . . friends. Who like holding hands a little. And maybe stare at each other from time to time. So what if I think she's perfect and I want to kiss her every time we're alone? I don't because it would fuck everything up. And I'm not what she *really* wants. And . . .

Damn. Theo is right.

I let my arm slip away, doing my best to make it seem casual and unintentional. Brooklyn glances at me, and I swear there's a furrow in her brow. Or I'm imagining it. Neither result is good.

She's wondering why I did that.

Fuck, now I'm overthinking literally everything.

"Thanks for the lift," I say as she presses her key fob. I climb into the passenger side of her massive Mercedes, and that gap between our worlds hits me a little more. It's not that I don't have means. My mom is successful, and I'll have no problems paying for whatever college I can get into. But my mom drives a Toyota, and she parks it in an uncovered lot because the garage fees are ridiculous. And my dad, well, he's got nothing.

I reach forward and turn the volume up on her radio, glad when a familiar hip hop beat hits our ears. We both start to rap along with the song, bold and loud when the F-bombs drop, and it clears the fog in my head some to see Brooky cut loose and act like a tough guy. And then she looks on at the freeway ahead, her mouth still moving with the words, her hand gesturing like she's some badass R&B princess. And I'm staring. A little too long. A little too hard.

Yeah. Brooklyn *is* different. And that's the problem.

Chapter 7

Brooklyn

My dad is always campaigning. Even before he decided to make a run for the senate, he was running for his next big whatever. Every appointment, honor, award he's gotten has been part of a long-term strategic plan. And outliers are his specialty. They must be dealt with, quickly categorized. Can they help the Bennett brand? Or will they be a deterrent?

Cameron became an outlier the minute he uttered the words "climbing partners." I started fielding messages from my dad about him the minute I pulled into the city hall garage after dropping Cameron off a block away.

DAD: *What's that kid's last name?*

ME: *Hass, and he isn't a kid really.*

I don't know why I added that part. That sounded defensive. There are no deleting things I send to him, though. He saves a record of *everything.*

DAD: *And he's graduating with you?*

ME: *Yes.*

DAD: *He's interning with Lowell and Howell.*

How does he know that?

ME: *I think so.*

I know Cameron is. The fact he dated Karl Lowell's daughter, McKenna, briefly was a big gossip fest at Welles. And when Karl picked Cameron for the internship spot, his daughter threw a major fit. I don't think there was a single resident of Hayden Hall who didn't hear her plight of having to work alongside a "dog like Cameron Hass."

I brushed it all off because McKenna Lowell has always been dramatic. Her dad and mine are good friends, however. And that means we are constantly thrown into circles together. Small circles, with zero chance of escaping. So I always play nice, and when she wanted all females at Welles to shun Cameron, I stood in solidarity. Actually, I simply avoided him at lunch for a week or so until McKenna let it go. If my dad calls up her dad to ask about Cameron, who knows what kind of stories he'll get.

DAD: *Do you know Michael Hass?*

I stare at that name, wondering if Cameron has a brother or if that's his dad's name. I've never met his parents. He doesn't talk about them. Ever.

ME: *No.*

The dots flash for almost a full minute so I wait for my dad's next message to come through, but eventually they stop.

I'm late to the mayor's office, which I know means I will be the one forced to make the coffee run. The sticky note with everyone's order is on the top of my computer screen, and it's long. I count seven drinks.

"Really? Seven? Glad I wore flats," I say, not expecting anyone to hear me. The mayor's assistant, Chuck, pops his head out of the office across from me, though, and smirks.

"Make that eight." He waves his own sticky note, which I know isn't an order for him, but for the mayor. Chuck is in his late fifties, bald, and built like a Patriots lineman. Every winter, he plays Santa for the staff and their families, and he's so nice that I sometimes wonder if he's really the jolly old man in hiding.

"I've never had a serving job, but I swear after a few months here, I might be good at it. Balancing hot coffee in cardboard while walking down Congress is no small feat."

"Well, like you said. At least you wore flats today," Chuck jokes, handing me the additional sticky.

I give him a wry smile before grabbing my crossbody purse and heading to the elevator. At this point I can practically make this walk with my eyes closed. I've been the fetcher about a dozen times. There are two other interns, both from the university, and they're usually working on bigger projects. Bottom of the totem pole, as they say, but I like working my way up. And I like that despite who my father is, this office doesn't give me special treatment.

I wouldn't mind fewer coffee runs, though.

I read the orders while I walk, mentally grouping them so I can rattle off my requests faster. That's another thing I've learned—the Congress Street Coffee Co. baristas are not very patient. I'm so deep in concentration that I don't realize the line is spilling out onto the sidewalk and I ram directly into an immoveable dark gray suit jacket.

"Oh!" My sticky notes go flying as I cup my nose with my hand, sure it's bleeding. It's definitely numb. My eyes water from the impact, but I spin around and search the ground around me for the tiny yellow papers.

"I got 'em." The jacket scrambles. The *familiar* jacket. Worn by a six-foot-plus young man with broad shoulders made for climbing, wavy brown hair, and the most infectious laugh.

"Cameron?" My voice is muffled, my hand still cupping my face. He stands, my notes in his fist, and gives me a crooked smile as he leans his head to the side and steps in close enough to inspect my face.

"Yeah, what are the odds? Here, lemme see." His palm covers mine and he slowly pulls my hand away from my face. I expect blood to gush out, but I guess by his deepening dimple that my face is fine.

"Is it broken?" I blink a few times, the burning sensation still very much there.

Cameron chuckles.

"No," he says, shaking his head. "You smacked yourself good, but I think you'll survive, Brooky."

I squint at him and grit my teeth at the nickname, which has zero deterring effect. He simply chuckles and spins me around to move forward to join the line.

"Let's compare orders," he says, pulling out his phone to read a text string. I take my notes from him and begin to read.

"Your coffees are all sweet and floofy," I say. "I mean, that one . . ." I point at his screen. "That's really a milkshake. Let's be honest."

"True, but I also feel like your orders could all be made in the break room. I mean, how many plain black coffees? Three? And two more with sweetener and cream?"

"Point taken," I say. "We may have uncovered some grand study about the differences between lawyers and public servants."

His eyes narrow and his lips purse.

"Public servants?" His eyebrow lifts with his question.

"Mayor's office? Elected officials?" I know what he's getting at, but I won't say it.

"And who gets elected?" he presses.

"Nope," I say, crossing my arms and shaking my head. We move another step forward in the line, and Cameron questions the woman who just stepped in behind us.

"Excuse me, ma'am, but can you help me with this word I'm trying to think of?"

I squeeze my eyes shut at his boldness. My cheeks are burning, but I know there is no stopping him.

The woman nods and Cameron begins giving her clues. It's what you would call people who become mayor, or maybe city councilmembers, or legislators, or—"

"Public servants?" the woman answers.

I spit out laughter and turn my back to them both so that the woman doesn't think I'm laughing at her. The opposite, really. I want to high five her.

"Thanks, but no," Cameron huffs, folding his arms around his body and moving to stand in front of me.

"He lost a bet," I explain to the woman, whose eyes were drawn in tight with confusion. She nods with raised brows, clearly wishing she was in any other line right now.

"I so love being right," I say, leaning into Cameron. His head falls back with a quiet laugh.

"Oh, Brooky. You were not right. She was wrong."

I punch his arm, which basically does nothing more than temporarily wrinkle his jacket sleeve. I think he might have been flexing underneath, and I like that he wants to show off. I won't say it, but the whole Brooky thing is starting to grow on me too. Kind of like he is.

"Hey, I'm sorry if I wasn't supposed to spill the beans about you rock climbing or whatever. I get that people probably want you to be cautious. Your dad makes me nervous. I think I've talked to him twice in my entire life, and the first time I was pouring rainbow sprinkles on top of seven scoops of ice cream." He holds up one hand to spread fake sprinkles over imaginary dessert.

"It's fine. My dad was probably just shocked to hear I did something so physical. My mom and I are more of the shopping type. Outdoorsy stuff was always for him and my brother." Part of me wonders whether my mom would like climbing as much as I did.

"You should let me take you camping sometime. Give you the full outdoor experience," he says, nervous, breathy laughter tailing his words. His eyes flit away, and I dare say . . . he's blushing.

"Yeah, me in the great outdoors. You just want to take videos of me blundering around a forest so you can monetize my awkwardness." The visual of being alone by a fire with Cameron's arm around me briefly invades my mental space, and my neck warms. Great. Now I'm blushing, too.

"I can't believe you remember my birthday party!" I say, changing the subject.

Cameron shrugs as we finally move inside the café.

"It was pretty epic. Were all of your parties cool like that?" he asks.

I think back to when I turned eight and my mom turned the alleyway behind our brownstone into a petting zoo.

"I see that grin. That's a yes," Cameron says, leaning into me again. I like the way he leans.

"My parents have always been busy with work, so they made sure our birthdays were over the top. My brother got to fly in a trick plane when he turned twelve. I was too young, but I'm not really into loops in the open air a thousand feet up," I say.

"I'd be down for that," Cameron adds.

"Uh, yeah. I know. You probably would have talked them into letting you skydive," I say.

"I have," he responds. I narrow my eyes at him with skepticism, but he pulls his mouth into a tight-lipped grin and simply nods.

"No shit! I'm pretty sure if a plane were going down I'd take my chances on surviving by clutching my seat-cushion floatation device."

Cameron laughs at my very honest response.

"I had to make my own fake ID, but if you go out far enough into the sticks, you can find a crazy guy running a small prop plane business just about anywhere who's willing to take your word for it to make a couple hundred bucks."

I can tell by his expression that he isn't joking.

Cameron Hass navigates danger like it's a tightrope and he's willing to fall to his death. It's a lifestyle I cannot understand, but there's a part of me that's a little envious of his willing to jump with both feet.

"How about you? Any crazy birthday parties?"

His smile fades a bit, and I think he's forcing it to stay put as his gaze moves down to the floor. His hands drop in his pant pockets as he shrugs.

"Nah. Never really had a lot of family around to throw parties and stuff."

There's an instant sadness to him, and I feel bad for broaching the subject with him. My pulse beats in my chest, rattling my neck and echoing in my ears. I want to pry more, but I also get the sense that this subject is off limits.

"You don't talk about your parents—" I start, only to get cut off by a familiar and rarely welcome face.

"Brooklyn Bennett? In the flesh?" Cole Masterson has known me since we were both five years old. His dad served with mine, and they both ended up working for the same engineering group. It forced Cole and me into a lot of the same social groups, which was nice for a while . . . having someone to talk to all the time. But somewhere along his trip through adolescence, Cole turned into a major douchebag.

"Cole, hi. What are you doing here?" He moves in to hug me, so I oblige, reluctantly. Cameron's gaze meets mine and his eyes twitch faintly as his head tilts.

"It's fine," I mouth to him. He nods, but his eyes remain on Cole, specifically his hands.

My hands barely pat his back as he ropes me into his tentacles and holds on a second longer than is socially acceptable. If our fathers had their way, we would be on our way to an arranged marriage. I've made it abundantly clear to both of my parents, though, that Cole—and his bleached-out perm, odd fetish of wearing cowboy boots around the city, and his fumigation-level use of cologne—are not my type.

"I'm taking a class at MIT. Probably going to go there." He sniffs after his brag, which is another annoying habit he learned from his father.

"Ah," I nod, not really wanting to open up his usual who-is-better conversation.

"Are you doing that famous Welles internship?" He's always mocked Welles. Probably because for whatever reason, he couldn't get in. His grades are fine, but he always seemed to blow the interview.

"I am, yeah. Mayor's office," I say, bracing myself for his one-up card.

"Cool, yeah. I had a meeting with her for one of our MIT projects. She made a proclamation for our class because our professor invented this new telescope piece. It's a pretty big deal." His eyes keep darting to my right, to Cameron, so much so I finally break down and introduce them.

"That's amazing," I say, my tone the same one used to cheer on a toddler who just stacked a few blocks. "Cole, this is Cameron. We go to Welles together. Cameron, I've known Cole for . . . ooof." I shake my head to indicate years.

"She was my first kiss. I mean, we were five, but it still counts, right? Nice to meet you." Cole jets out his palm and Cameron's lip ticks up as he briefly pauses before shaking it. His wrist flexes, and I'm pretty sure he's squeezing extra hard.

"Nice to meet you. She was my last kiss, so I guess we have something in common. Excuse me, I'm up," Cameron says with a tight-lipped smile and a nod toward the now open register. My body feels numb as he leaves me there with douchebag Cole and a very well-played one-upper.

"You dating that guy?" Cole gestures toward Cameron, who is busy rattling off his own set of drink orders. His head is cocked just enough that I'm pretty sure he's keeping one ear invested in our conversation.

"Oh, dating? Uhm . . ." The conundrum is the link Cole has directly to my father's ear doesn't include too many telephones. It's basically just one—his dad. And if he's feeling bold, he'll call my dad directly. I'd love to mess with him more, but it's better I don't.

"He was kidding," I say in a hushed tone, hoping it escapes Cameron's ears.

"Yeah, I figured," Cole boasts.

Now my turn to order, I step up to the counter, no longer prepared as I had planned to be during my walk to the cafe. My attention is divided just as Cameron's was, my ear eavesdropping on the exchange between Cole and him. I find myself silently rooting for Cameron to bury his ego hard.

"Tell me, Cam. Can I call you Cam?"

"No." I hold in my laugh at Cameron's fast rebuttal.

"Oh, don't be like that, Cam. I'm curious is all. What's it

like being a *Welles boy?* Are you one of those legacy students? Did your old man go to Welles and that's how you got in? I ask because I know a lot of people our age in this city —the ones who are going to be important someday. What's weird, though, is I don't know you. And there are two kinds of people at Welles—important ones and legacies mooching off of daddy's foot in the door."

My mistakes are pissing the barista off, but I can't answer her questions and listen to the drama behind me at the same time. She's already tossed two cups in the trash because I made her write, rewrite and scribble orders on them too many times.

"Just give me your sticky note," she finally insists, holding out her open palm.

"Oh, that's smart!" I hand it over happily, which I don't think was the reaction she wanted but I'm too busy making sure Cameron doesn't throw Cole through the café window.

"I guess I'm not the kind of guy who hangs out at boring parties. Maybe that's why our paths haven't crossed," Cameron says, unwrapping a stick of gum he pulled from his jacket pocket and placing it on his tongue with extra flare before biting down and grinning at Cole.

I scan my credit card and take my receipt, rolling it up and tucking it in my purse while I join Cameron and Cole by the display of fancy teas and gift tumblers.

"More like you've never been invited to one," Cole says in his on-brand quiet but snarky tone, an insult he lobs so quietly Cameron may have missed it.

"Brooklyn, always nice running into you. Say hello to your dad for me," Cole says, stepping across Cameron on purpose so he can force another unwelcome hug on me. I pat his shoulder with an open palm the way a nervous child might pet the top of a turtle. I glance to Cameron and catch his jaw twitch twice. He definitely heard Cole's last shitty comment.

"Real classy company you keep," Cameron says as soon as Cole is out of earshot.

"He's an asshole, and I wouldn't classify him as company. He's . . . a few degrees of separation," I defend. The way Cameron glares at Cole across the café then turns his focus to me makes my chest hurt. He's lumping me in with him, and that's not fair.

"Besides, you didn't have to play his game," I add.

"I don't play games," he says, his usual playfulness gone from his voice.

"Oh, yeah? What was that bit about being your last kiss?" I whisper my response at him, glancing left and right to see who's listening because I don't like attention when it comes to personal things. I step in close, under his chin, and his mouth curves in that amused way I was starting to find sexy but am suddenly finding irritating as hell.

"That was an impulsive *thank you* I gave you on your cheek. Not a real kiss. *Not a real kiss!*" I lean in close, poking his chest to make my point then rock back and hug myself, my body growing hot with anger. I like Cameron so much better when he's being cute and flirtatious. Jaded and jealous isn't a good look on him.

I blow up at the few loose hairs that have escaped the pins holding my hair in a loose bun. Cameron rolls his eyes as he abandons me to retrieve his order, and I take the opportunity when he's gone to scan the café for Cole. I'm relieved when I see he's gone.

This morning has been one giant disaster. My dad's flight was cancelled, and he thought to use it as a chance to spend breakfast with me. I was foolish enough to get excited when he called and woke me an hour before my alarm. I was even feeling the positive energy enough to leave a note for Morgan saying that I was truly sorry I lied. I was still hurt by her opinion of Cameron, but even those feels were muted in the morning sunlight.

My cheerfulness lasted about twenty minutes, ending the second I met my father in the Welles alumni lounge. I should know better by now after years of letdowns. These chance moments are never really about spending time together. Instead, he ran me through the list of people I need to be sure to say hello to at the gala in two weeks. That was after reminding me to be careful with my leg, noting that I should be wearing my brace, especially if I'm going to work out at night. I don't like talking about my surgery and my recovery around him. He wasn't there for any of it, and it makes me resent him. I don't want to resent him despite the fact I so often do.

"You're right." Cameron breaks through my moody thoughts, his mouth incredibly close to my ear. He must have stepped up behind me while I was looking for Cole and daydreaming. I spin around fast and find myself facing his chest, the drink holder balanced in his palm to make room for me.

"About what? That you gave it as good as you got with Cole?" My nostrils flare as I peer up at him. He hits me with that stupid crooked smile.

"No, Brooky. That we never shared a real kiss. When we do, believe me—you'll know."

I blink up at him, mouth open, wanting to spar but also . . . *when we do?*

"Brooklyn, your order is ready!"

I look in the direction my name was called for maybe a breath, long enough for Cameron to skirt around me and leave the café. And to top it off, I count seven drinks in the carrier, not eight.

Goddamn mean-ass barista.

Chapter 8

Cameron

Admittedly not my best moment. That Cole dude pushed every single one of my buttons, though. First, what the fuck is up with wearing boots with a suit? No way that guy has ever stepped foot in real dirt, much less been near a horse, to earn the right to walk around in ropers. And I'm sure that was Armani he was wearing, or something like that.

Still, I could have handled it all, blown him off or buried him with my own brand of *nobody cares.* But he started talking about fathers as if there is some scale for comparison of privilege and shit luck. That's where my line is carved deep in the sand. I don't talk about my dad with anyone. And yeah, for lots of reasons that maybe aren't noble, but mostly because the relationship I have with my dad is between us, *me and him,* and fuck everyone else.

The whole interaction put me on edge. I wasn't much help at the firm today, and I even volunteered to grab lunch for everyone. Nobody volunteers to be the gofer twice in one day. I needed out, though. I still do. I'm not in the mood for

McKenna Lowell's passive aggressive guilt trips. I went on four dates with her—I enjoyed zero of them. I did it as a favor to make people in my family happy. I did it for her dad, who is now my internship boss, which makes everything super uncomfortable and weird.

He and I actually hit it off first at a Welles alumni event. He thought I would be perfect for McKenna, or at least, he wanted me to be. But how do you tell a guy you respect that his daughter is high maintenance, a narcissist, and likes to make up rumors about other girls just to watch their social circles burn?

I tried to let her down gently with the whole "it's not you, it's me" thing, but when you've burned as many girls as she has, allies are hard to come by. Other than her immediate circle of friends, the rest of the Welles world leapt at the chance to pile it on. Which made her resentment of me skyrocket. Somehow, through it all, her dad still loved me. It's how I got this internship. My grades are mediocre compared to the others in my group, which is meaningless in the real world, in my opinion. I guess Karl Lowell agrees.

I text our political science teacher, Mr. Dax, that I won't need a ride back in the van then head in the direction of city hall. Brooklyn is always there late. She puts in the work, more than any other student at Welles. I hope all of the over-achieving gets her where she wants to go, but my jaded self has doubts.

"Well, would you look at that; it's Welles Boy Cam!"

I've met Cole once and the sound of his voice is forever etched into my memory, like a track laid on hot wax in my brain. My back to him still, I tuck my chin to bury my smirk, glad I'm not yet with Brooklyn. She doesn't need to see this side of me.

"What a pleasure. Harassed by a privileged wannabe

surfer cowboy twice in the same day!" I turn slowly to meet the expression I was expecting. His nostrils flare like a bull as he pushes up the sleeves on his oddly metallic-looking jacket.

"You're one to talk about privilege, Welles boy. That's a real smart mouth you've got on you, too. You learn that in school?" He's swaying on his feet, which triggers my instincts that he probably wants to fight. Nothing like throwing down outside Boston Common on a cold fall afternoon as the sun sets. Almost poetic. Perhaps I should be wearing cowboy boots too for our duel.

I breathe out a short laugh at his absurdity and my own amusing thoughts then run the back of my hand over my bottom lip, prepping my muscles just in case.

"Dude, you know zero about me. I'm sorry we had to meet, but Brooklyn's professional like that I guess. Probably best we pretend we didn't and move along, yeah?" Tongue tucked inside my cheek, held by my teeth, I size up his body language in an instant. My guess is he's had the same pining crush on Brooky that I have, only he's got zero shots and he knows it.

"Her dad meet you yet? He's a real hard ass about the company she keeps. Maybe I'll put in a good word for you." His smirk is fucking obnoxious, and for whatever reason, it's the thing that sets off my irrational side, not that I have much of a reasonable one to begin with.

"Yeah, all right," I say, spitting at the ground to my right as I cock my left arm and take a full-bodied swing at his jaw.

My punch, however, never lands. Fucking surfer cowboy dodges it then swats my arm away with his palm, completely throwing me off-balance as his knee comes up to nail me in the gut.

"Black belt. Among other things," he says, spitting on the pavement where my eyes are zeroing in on a few scurrying ants. I try to laugh out in disbelief that this is happening, but it's useless. He's knocked the wind from me.

"I'll be sure to mention to Mr. Bennett that Brooklyn's buddy Cam isn't much of a fighter," he says, his mouth way too close to my ear. I lift my head up in a jerk, smashing the back of my skull into what I think is his mouth. The bloody gash on his lip when I right my vision confirms it, and that laugh I've been waiting on finally makes it out of my mouth as he spits a little blood this time.

"Street fights and pick-up hockey, among other things," I say. My stomach is twitching from the impact, and I might throw up, but I have a few good swings left, if I need them.

"Hi, how you doin'?" I nod to a woman who passes us, veering out into the gutter to avoid us as best she can. I'm used to the glances I'm getting from people passing by. I do a lot of things that earn me these expressions—granted, usually it's a stunt or a dare I've taken on, like the time Theo said he'd give me twenty for climbing up and riding the Paul Revere horse statue by the Old North Church. I got an extra twenty for shouting "Ya!" while smacking its bronze ass.

I rush Cole the minute sidewalk traffic eases, grabbing his shoulders while I try to push him off balance. He wasn't kidding about that black belt thing, but he's also never fought a lunatic like me, which I use to my advantage, catching him off-balance with the help of a fire hydrant.

I'm celebrating his fall with a good belly laugh when he springs to his feet in a blink and throws a fist at my face so fast I see not just stars but literally the entire Milky Way. I spit on my feet and stumble toward the nearby wall, leaning into it for balance while I hold my sleeve to my nose and lip to test the bleeding. Dark red seeps into the material in seconds. I'm stunned, but also a little high from the rush.

"Tell Brooklyn I'll see her over Thanksgiving," Cole says.

I lift my head in time to see him straighten his own jacket. He limps as he walks away, but I'm clearly worse off.

I cough a few times, my lungs burning, and a rib maybe cracked. A younger man with a leather satchel tucked under one arm rushes to my side. He's clutching his phone.

"Hey, are you all right? I saw that, and I will be your witness. I took video," he says, pushing my arm around him so he can help me stand. I use him for balance for a few seconds before quietly laughing over the last few minutes of my life.

"I'm all right. I probably deserved that. But hey, can I have that video?" I say, reaching for his phone.

"Yeah, sure. But . . . you maybe want me to call the police? File a report."

"No, no. I'm fine. Really," I say as I punch in my number and send the video to my phone. I feel it buzz in my pocket, glad that my phone is still there and not lying cracked on the sidewalk.

"Thank you," I say, untangling from the good Samaritan. I hold out a hand for him to shake, but recoil when I see the blood on my knuckles. I nod at him instead and force myself to move along.

This is not how I wanted to apologize to Brooky. *Hey, sorry about my cave man behavior earlier. I made up for it with, well, more of the same.*

I could probably catch the train if I hurried, but the nearest station is right by city hall anyhow. Assuming she has to park at the bottom level, I take the garage stairwell down as low as it goes. Her Mercedes is one of maybe five vehicles left in the sub-basement level. I take a seat on one of the concrete stops near her vehicle, stretching my legs out slowly when I realize there's a rip in my right pant leg and the material has glued itself to my scraped-up knee.

I pull out my phone and find the text I sent to her

number during our drive in this morning. She replied after dropping me off with a thumbs up. That was all before the next nine hours unfolded. Hopefully I haven't been blocked.

ME: *I'm gonna need a ride home. Missed the van again.*

I read my words and decide that even the small lie is one more step in the wrong direction with her and delete

ME: *Can I hitch a ride home? Sorry.*

I pause on that last word and decide to delete that, too.

ME: *Can I bum a ride.*

A quiet laugh shakes my chest as I drop my phone in my lap after sending. If my hands, sleeves, and legs are any indication of what my face looks like, Brooklyn is going to walk up and find a horror show when she gets to her SUV.

My phone buzzes so I tap the screen in my lap.

BROOKY: *Admit I never kissed you. Then we'll talk.*

Ha. I stare at her stubborn words for a few seconds and shake my head, reaching into my jacket pocket on a prayer that there's a napkin or tissue in there. I feel the envelope for the gala, but nothing else. I pick my phone up to type.

ME: *Pretty sure I already did that, but one more time with feeling. No, Brook. We never kissed. When we do, you'll know.*

I hit send before overthinking this time, which is probably dumb, but I haven't exactly had a great day. I'm hoping she'll cut me some slack. My phone buzzes again, and I tap the screen to reveal a gif of some famous actress rolling her eyes.

ME: *Does this mean I can get a ride?*

BROOKY: *Fine. But you have to ride in the back. I'm mad at you.*

"Ha!" My laughter echoes around the empty garage floor.

ME: *Get in line, sweetheart. You may actually want to put down a towel . . . or plastic. And bring a few tissues with you. Or a roll of paper towels? I'll wait by your car.*

I pop on the camera app on my phone and reverse the

view to take a look at what I'm dealing with. The good news is the blood I thought was gushing out of my right nostril seems to have stopped, but it's still a crusty, crimson mess. And my lip is puffy as hell, plus there's a lot of bruising on my chin and cheek.

My phone buzzes in my hand and I swap out my image for Brooklyn's text.

BROOKY: *You just freaked me out. I'm on my way. With a roll of towels for . . .?*

I survey my body and chuckle lightly.

ME: *You'll see.*

I get to my feet and pocket my phone, doing my best to tidy up the mess that I am. I lick at my upper lip to test how it feels and taste the iron and salt over the plump surface. There isn't much to be done about that, so I go to work on my pants, dusting off dirt. I take my jacket off and fold it over my arm, hiding my jacked-up left hand before rolling my shoulders and stepping up to the large back window of Brooklyn's SUV. My reflection isn't half bad, but I think the devil might be in the details that you can't see in dim garage light and window tinting.

When I hear the garage door slam shut behind me, I turn slowly, hoping my appearance doesn't freak her out. She stops in her tracks when her gaze reaches my face, staring at me with an open mouth that shuts after a few seconds. Her head falls to the side slowly as her mouth forms a tight straight line. I hang my head because Brooklyn's not stupid, and she knows me well enough.

"Did you literally follow him from the café or was this a coincidence?" Her tone is wry.

"You say coincidence, but I would classify it as rather fortuitous," I respond.

"Damn it, Cam," she huffs, dropping her bag on the

ground at her feet after pulling out a roll of paper towels. She unwinds several feet of it, which makes me wonder if I look worse than I thought.

"I got it," I say, reaching to take the pieces from her. She jerks back and shoots me a stern look.

"Get in the car and let me take a look, you dumb idiot," she chastises with a slight rolling of her eyes. I smile in response, which basically confirms what she called me. I can't help it, though. She's cute when she's irritated.

I move to open the backseat door, figuring now that she's seen me, she's probably serious about putting me back there. Hell, I may end up in the cargo area.

"Don't be a martyr. Get in the front seat," she says. I let go of the back handle and move to the front, but she cuts me off, opening the door and sticking her arm out to block me from getting in.

"Give me your jacket," she commands.

I hand it to her, and she lays the inside on the seat before taking a step out of the way and holding an open palm out to welcome me in.

"I don't have any blankets or towels in here, and yeah . . . you're a mess."

I smile on the side of my face that isn't throbbing and slide into the seat.

"I'm glad you find this amusing. I'm the one who'll have to field the litany of questions my dad is going to have because, sadly, Cole's dad and mine really do talk all the time. And I'm sure by now Cole has turned this into an epic tale." She swats my hand away from my face, so I let her go to work on me without interference.

"I wish I could say you should see the other guy, but that raggedy-ass chump is scrappy." I wince when she touches my eyebrow. I didn't even know he hit me there. Maybe that was the ground.

"He's a black belt, and he went through some combat training thing. I don't know what it was called. But when you're an asshole like Cole you need to have tools to defend yourself." She retrieves her bag, bringing it to her car and setting it on the floor, pulling out a water bottle and a packet of Advil.

"I don't need that," I say, taking it from her hand and tossing it back in her bag.

"Lemme guess, you'll use the natural stuff?"

I shrug as she purses her lips to scold me.

"It works better. Just does," I say.

"Whatever," she grunts, pouring water from her bottle onto a folded paper towel. "Hold still."

She presses the makeshift compress against my eyelid, holding it there through the sting. She pulls it away and I see how pink it is from blood. I'm in worse shape than I thought. She repeats the process a few times, eventually getting to my busted lip.

"It's pretty bad, Cam. Coach is going to have questions," she says.

My lip twitches at her touch and she pauses, her fingertips hovering millimeters away from my skin as her eyes flit up to meet mine.

"I'll tell him I was defending a woman's honor," I say, my chest collapsing when her eyes soften, and her shoulders fall a tick.

"Is that what happened?"

I lick my bottom lip, a nervous habit that isn't great in this condition, and take a ragged breath. I can't lie to her.

"Not exactly," I admit, which brings all of the ire and resistance back to her expression.

"Nice, Cam. Real nice," she says, her stare suddenly cold. It breaks away and she focuses instead on my cheek and jaw, cleaning up my skin while her jaw flexes from holding in all of the words she probably wants to scream at me.

After a minute, I can't take the tension between us anymore, and I wrap her wrist in my hand, willing her to look me in the eyes again. Her arm flexes when she freezes, and her eyes narrow with the brewing storm behind them.

"This is all a bunch of grade school cafeteria drama, Cam. What is wrong with you?" She starts to back away, but I hold her hand in place, our eyes locked as I do my best to wordlessly express how sorry I am. When I feel her relax, I let go. She dabs at my lip again softly, and all I want to do is kiss her touch.

Her gaze skims my face, her mouth set in a disappointed frown, faint but there, as she purposely avoids direct eye contact again. I don't always think before I act. In fact, I rarely do. My mom says my impulsive nature comes from my dad. But I think even he thought through what he was doing when he walked into a bank as a barely legal adult with an unloaded gun and ski mask. He was thinking he had no other way out. He was young and in love and desperate to hold on to the fragments that made him fucking happy.

"You said you wanted pistachio," I say, my eyes unflinching as I wait for her gaze to meet mine. She stops moving, but she doesn't change her focus. Her lips part with a soft breath as her tongue peeks out. She bites the tip.

"What?" she whispers. I can tell. She remembers.

"Earlier, when I mentioned your thirteenth birthday party to your dad . . . I've been thinking about it all day. You had every ice cream flavor at the tip of your spoon, but you wanted pistachio." I lean back a little, laughing quietly at the memory. "You tried so hard to pretend you were happy. Shoveling spoonful after spoonful of mint and vanilla into your mouth."

Her lashes flutter as she looks down, the corner of her mouth twitching with the threat of a smile.

"You mashed up almonds and mixed them in coffee flavored ice cream as an alternative." She remembers . . . *almost.*

"They were cashews, but close," I say.

Her lashes flit like butterfly wings before she peers up at me and stops my heart.

"Why did you care so much? I was acting so entitled." Her brow draws in, denting her forehead.

I smirk.

"You weren't entitled. You were spoiled," I say.

She scoffs and looks out at the near-empty garage.

"Thanks," she grumbles.

I reach forward and brush my fingertips along her arm, and her gaze darts to the spot.

"You know why I did that?"

She shakes her head no.

"There are so many reasons—I didn't want your parents to cancel the party, I was curious what my concoction would taste like, and Theo dared me to see if I could make pistachio ice cream," I say.

"All very good reasons," she jokes. She leans against the door frame, just on the other side of my knee. If I had any guts I would pull her in front of me to stand between my legs so I can run my hands up her curves and push her hair back as I kiss her. I just got my ass kicked by a bleach-blond urban cowboy, though, so tonight I'm going to have to use my words.

"There are two other motivations that truly marked me," I say.

"Yeah? What are they?" Her head falls against the metal of the car, and I breathe a little easier knowing she's relaxing.

"You're not ready for one of them," I say.

Her eyes narrow as we have a mini stare-off.

"I think I know what I'm ready for," she says.

I breathe out a short laugh and smile on one side before shaking my head.

"Not tonight," I say.

"Fine. What's the other one?" she gripes.

I push my lips together, testing the pain, wishing I could chew on them a little before sharing something so big with her. I'm completely lucid right now—no pot in my system, no drinking, zero adrenalin. I'm about as flat as I've ever been and things in my life seem so clear. My gut is rarely wrong. I've always felt Brooky is the one I can trust. I need a person, and she doesn't have to see me the way I see her to hold my secrets. She only needs to understand them—to help me carry them a little.

"I've never had a birthday party."

She shifts, lifting her head from where it rests as her hands reach toward me tentatively. While I would love for her to touch me, that's not why I'm doing this. And if she does, I might stop my story there.

"No, it's okay. Really."

"Cam, it's not. How did I not know this? I'm such a shitty friend. I never put it together," she says.

"Friend," I mutter.

Her eyes move to mine, her brows pulled tight in question. I won't repeat that. It was a slip.

"My birthday's in June. But that's not why," I say, closing my mouth to take a deep breath through my nose. I bring my palms to my eyes and rock back, letting out a low growl. "Gah! This is hard."

"Cam," she says, her hand covering my bicep. I squeeze my eyes shut tighter. My chest burns and it feels like gravity is pulling me through the garage floor.

I shake my head with my eyes closed, refusing to chicken out. My story is safe with Brooky. I feel it.

"I don't have the kind of family you have, that Theo has or Morgan or James or . . . *fuck!* Anyone at Welles!" My lips feel numb as I speak, and I know it isn't from being punched. It's anxiety threatening to strangle me and knock me to the ground.

"Cam, nobody's family is normal. We're all messed up in our own way—"

I shake my head and cut her short.

"No. Uh uh. Not like me," I implore. I lean forward, pressing my forehead to my fists that rest on my knees, and Brooklyn's palm glides to my back. She rubs it slowly, her touch so goddamn soothing, so comforting. I bet her mom did this for her when she was sick as a kid. I would have given anything for this kind of affection.

Resolved to break free of these invisible chains that I've been trained to wear, the talking points I've been made to repeat, the boundaries set by myself, by my mom . . . my family, I lift my head and find her waiting gaze for comfort and strength. When it's there, I let go.

"Brooky, my dad . . . he's in prison."

She doesn't blink. Neither do I. Our gazes locked in this sudden shared reality, we simply sit in the humid chill of a basement garage far away from all the people I can't tell my story to.

"Since when? How? Why?" Her questions scatter from her mouth, and I offer a pathetic smile because I can't even answer them all.

"I'm not ready to share the why yet, if that's okay," I

admit. My heart feels dulled, like a tiny pebble beating deep inside. Everything seems muted, and I'm hot.

"Of course," Brooklyn says, moving her hand that has been on my shoulder this whole time. I turn to my right to look at it, and before she can pull it away, I cover it with mine.

"Please," I utter. Her touch sinks in and my head falls against both of our hands.

We stay in this quiet cocoon for nearly a minute before she solves the puzzle.

"Cole was going on and on about your dad, about his, and mine," she says.

I look up and give her a small nod. Her eyes gloss with sympathy, and while I didn't want to make her sad, it feels nice to see it. That's how I feel inside sometimes, but I can't seem to ever let any of it out.

"I hope you got a few good ones in," she finally says.

I smile on the side of my mouth that isn't busted up.

"I surprised him, I think." *He sure did surprise me.*

She nods then squeezes my shoulder once, slipping her hand away and gathering up the paper towels from the ground and floor of the car. I shift my body to sit in her passenger seat, and the entire way home, I feel lighter. I feel closer. I feel ready to tell her more.

Chapter 9

Brooklyn

I could smell Cameron's *herbal medicine* from the lawn below McKinley Hall. He and Theo are only one floor up, and Welles has a pretty strict policy about substances, especially after the accident last year. Theo keeps saying his room is immune to authority and inspections because it was his sister who died. For a while, I assumed he was making a fairly crude joke about it, but I'm beginning to realize he was simply being honest.

Class starts in thirty minutes, which doesn't necessarily mean Cameron Hass is awake. But I doubt it's Theo blowing that scent out into the courtyard. I wait for one of the McKinley boys to let me in on their way out then make my way to the far stairwell and up to Cameron's room.

Now that I'm standing outside his door with a blueberry muffin I bought at the mobile café near the library, I feel juvenile. I want him to know how much telling me about his dad meant to me. More than that, I want him to know he can trust me, that he can tell me more . . . if he wants to.

Faced with either turning around and eating the damn

muffin myself or knocking on his door, I form a fist and rap three times. I take a step back and hold the muffin box in both palms out in front of me like an offering. Cameron coughs on the other side of the door and I catch the sound of a fan being blasted on high. I suck in my lips to stifle my laugh but can't help but let it out when he opens the door and sees me, suddenly relaxing.

"Shit, I thought you were—" He closes his eyes and shakes his head, still shaken, and probably a little irritated that I'm laughing at him.

"Headmaster? No. I am the muffin man, however." I look down at the box and his eyes follow.

"Sweet Jesus, please say that's for me." He takes it from my grasp, assuming it is. I follow him into his room, which is littered with clothing and shoes and practice jerseys.

He's sitting on his bed wearing nothing but a white T-shirt and the famous Grinch boxer shorts. With his long legs folded up like a kid in circle time, he pops the lid on the muffin box and pulls a bite off with his fingers, shoveling it in his mouth.

"Oh, my God, this is amazing," he hums as he chews.

I laugh, enjoying seeing him so damn delighted over something so simple. I kick a cleat out of my way and toss a sweatshirt onto his bed from his desk chair so I can sit.

"Sorry it's messy. I wasn't expecting company," he mumbles, going in for another fistful. Crumbs fall down his chin and into his lap, and he brushes them away . . . *onto his bed.*

"No wonder nobody notices your weed. How could they smell anything over . . . this!" I wave both hands around the room.

"Hey, most of that is Theo," he says. I inventory both sides of the room and they seem about even to me.

"Sure," I say.

He coughs out a short laugh, more crumbs tumbling from his lips.

"How are you this morning? The . . . everything?" I point to my face and circle it.

Cameron discards the now empty muffin box to the side and kicks his legs out so they hang off his bed. He looks better than he did last night, but the bruising on his face is obvious.

"Everything's sore, but I've had worse," he says.

He stands and I avert my eyes, not wanting to catch anything *extra* in his boxers. I can't help but mentally unravel his answer to make it fit. How has he had worse? Did his father hit him?

"I thought you don't fall," I say, using his own assertion against him.

"Ha, yeah. I mean, I guess I *do* fall, but only when I'm expecting it. I was really into skateboarding for a while, and then I tried some of those BMX parks, flipping tricks and stuff." He glances at me and twirls a finger with one hand and tugs at his boxer short band with the other.

"Oh, uhm. Okay," I say, sweat instantly beading on my neck. I spin in his desk chair and put all of my attention on the doodles on his notebook. One of them looks like the game of hangman, and the answer is filled in as DUMBASS.

Why do I have a crush on this guy again?

The sound of zipping pants is followed up by the clanking of a belt buckle.

"Okay, all clear," Cameron announces.

Still, I turn cautiously.

"What, you think I'd trick you so I can flash you like some creep, Brooky?" He smirks and slips his arms into a white button-down.

I glare at him with tight lips.

"Why Brooky?"

He laughs as his hands work through the buttons, shutting down my view of his near perfect chest. He took a good beating from Cole, but looking at his ab muscles, the way they flex with every tiny movement he makes, I can't fathom how Cole walked away at all.

"Habit, I guess. I liked that it bothered you, but now I can't stop. I hope that's okay." He picks up a tie from the top of his dresser, the knot already made. I smile because that's kind of smart. All Welles ties look the same. Why start over every day?

"I don't think I have a choice," I answer.

He chuckles.

"Probably not." He reaches into his closet for his Welles jacket and sinks his arms into it before running his hands through his wild hair. I become fixated on the staticky pieces that simply won't obey.

"Here," I say, standing up and pulling my conditioning lotion from my bag. I put a small dollop in one palm and rub my hands together before lifting up on my toes to reach Cameron's hair.

"A little help?" I ask.

He tucks his chin and I sink my fingers into the silkiest sensation I've ever felt. I run my hands through his locks four or five times, wishing I had an excuse to do it more, and when I'm done, his wild strands are in order.

"Thanks," he says quietly.

He holds out an arm, I assume to escort me to our economics class, and I take it as he leads me out of his room and down the hall to the stairwell. I let go as we take the stairs and do my best to avoid him offering again. I'm not willing to face the rumor mill and gossip scrutiny of Welles right now. It's enough that Cameron and I are walking together into the same classroom he showed up in half-naked a couple of days before.

He gets hit with questions about his bruised face the moment we step into the room, and rather than shirk the attention away, he feeds it, showing off his busted knuckles next as he talks about some preppy boy who went all Cobra Kai on him. He never once says where it happened and he keeps Cole's name out of the story, I think maybe out of respect for me and not wanting to involve me in this growing story that will have turned into a major boxing match by the time lunch rolls around.

Watching the stress roll off him, I'm struck by how different he seems this morning. Everything about him is lighter than when he told me about his dad. The weight of his secret must be an awful burden. I wish I could make him feel more comfortable when talking to me about the heavy things. Maybe, with time, I can. There is so much I want to know.

Even though his confession was about his dad, I spent most of the night thinking about his mom, wondering how she fits into his complicated puzzle. I've met her once or twice, briefly, at Welles functions. She never stays long when she does show. Mostly, though, Cameron has marked his school milestones without family there to celebrate with him. He's said in passing that his mom is incredibly busy, her teaching schedule full, and maybe that's the case. I understand being the daughter of someone ambitious. My mom has found her own path in my father's shadow. She says philanthropy gives her purpose, but I do sometimes wonder if it fills the void of a rather one-sided marriage. My dad misses a lot of things. He missed my surgery. My recovery. My return to school.

Small sacrifices for the big picture, though. I believe in him. He has it in him to help a world that is hurting and in need. I hope I can learn to showcase that same leadership one day. I'm less of a spotlight dweller and more of a behind-the-curtain person so far, but I'm young. A lot of what my dad has can be learned.

Mr. Philips lets the hallway door fall shut with a bang, his favorite way to startle us all into our seats with our eyes on him.

"Mr. Hass, I see you decided to wear pants today. I think I speak for us all when I say *thank you.*" Our teacher pushes his glasses up his nose with the tip of his pen, not realizing that it's clicked with the ink out, not in. The result is a blue line on the bridge of his nose that progressively smears into a larger mark as he reads through the attendance sheet.

My phone buzzes in my bag, which is tucked between my feet, so I bend down and turn the screen so I can see it without being obvious.

CAM: *Someone should tell him.*

I smile and glance to my left to find Cameron's gaze waiting for me. He taps his pencil on his phone, which is sitting on his desk. I look back to the front of the room and contemplate bringing my phone out. It's against school policy, but also, I may be the only student who follows the rule. As a compromise, I bend down and slip the phone to my lap, camouflaging it in the plaid folds of my skirt.

ME: *You should tell him. You need brownie points.*

I glance toward him as he reads. When he's done, his head pops up and his eyes flash to me as his mouth forms a very clear but silent *no way* as he shakes his head. He returns his focus to his phone, tapping out a message with one finger.

CAM: *He'll send me to the office.*

I twist my lips in doubt and shake my head as I type a return message.

ME: *Why would he do that? It's the nice thing to do. I*

can't believe nobody else has. The man has a Smurf nose at this point.

Cameron chortles, quickly masking his laugh with a cough as he shifts in his seat.

CAM: *I don't see you raising your hand.*

I stare at his very valid point for a few long seconds. I'm not letting him know because if I do, it will be one more checkmark in so many people's books that I'm a kiss-ass. I hear it a lot, even if never directly. I follow rules, work hard, get recognition, volunteer for assignments, act as a group spokesperson—I'm the model Welles student. It's all I know to be. When you're a Bennett, your brand is perfection. I don't just meet expectations, I obliterate them. And yeah, given all of that, I probably should let Mr. Philips know his nose is covered in blue ink. But I'm also an eighteen-year-old girl in a school that thrives off judgement of others. I walk a very fine line between being a pretentious snob and simply being well-respected.

ME: *How about a bet.*

CAM: *Oh, you devil. You know I can't turn that down. Terms?*

ME: *You let him know his nose is inked. If he thanks you or simply cleans it up without any reprisal, I win. If he sends you to the office, you do. Loser has to get coffee for both your office and mine tomorrow.*

He chews at the end of his pen, his mouth curved into an intrigued smile while his teeth chomp at the pen's clicker. Finally, he flattens the pen on his desk and smirks as he types.

CAM: *Deal.*

Before I have time to respond, or even to react, his hand jets up and he sits forward in his desk, mouth quiet. Mr. Philips reads two names before glancing in Cameron's direction and seeing his call for help.

"Mr. Hass, whatever could it be?" he asks. I sink down slightly in my desk, suddenly not so confident that I'm right.

Cameron clears his throat but leans in, hands folded on top of his desk, heels crossed underneath.

"Sir, you have some ink on your nose. It's rather blue, and I thought you would want to know." That's it. A simple courtesy extended with respectful intent. This scene between any other two people might go my way, but this is Cameron Hass. And he was bloody right.

"I'll be sure to rush out to the teacher's lounge in search of a mirror, Mr. Hass. Why, thank you for this very unnecessary distraction. Perhaps you would get more out of spending this hour up front seeing what help Karen may need while you wait to talk to the headmaster." Mr. Philips hasn't moved from his spot since he called on Cameron, and he hasn't once touched his nose.

"Is this an optional suggestion?" Cameron says, glancing my way briefly and lifting his brows.

"It is not," Mr. Philips says, tearing a pink sheet from the small pad on his clipboard.

Cameron looks down at his desk with a tight smile, nodding—and laughing silently, though I think only I can tell. He gathers his things and steps to the front of the class, taking the pink slip without even making eye contact with our teacher.

"Thank you, sir," he says, prompting Mr. Philips to sigh and push his glasses up again, leaving another mark. The entire class rumbles with choked laughter, and as Cameron pushes his back into the door, his eyes meet mine, his mouth very clearly forming the word *mocha*.

My head falls to my desk with a thump as he slips through the door on his way to the office. *How did I get that one so wrong?*

"All right, history of the stock market. Let us first look at the East India Company in the sixteen hundreds," Mr. Philips begins.

My classmates shuffle papers around me. I grasp my phone to return it to my bag as I reach in for my notebook, but it buzzes before I let go. Glancing up, I scan to make sure Mr. Philips is still facing the white board. I assume it's Cameron texting me to gloat on his way to the headmaster's office. I pause when I see it's actually a message from my dad.

Pulling the phone up to my desk, I tap my father's message open and slide my phone under the shield of my notebook. My pulse fires away as my body rushes with anxious tingles, and I'm not certain whether I'm all of a sudden worried or scared. My dad is at a summit in Canada, and he doesn't divide his time to send me messages when he's working. Not unless it's something truly important. A death, maybe. Legal trouble? Something with mom or my brother?

I feel faint, so before my panic fully takes hold of my body, I bend the edge of my notebook and read my father's message.

DAD: *You and Cameron Hass cannot be connected.*

My heart drops. No beat. My skin feels sticky with instant flop sweats. My fingertip hovers over the keyboard to type back *why?* But I know I can't. He wouldn't answer that question anyhow, not in a text. And I know why. Because Cameron's dad is in prison, and my dad is running for Congress.

Chapter 10

Cameron

That bet I made with Brooklyn was almost unfair. Mr. Philips and I have a long history of me pushing his buttons just a little too far. It started my first day in the Welles cafeteria. He was the teacher on duty, and well, I had quite literally consumed my weight in orange-flavored Hi-C mixed with a dash of Sprite and Dr. Pepper. I started an unsanctioned game of tag in the lunchroom that resulted in several tossed trays of food and one Morgan Bentley with a lap covered in Yoo-hoo. It all culminated in me standing in front of Mr. Philips, awaiting my sentence, then suddenly vomiting a gallon of my soda-machine concoction onto his shoes. The self-serve drink dispenser was removed from the cafeteria by the end of the week, and Mr. Philips has had trust issues with me ever since.

I knew he wasn't over the boxer shorts ordeal. I could have coughed too loudly and gotten myself sent to the office.

When I texted Brooklyn before football practice and told her to meet me at the same trail as last time, I had a feeling she was relieved I wasn't messaging to delight in all the drinks she will have to carry up and down Congress Street tomorrow morning. She's not going to like my gift for her when she gets here, though. She might even throw a punch my way. I'll take it. This growing connection between us has been the one thing I look forward to when I wake up every morning. I started making mental notes throughout my day of stories to tell her whenever we're alone. And I'm also constantly searching for ways to be alone. There's something about her personal attention, of having her all to myself, that feels . . . special, I guess. It's more than the crush I've had for years. I feel a freedom when I'm with her, like it's okay to be myself and tell her things. I told her about my dad, and what shocked me is I didn't regret it at all. In fact, I'm dying to tell her more. I just wish she'd get here.

I leap down from the middle of the rock wall, my feet landing in a *thud* on the ground. My bag is packed with the harnesses as well as some spare clothes in case I can talk her into trying something else tonight. I pull my phone from my bag and check for missed messages, but there's nothing but the notice that she read my text about tonight.

She's fifteen minutes late, which is odd for her. Brooklyn Bennet has a schedule for everything. She even has one at parties, knowing exactly how long she'll stay out, how much she'll let herself drink, and what time she needs to be in bed to get up and be responsible in the morning. Maybe she forgot to text me that she couldn't come tonight.

Scratching my head, I start to type a message to her, asking if she's all right or wants to skip it tonight. I delete two attempts before finally dropping my phone in my bag and pacing in circles as I let out a growling sigh. I look desperate. Needy.

Because you are, dumbass.

"I'm sorry I'm late," she wheezes, breathing hard as her feet slow to a walk.

My chest expands as if I've been holding my breath for hours and am nearly dead. I practically bound over to her but stop myself short of picking her up and swinging her around in my arms.

Christ, Cameron. Get a grip!

"I was starting to worry you got lost," I lie. Sort of. I mean, that thought did cross my mind but only as an excuse to keep myself from believing she stood me up or is flat-out avoiding me.

Her chest heaving from her run, she threads her hands behind her neck and works to slow down her breathing before finally uttering "Family thing. Long story."

"Enough said," I say, glad she's here. "What do you think? Are you ready to do this?"

I bend down and pull out the gear then lift my head to meet her wide eyes.

"Or maybe we need to do some cardio?" I tease.

Her mouth twists and her eyes narrow. I think if she had something to throw at me right now, she would. But other than her phone and the shoes on her feet, she's accessory-free.

"I get nervous running in the dark, and it's colder tonight. I don't know how two days made that much difference, but it did," she says.

"Because it's October in New England. It gets wicked cold here, yeah?" I puff out a laugh that accentuates my point when my breath fogs.

"Okay, let's do this," she says, forming fists at her side and taking in two deep breaths to reset her heart rate. She'll be breathing hard again in ten minutes, but climbing is a different type of exertion. Being able to keep your heart rate steady while scaling takes time. Like earning a black belt. *Fuck that Cole guy. He still pisses me off.*

We get suited up and Brooklyn is finding her footing within minutes. She follows the same route as before, placing her hands in all the same places and using her legs to ascend, her upper body to steady herself. She clips the rope easily into the hooks, and we make it to the same spot as before in about half the time. She giggles when my hands wrap around her calves.

"Ticklish much?" I lean my head out to the side to catch a glimpse of her face. The moon is full tonight, lighting up her profile with a blue-silver glow. She flattens her check against the wall as her laughter grows more manic, her eyes squeezed shut. I'm not sure if she's smiling or weeping.

"Hey, are you all right?" I switch my hold on her right leg to a gentler, more tender touch, rubbing her muscle.

Her body shakes with her emotion for a few more seconds before she howls into the night air so loudly I'm a little worried people are going to come looking for us.

"Is that a yes?" I say through a breathy laugh.

She drops her chin, and our eyes meet.

"I can't believe I'm doing this. Thank you, Cameron. Just . . ."

She swallows hard and I move my hand along her calf again to comfort. To adore.

"*You* are doing this. Thank you for letting me be a part of it," I say, unable to stop my smile from spreading to both sides of my face.

I hold on to her gaze, wanting to lock down this moment for as long as I can, my touch on her leg light and tender, my thumb trailing behind my palm with the slightest lingering touch as I caress up and down.

"Higher?" I ask.

She nods emphatically, her eyes glistening as she smiles. "Yes. Higher, please."

I pat her leg and tighten my grip to brace her as she shifts her body to search for her next landing. She sees the same ridge as before, the one she slipped from, and without hesitation, she grabs hold, her right leg scaling the wall a second after, the left following when she quickly finds a nook. In seconds, she's risen another foot, hooked in the rope, and this time I'm the one to yell out, "Woot!"

"One more. Maybe two," she says. I can feel her muscle quivering under my touch, fatigue setting in.

"Don't overdo it," I preach.

"One more," she insists.

I spread my fingers to give her muscles as much support as I can then let her call the shots.

"Where to?" I ask.

"I think I need to use that crevice," she says, jerking her head up to point. I know the one. She's right, but it won't be easy.

"Okay, reach inside with your right hand first, then follow with your right foot. It seems counterintuitive, but it's the best way. I promise."

She nods and flattens her palm against the rock, inching it upward toward the two-inch gap above her head. When she finds it, she sucks in a hard breath, and I step up to cover more of her with my chest for reassurance.

"You've got this," I say. I'm merely reminding her. This is a new Brooklyn, one who believes she can.

"Will you hold my foot until I say?" Her voice wavers, but I still sense her determination.

"Of course."

I wrap one hand around her right ankle and wait until she decides it's time to move. I can tell by the way she's slowly sliding the toe of her shoe along the surface that she hasn't found a spot yet, and as much as I want her to see it on her own, I also want her to have this success. I nudge her, ever so slightly, hoping she doesn't realize, and when the hard rubber bottom of her shoe rubs against a sharp ridge, she nestles her foot in close.

"Now what?" She's panting hard. This is when the climbing makes or breaks you. It's about decisions and committing. And to an extent, you have to be all right with failure.

"Lean into it. To your right. Your leg is going to work hard, and if you feel uncomfortable, all you have to do is say *done* and I will leap down and catch you. But I don't think you're going to need me to, Brooky. You've got this."

She grunts as her body angles to the right, her left hand letting go of the comfortable ledge it had been gripping to join her right hand in the wide crack in front of her face. I remain right behind her, only touching her for support, letting her do this last step on her own. She lifts with her right leg, growling as she moves up the wall, now a good ten to twelve feet from the ground.

"Don't . . . call me . . . Brooky!" she shouts. Stretching her body into a stand, her back muscles waver with her lungs, her pulse beating so hard I feel it in her veins.

"Yeahhhhh!" I shout. I slap the wall next to her waist and a second later she slaps the wall by her face, her left hand clinging to the crevice to hold her against the surface.

"Oh, my God, Cameron! I can't believe I did this!"

I step up on the ridge just below her and rest my forehead on her shoulder blade, my mouth wanting so badly to kiss her. A small peck, a token of my praise, my friendship and affection. Instead, I breathe with her, chasing her rhythm.

"I'm so proud of you, Brooky," I say, causing a raspy laugh to break through her chest.

"Asshole," she teases.

I smile against her shoulder blade and inhale the lavender scent on her shirt. The tips of her hair tickle my nose as her ponytail hangs down the center of her back, and I jokingly blow it. She swivels her head to whip me with it a few times, and for a beat, I imagine wrapping it around my hand and holding her still so I can study her face and tease her mouth. That inconvenient thought hits my dick before I have a chance to tame it, so I step lower before Brooklyn's thigh becomes aware.

"I'll guide you down," I say.

"Can't I just fall like last time?" she laughs out.

"I mean, I don't recommend it."

I brace myself in case she isn't kidding.

Her hands retrace their paths, followed by each foot, and she grows more comfortable moving down the cliff face with each new grip. My feet hit the ground seconds before hers, and I'm not fully prepared when she spins and leaps at me, wrapping me up in a bundle of mildly-freaked-out-but-proud-yet-exhausted limbs.

"I did it," she says into the nook of my neck.

My palms flatten on her back, my mouth open in disbelief. I could carry her around for days like this.

"You did it," I say, mouth right at her ear. My lips buzz with temptation that I lick away as I slide my hands along her back, nearly doubling her up in my arms.

I walk her around in a slow circle, soaking up every last drop of her elation, her gratitude to me, however unearned and deserved I think it is. The metal clips from our harnesses clank against one another, and eventually she loosens her hold around my neck. I'm tempted to cling to her a little longer, but there's no way it wouldn't lead to trouble. I'm already praying my erection doesn't make contact as she slides down my body.

Our eyes lock for a breath, and her gaze moves to my lips next. Her tongue peeks out, tasting her lips before she sucks them in. My fingers curl in response, practically clawing against the fabric of her leggings and shirt as she cascades from my hold. When her feet hit the ground, she instantly turns away.

"Do you need me to help with the harness, or—"

"I got it," she says back fast.

I watch her fumble with the straps for a few seconds, but eventually she gets them to loosen and slips the gear down her legs. I take mine off and pile both sets together in my bag, pausing with my hands on the spare clothes I brought. I'm no longer sure this next part is such a good idea.

"What's up?" she questions after I've been kneeling with my hand in my gym bag for several awkward seconds.

"I wanted to have you try something else. But . . . I don't want to push you." *I don't want to get into trouble and cross a line you might regret, and I think talking you into putting on a pair of my shorts, which means you stripping in my presence, will literally catapult me over that boundary.*

"Maybe you could tell me what it is and let me decide?" Her head falls to the side as her eyes blink wide once and she makes a popping sound with her tongue against the top of her mouth.

Point made—she's a big girl. She can choose our fate. Honestly, it's so much easier to let her decide everything.

"Have you ever done a cold bath?"

Her brows shoot up to her hairline and she shakes with a single laugh before folding her arms over her chest.

"I am *not* bathing with you!" she protests.

"Uh, well, yeah. And . . . wow, hurtful," I say, oddly a little dejected by her insta-protest.

I toss my spare shorts to her and she catches them against her midriff.

"I meant in the stream. There's a really great spot that's an easy climb down, and you'd be surprised what natural water can do for sore muscles and healing." I sound like one of those woowoo freaks when I talk this way, but I swear this water has always done more for me than the training staff at Welles athletic department.

"Are you high right now?" she asks.

I laugh, but then pause and look off to the side to really consider her question. Huh. I'm actually not. I haven't smoked since this morning, which, sadly, is rare for me. I'm in the habit of bookending my academics with a little herbal help. I didn't even consider it this afternoon. I was too excited about *now*.

"I'm totally straight. But if you want," I tease, pretending I have a joint in my bag.

"Maybe next time." She laughs.

Brooklyn stretches my black workout shorts out in front of her, eyeing them.

"They're small on me. I don't wear them anymore, and I thought if you rolled them . . ."

"The size is fine," she says in a hushed tone. She chews at her top lip as her gaze skims the fabric.

"I won't watch you change. I promise," I say, crossing my heart.

She breathes out a faint laugh and flits her gaze to me.

"I know you wouldn't. I trust you," she says.

She trusts me.

"Is it . . . water? From the accident? I didn't even think. Brooky, I'm so sorry. This was a dumb idea." I reach for the shorts, but she hugs them to her chest, her eyes trained just below mine.

"It's not that. I promise. It's . . ." She squints and tightens her mouth, her sudden reluctance this palpable feeling that resonates with me. I was in her shoes merely twenty-four hours ago when I told her about my dad.

"Whatever it is, it's all right. You don't have to tell me. Unless you want to. And we don't have to do this . . . unless you want to."

"I don't show my skin," she blurts out. Her gaze darts to mine then flits away again as she mashes her lips together nervously.

"Brooklyn, you are beautiful. I've seen you in a bikini I'm pretty sure, and not to make you blush, but—*woo!*" I fan myself as her stare comes back to me. Her mouth inches up on one side for a split second before falling back to her chin.

"I'm not like I was," she confesses.

On instinct, I scan her body, following every perfect and beautiful angle from the tip of her nose down to her ankles and back up again.

"Brooky," I sigh. "You're perfect."

Her eyes soften, then scan to her left as her mouth twists in indecision.

"I swear I won't look. I won't even let my vision dip below your neck if you don't want it to." *Which will be hard because staring at every beautiful goddamn piece of her has been my silent pastime from afar for years.*

"Let me change," she squeaks out.

I turn my back to her.

"Really, Brooky. It's okay." I give her one more out, my gut suddenly swollen with guilt. She was on such a high. I feel like I crashed her.

"You're seriously never going to stop calling me that, are

you?" she says, easing my remorse a hair. It's so damn amazing to hear her laugh, to banter with her like this. To grow up with her.

"Not a chance," I admit. That's my name for her. It's *ours*. Even if she doesn't realize it. I made it, so the first time she protested—and knowing nobody else would dare use it—made it special. Made a tiny piece of her mine.

"Okay," she croaks.

Keeping my promise, I turn to face her, staring her right in her eyes. She reaches forward to hand me her leggings, which she's rolled into a ball that I tuck into my bag to keep from getting dirty. I hold out my hand when I stand, eyes still on hers, and she gives me her freezing fingers. The back of her hand is rough, likely scratched from climbing, and I graze it with my thumb.

"Looks like we match," I say, my knuckles individually wrapped in athletic tape.

"Ha. Hardly," she huffs.

I smile because she does.

I turn to lead, still holding her hand behind me as I guide us down the gentle slope. It's a small switchback covered in dry brush that turns to fine rock and sand. The bubbling sound of the water welcomes us.

"Are you okay taking off your shoes? I've walked around this water a million times. The rocks are smooth. Slick, actually. You'll want to tread carefully."

"Okay." She nods.

"Just, don't let go, okay?" she adds, gripping my hand tightly as she pulls off one shoe and sock then then other set.

"Never." My voice cracks at the word. Brooklyn swallows.

I kick my shoes off next to hers, and since I rarely bother with socks, I don't have to let go even now. I'll keep this promise, for the night. I'd keep it longer, but I don't think that's what she meant.

I walk backward into the shallow water, and Brooklyn reaches for my other hand. Our fingers interlock and I steady her as we toe our way into the stream, stopping at a wide, smooth rock that's not quite knee deep.

"Can you handle this?" I ask, unable to ignore her chattering teeth.

"It's New England, he says." She mocks my answer from before. We both laugh.

She nods and I bend down, steadying her as she lowers herself with me. I don't mean to look. And Brooklyn doesn't see me do it. I move my gaze to hers within a second, maybe less. But I see enough.

The scars are deep and jagged. The skin is pink and a muddied red where they cut her. Not every mark is from the surgery, and I can tell. Some of that was skin that tore in the accident. The damage was severe, leaving behind a massive permanent reminder on her body. This is what she hides from the world. She probably hides it from herself most of all.

Pushing what I saw to the back of my mind, I help her find her balance and finally sit with her legs stretched out next to mine. The freezing water cascades around us, hugging our skin and kneading our muscles. I keep my focus trained on her expression, holding my breath as she holds hers, coming to terms with the frigid temperature.

"Ho-holy sh-sh-shit," she stutters.

My head falls back with a laugh.

"New England's a real bitch, yeah."

She pulls her hand free for a second to swat at my arm but then quickly rejoins our hands. She doesn't need me, but I love that she thinks she does.

Her hand squeezes mine tightly, her body stiff and immobile while she exhales sharp pants that practically whistle their way out of her lips. After nearly a minute, her breathing slows. Her body is acclimating. I've always loved the rush of the instant cold on my skin, the way it attacks my stomach and kills my breath. It's like being reborn.

"How do you feel?" My eyes trace her profile, her lashes kissing her cheeks while her nervous system catches up. A trembling smile plays at her lips.

"Well, my legs aren't sore anymore. I can say that with certainty. Because . . . I can't feel anything from my belly button down," she laughs out. Her teeth knock together so I move closer, our thighs touching, and boldly put my arm around her.

"Give it five minutes. Can you handle five minutes?" I'm so close. It would be so easy for our lips to touch. I taste my bottom lip and her gaze dips to catch my involuntary movement.

She can read my thoughts.

"I can handle five minutes." Her voice is steadier, though breathy, as her gaze lifts back to mine.

I rub my palm along her arm to warm her, and her smile grows.

"Is this okay?" My goddamn tongue slips through my lips again. I catch the tip with my teeth, but it's too late. Her eyes are focused on my mouth.

"*Uh huh,*" she hums. Her lips part and a tiny cloud from her breath fills the slight space between us.

Focus on your hand, Cameron. Keep her warm. Remember her legs. Show her how to recover. Keep her from falling. Do not fall yourself.

I never fall.

Except with her.

"I'm really sorry about getting in a fight with Cole," I say, my shame screaming at me from inside. I feel like an idiot for letting him get to me like that. No matter what he said, I should have been able to keep my calm. Her dad and his dad are friends. I'm sure this is causing a problem for her, and if it hasn't yet, it probably will.

"Don't be. I told you, he's all asshole. I'm sorry he's a better fighter than he looks like he should be." Her gaze holds on to mine as we both quiver with a mixture of cold and laughter.

"He really is," I say, a slight shake of my head. I never let my gaze stray far. I'm too enraptured with her expression, with the focus of her eyes, her attention given to me. Her complete attention. *For me.*

"Hey, Brooky?" I swallow what feels like razor blades. The cold air dries my mouth, but nerves have zapped me completely.

"Yeah," she responds.

"You know how I said when we kiss, you'll know?" My brow draws in with a desperate yet hopeful dose of adrenaline. I bite my lower lip and stare at her mouth, praying for the right words to come out.

Instead of speaking, she nods, lips parting for her tongue to taste the cold pink skin.

"Would it be bad if I gave you a heads up when it's coming? Because I really want to kiss you right now. Like, a real kiss. None of that cheek bullshit."

Her mouth stretches into a teeth-baring smile as her body quivers with bashful laughter.

"I told you that one wasn't a real kiss," she says.

My focus trails from her mouth to her eyes. Her smile reaches them, her cheeks rounding and pushing up on the sides.

"Yeah, you did," I say.

I hold her stare for several silent seconds, both of us breathing ragged with the cold—*and the heat.*

She turns slightly and I move to allow her room to move closer, praying she will. Her hands reach toward me, grabbing fistfuls of my damp shirt as she leans into me, lifting herself onto her knees before swinging one leg over my lap.

My hand trails from her arm along her back and finally skimming up the curve of her neck and into her tied back hair. I weave my fingers through the strands, destroying her ponytail when my other hand follows suit, fingers curling against her scalp as she settles onto my lap.

"Brooky, you have no idea," I say, my eyes searching hers.

She pushes against my chest as she lifts herself to close any gap between us, and I break my promise, letting my gaze scan from her mouth down her neck, along the curve of her breasts to the place where she now sits on my hardon. I can't stop the stuttered breath that falls out of my mouth as she rocks against me. My hands abandon her hair and move to cradle her face, pulling her mouth to mine. Our mouths fit together as if they've found missing pieces, her plump bottom lip sinking between my teeth. I nip at her playfully, encouraged as her lips stretch into a coy smile.

"Brooky, huh?" she teases.

I nod and suck in her top lip, letting it go with a snap.

"You've always been Brooky," I say, running my thumb along her cheek as I lean back enough to see her angelic face. She's so soft, every curve of her. She's art; nature drawn to perfection. Her dark hair falls loose and frames her face, cascading over her shoulders, and I wish more than anything I could pull off her shirt so I could see whether her hair is long enough to reach her breasts.

I dare enough to move my hands to her shoulders, then arms. She lets go of her hold on my shirt and her hands drop to her thighs, allowing my touch to travel lower. My thumbs skim the hard peaks of her breasts, causing her to gasp. Her head falls back, exposing her neck. Her skin is pebbled from the cold, but it's so damn inviting to my mouth. I press long, needy kisses into it, dragging my lower lip over her chin until our mouths meet again.

Rocking into me again, she moves her hands to my hair, winding her fingers in and holding on as we kiss so hard I'm sure both of our lips will be raw by the time we leave this stream. My dick is so hard there is no way Brooklyn can ignore it. She swivels her hips, which only adds to the pressure, and I swell against her.

"Okay," I say, holding her face in my hands and pulling our lips apart for a bit.

Panting, our hot breath mixing in our intimate space, we sit on this precipice trying to decide where we go from here. This is already so far over the line I thought I'd never cross, and if she has any regrets from this night, it would kill me.

"I should get you out of this water," I say as her forehead falls to rest on mine.

She nods.

"Okay," she whispers.

Still, we don't move. I want to live out my fantasy, to wrap her hair in my fist and push up into her. I want to see her bare tits in the moonlight, her nipples so hard from the cold that the only way to warm them is with my mouth covering them. I want to sink into her and worship every inch of her body, especially the parts she feels she needs to hide.

But that can wait.

Yes, Cameron. You can wait.

My eyes flutter closed, and I shift my hands to her hips, tempted to pull her closer one last time. Instead, I lick my bottom lip and chuckle softly.

"I got a little carried away there. I apologize," I say, not sorry at all. Not one bit. I nudge her weight up and she lifts on her knees, finally taking my hands to get on her feet. Her leg in front of me, I consider for a second leaning forward and pressing my lips to her scars. But I promised her that I wouldn't even notice, and this small piece of magic deserves to remain untainted with any negative feelings. This, too, can wait.

"Don't apologize," she says as I get to my feet next to her. Her hands held in mine, I walk backward as she follows, her gaze darting from my eyes to the water at our feet. She's blushing. I don't need the light to know it. I see it in the way she sucks in her lip and tries to keep her smile in check.

"You said when we finally kissed, I'd know," she says, our feet finally on dry land.

A wet strand of hair has fallen over her eye and I move it behind her ear, the back of my hand hovering for a moment against her cheek. I run it along her jaw then stroke her mouth with the pad of my thumb. Her lips part with the sweetest exhale.

"I did," I say, again fighting temptation.

She swallows, her body shivering.

"That sure wasn't some of that on the cheek bullshit." She throws my words back at me and we both let out an airy laugh.

"Let me get you a sweatshirt," I say, moving my palms to her biceps. I rub up and down a few times then skip up the slope to my bag where I tucked my Welles Football sweatshirt after practice. She manages to scale her way up to me on her own. I help her slip into my sweatshirt then indulge in one final kiss before walking her back to her dorm.

I sense she's not ready to share our secret with others and I respect that, letting go of her hand when I feel her fingers itch to be loose. She says good night and turns to jog up the steps of Hayden Hall.

"Wait, I almost forgot," I say before she gets too far away.

She comes back down to the first step, her eyes scanning the empty campus around us. If anyone is out here tonight, it's likely Lily and Theo or Morgan and James sneaking off to the stupid library lair. I quickly reach into my bag, not wanting her to feel nervous, and pull out the folded list of coffee orders along with a crisp hundred-dollar bill. I hand it to her. She blinks at it a few times, finally unfolding the paper to read the various words:

Unsweet mocha, venti

Regular coffee, half almond milk

Carmel macchiato, large (2)

Medium coffee, four Splenda, two pumps of sugar-free vanilla

Pumpkin spice cold brew

Pumpkin spice hot brew

And about seven more orders. Her mouth hangs open as her gaze pops up to meet mine. I grin with closed lips and nod toward her losing bet in her hands.

"Maybe give me a lift in the morning again and we can negotiate whether or not I am willing to bend the betting rules to help you carry these."

She huffs out a hard laugh, and my lips twitch into a lopsided smile.

"Good night, Brooky."

I wink and turn my back to her, jogging across the main lawn to my dorm. My phone buzzes in my bag when I reach the steps, and I turn to see if she's still standing on hers. She's not, but the message on my phone is from her.

BROOKY: *Negotiation time. You help me with both*

*orders tomorrow, and I'll let you drag my ass into that cold
river to make out again.*

I smile at her words, my fingertip touching the raw spot
left behind on my lip. I knew that kiss would hurt in a
good way.

ME: *Fuck the river. I want you in my bed.*

I hit send before thinking it through, and my eyes widen
when it dawns on me how that sounds.

Shit!

I meant somewhere warm, like inside. And there aren't a
lot of places around here, and *shit, shit, shit.*

My phone buzzes and I squeeze my eyes shut, praying I
didn't ruin this night. Turns out, this night only gets better.

BROOKY: *Ok.*

Chapter 11

Brooklyn

I barely slept. Correction. I did not sleep.

My mind was on a continuous loop that swung from elation and swoon to panic and regret. It's that last one that hurts. That's the burning emotion that kept me awake. It's what has me lying in bed still this morning, long after my roommates have left.

Regret.

I don't want to regret kissing Cameron. So much of me doesn't. But that tiny voice, the one that echoes my father's request, scolds me. It says I messed up. It's a confusing barrage of thoughts battling for top honors, too. It's not fair to put Cameron in some category based on something his father did. It's also the way the world works. How the press works. How the other campaign works.

Walden Bennett Soft on Crime.

Walden Bennett Lets Daughter Date Convict's Son.

Walden Bennett Wants to Empty the Prisons.

I press my palms to my eyes and groan, ashamed of those thoughts even though they are exactly the types of headlines

I would expect—that my father was anticipating with his warning. No matter how unfounded the words are, they get used. Politics is mostly the dark side. It takes work to maintain the light. Even Walden Bennett sinks below the line from time to time, and I see how it weighs on him. It's trained him to see things coming, however. It's why he texted me what he did.

None of this is fair, and mostly to Cameron and his dad. I don't even know what his story is. And I haven't spoken to my dad since his message, which I didn't respond to. I'm operating on *what ifs* without any details, and I'm spiraling to the most negative places my mind will go. Meanwhile, one of the kindest boys I've ever known kissed me last night in a way that made my heart explode with happiness. And when he hinted that maybe we do more—*more kissing . . . and other things*—I said yes. I was swept up by it all. I was happy. Still am. It's buried, however, underneath all the shit.

Knowing I have to get my ass out to my car soon, I rock myself to a sitting position, expecting my legs to be sore. And they are. Only, not as badly as I expect.

"Son of bitch, that cold water works," I mutter to myself.

I ball my hands into fists and press along my thighs then grip at my knees and squeeze. My lower limbs are definitely fatigued, and the muscles hurt, but nothing like that first day after climbing.

I slip out of my sweatpants and Cameron's sweatshirt, which I bury under my pillow, not quite ready to give it back. I'm putting off the inevitable, perhaps, but sleeping in something of his felt nice. I want that option for one more night.

It's a good day to wear a sweater tunic, boots, and leggings. I complete the office casual ensemble with a messy bun then grab my tote bag and phone just as it buzzes with a message from Cameron.

CAM: *What's wrong? I should never be earlier than you.*

My stomach sinks. First with panic that I'm late and second at the reality I'm going to have to sort through in the next few minutes. I'm about to drive into the city with him. I'm going to spend extra time with him getting coffees. And then I will spend my entire day thinking about the time we'll be together on the ride home.

I want to be with him. I want to be excited about it. I want more kissing. But nobody wants us to go down this path. I can't even tell my friends about it because their opinion of him is so tainted. They see someone who isn't serious.

My chest burns with the threat of self-pity and gloom. I cut that feeling off fast, forcing a smile on my face as I snap a quick selfie and send it to Cameron with my message.

ME: *Heading out the door.*

CAM: *Beautiful.*

I stop upon reading his instant reply. Thing is, I think he means it.

My head conks on the door, just below the BTS poster Morgan put up when we moved in. I kick the bottom with my boot a few times, cursing under my breath. Shoving my phone into my bag, I give it one last check to make sure that the coffee order and hundred is still inside and head out with my key fob in my hand.

I press the remote start and unlock when I'm within range and Cameron is already sitting inside comfortably by the time I reach him. If it's even possible, he's somehow more adorable today. Maybe it's the post-kiss-bliss coloring my lenses, but I swear he put in extra effort today, unlike me. Black pants, crisp white shirt, skinny black tie, and suspenders—he looks ready for a charity auction where *he* is on the docket. He pulls one foot up when I open my door, resting it on the dash, and I smirk at his Mickey Mouse socks and white Vans.

"I'd tease you about being a little liberal with the whole *office casual* thing, but you had me at Mickey." I hold a hand over my heart and tilt my head, temporarily forgetting all of the turmoil that dooms us.

Crooked smile. Wink. *Sunk.*

Five minutes late to the freeway and the traffic into the city is a whole different environment. I hate being late, and I'm terrible at hiding my stress. After the fourth lane change and twenty minutes of sitting as close as possible to the steering wheel, Cameron calls me on it.

"I'm gonna suggest you skip the coffee today," he says.

"Why?" I ask.

He simply nods toward my hand, which is beating the top of the steering wheel with the speed and force of the drummer in a metal band. I halt it immediately.

"Oh."

"Yeah," he says through a soft chuckle. His foot still on the dash, he's practically lounging in the passenger seat without a care.

"We're going to be late," I shrill.

His laughter picks up and he holds out his open palms.

"And?"

I glare at him with wide eyes for a second then look back at the bumper-to-bumper traffic ahead of me.

"And that's not professional," I explain. "Cameron, I work at the mayor's office. This is important to me. Maybe your internship doesn't mean anything to you, but mine—"

"Stop there. You are going to say something you'll later regret, and I don't want regrets near us. Regrets are dangerous."

His sudden serious tone pulls me out of my manic state,

and my mouth snaps shut as I glance between him and the red taillights glowing in front of me. Cameron shifts in his seat, both feet now on the floor, his elbow on the passenger windowsill, thumbnail between his front teeth.

It starts to rain. My wiper blades automatically clear the window, the first few passes rough screeches against the glass. My instinct to panic threatens to boil over again, knowing this will put us even further behind, but I stop myself, instead looking to my right where Cameron stares out the window.

Without realizing what I'm doing, my hand reaches across the console toward him, my movement enough to catch his attention. His hand meets mine in the middle, fingers grazing over my palm until we're locked together. The softest smile hits his lips, which prompts one of my own. I'm in this now. No regrets.

Cameron pleaded for me to drop him off at the coffee shop and do one lap around the block. By the time I got back, he had secured both of our orders, which required quite the feat in drink-holder construction. I'm not even sure how he managed to work the cardboard boxes into something that held a dozen drinks each, but he nestled the orders heading to my office on the passenger floor and insisted I head in while he walked to his building.

I still feel guilty about it, but the cheers from my office-mates for bringing in their usuals without being asked, sparing them a walk in the rain, seems to have made showing up thirty minutes late a non-issue.

Despite my insistence that nobody pay me, everyone does. When I'm finally settled at my desk, I sort through the random bills in my purse and send Cameron an e-payment. To be funny, I tag it with a note that says it's for the strip club, then slide my phone to the side when Chuck walks up with a notepad covered in the mayor's awful handwriting.

"What do you have there?" I say, sitting up tall to peek at my next task. He sets the notepad down by my phone and sighs.

"I swear you can never leave this office because you are the only person who can decipher these puzzles. She wants us to find some images in the archives. I think this one says POTATO?" He pulls his glasses down his nose and bends over trying to get a different read on the scratched letters.

I squint at the word.

"Podium. That definitely says podium." I smile up at him as he chuckles.

"I guess that makes a lot more sense. I was trying to recall some union speech or a trip to Iowa—"

"It's Idaho. Idaho is the potato one. Iowa is corn."

He smirks.

"Mind decoding her messages and then pulling together a shot or two for each?" he asks.

I salute him just as my phone buzzes between us. My text screen still open, there's no preview setting to cut off Cameron's words.

CAM: *It's going to cost you more than $47 to get me naked.*

My eyebrows shoot up as I slap my palm over my phone and literally sweep it into my purse on the floor below. My gaze shoots up to check Chuck's expression, which is highlighted by red cheeks and wide eyes. He clears his throat, eyes still fixed on the spot where my phone just was. I wish I could make myself tiny so I could dive into my purse and hide there with my phone.

"That was . . . he was joking," I stammer.

My eyes flutter shut as I spread my fingers wide as I cover my face with my hand. I want to die. I'm sure it's only a few seconds of quiet, awkward lingering, but it feels as if he's been standing here at my side for an hour.

"That's good," he finally says.

I nod, still shading my eyes, unable to drop my hand until he walks away.

"I mean, forty-seven is the going market rate," Chuck says over his shoulder. I catch the snorted laugh that pops from his chest before he gets to his office.

My head falls down to my desk, my gaze darting to the glowing phone screen in my purse. I pull it out and hold it in my lap while I remain crouched over to ensure nobody ever sees a message on my phone screen again. I type fast.

ME: *My boss just saw that.*

The dots that show his typing lasts for almost a minute until finally I'm hit with a gif after gif of comedic male strippers. The last one is my favorite. I recognize that skit from *Saturday Night Live.* My dad says it was a classic with Chris Farley and Patrick Swayze.

CAM: *Really, though. Sorry. Forgive me.*

My chest fires up at the sweetness he displays. Our morning didn't start off so great, mostly due to my issues. And yet he's still here, still trying at whatever this is he and I are beginning.

ME: *No. Forgive me.*

I send that message off and wait a minute to see if he responds. I can tell he read my message, and that's enough. I put my phone away again and go to work on the mayor's mystery list. It takes me most of the afternoon, including working through my lunch thanks to a sandwich at my desk, but by the time I leave the office, I've pulled together sixty images that I think hit the mark.

My mood during our drive home is a full one-eighty from what it was in the morning, and in reaction, so is Cam's. Part of that is from feeling accomplished for the day. I respond well to praise, and Chuck seemed genuinely relieved when I handed over a rewritten list of images with each search term checked off.

But mostly, I was excited to see Cam again.

Cam.

I decide I like saying his name that way, and if he gets to call me Brooky, I deserve a little leeway to make up a nickname of my choosing.

"How was your day, *Cam?*" I try it out.

"My day was splendid. And how was yours, Brooky?" His right brow raises as he turns to face me head on from the passenger seat. I glance from the roadway to him a few times before laughing.

"It doesn't even bother you in the slightest, does it," I say.

"Nope. I love that you have a pet name for me. Granted, pretty much everyone I know calls me Cam, so really, saying my full name is what's different." He shrugs before settling back into his seat and propping his foot up on my dash like he did this morning.

"Gah! Okay, I'm going to come up with something else then. But I like Cam. So I'm going to use it."

"Cam likes Brooky," he throws back.

My lips pucker into a bashful smile as I keep my focus on the road. He likes me, which . . . *duh.* But how cute are those words? Hearing our names together like that, playful and flirty and connected, makes me feel warm inside.

"Hey, seriously for a minute." I glance to his shoe and his cartoon socks. "How do you pull off this outfit at a law firm?"

Cameron lifts his pant leg up a few inches and admires the tiny, famous, red, and yellow mice on his sock.

"It was a basement day. I knew it going in, and they said to wear comfortable shoes." He wiggles the toe of his sneaker.

"What's a basement day?" My stomach tightens remembering how I insinuated his internship wasn't important this morning. I hope he doesn't think I'm questioning the value now.

"Well, it's a day . . . that me . . . and others at the firm . . . spend in the—"

My brow pulls in and I grimace at him. "Basement day. Clever. Got it."

He laughs, so damn proud of himself for teasing me.

"Seriously, Cam. I want to know what kinds of things you do."

He clears his throat and drops his foot to the floor.

"Okay, well, basically, I work with a lot of the paralegals and aides all day pulling together research and collating papers. Sometimes it's really boring stuff, like today. One of the attorneys is working on a tax case and she needed about forty different files from the boxes in the basement."

"Ah, *basement day,*" I say.

"Exactly," he says. "Me and two of the aides lugged boxes up and down the elevator all day while a team spread them out in the conference room in search of the perfect documents."

"Sounds frustrating," I admit.

Cameron's head wiggles side to side in response.

"A little. Mostly because this would be so much easier if some of the older partners would get with technology and have their files converted to digital. They're old school, though."

I think about my father and how that description fits him, too.

"My dad has every speech he's ever made saved in spiral notebooks. They are all labeled and in this massive file

cabinet in his office at home. Of course, they are spiral notebooks, so those labels . . ."

"Can't be read on a spine," Cameron says with a laugh,
following my drift.

"It drives my mom crazy because he's always asking her
to find one of them so he can pull out a quote or make sure he
isn't repeating himself. The last real argument my parents
had ended when my mom threatened to drop a match in one
of the metal cabinet drawers."

Cameron's mouth forms an O.

"Okay, good to know the Bennett women mean business." He scoots closer to the passenger door and forms a
cross with his fingers as if I'm a vampire.

The easy flow between us is as smooth as the traffic out of
the city. Everything that felt wrong when I woke up seems so
irrelevant now. The only sense of doom remaining is that text
my father sent, and I decide to handle it frankly with him. I
won't go in unprepared. I've been taught politics well, and it's
important to have talking points for debate. I can only specu-
late on my father's disapproval of me having a relationship
with Cameron, but I have a good sense for the things that
concern him, and I'm sure everything centers on his dad's
incarceration. The one bridge I will have to cross that might
be hard is with Cameron. I'll need to warn him that his father
will be brought up—in debates, in mudslinging articles, on
social media.

It hits me all of a sudden. The realization so hard and fast
that my body tingles with anxiety, my pulse racing as sweat
beads on the back of my neck. What if Cameron decides
being with me isn't worth it?

That thought sits heavy with me throughout the end of
our drive home. I do my best to keep up the façade, but I fear
my fake smiles are pretty transparent. To add to my worry,

campus is buzzing with people when I pull into the parking lot. It hailed recently, which left a layer of crystal-like ice on the main lawn and several people are out pretending it's snow. Cameron's smiling as he looks on through my windshield, the carefree kid that is always close to his surface probably dying to run out and slide along the slick grass with his bare chest. I can't ruin that.

He exits my car and I snag my bag from the back seat then join him. He's waiting a few steps in front of my SUV, and I'm paralyzed. My hand itches for his. My fingers literally stretch with want at my side before I ball them into a fist. No longer able to mask my thoughts, I blurt them out before Cameron turns around to read my face.

"My dad doesn't want me connected with you."

I cup my mouth with both hands. Cameron remains perfectly still in front of me, his black tie blowing over his shoulder, his hair wild in the wind. I'm so ashamed. I'm not even sure what embarrasses me most. That my father's opinion matters. That my father's opinion is what it is. That I would even suggest that his circumstances are something to be hidden—erased. What's worse is it's clear that's what he's been forced to feel. Otherwise, we all would know his story. *His complete story.*

Cameron is so beautiful. His sleeves rolled to just below his elbows, his forearms defined, every inch of him flexes in reaction to my words. All I want to do is step up behind him and wrap my hands around his chest, pressing my face to his broad back while I inhale his scent. He's whiskey and cinnamon, but the rarest kinds. I would never be able to match his formula, even with all the ingredients in the world.

Cameron's head turns, his eyes not quite reaching me as he drops his hands in his pockets. His mouth opens, his breath fog in the air. My eyes are trained on his lips. My fingertips linger on my own as I hold on to the memory of how they felt.

"Thank you for the ride, Brooklyn."

He doesn't wait for a response. I wouldn't have one for him now, anyhow. Not the right one. I would be blinded by this aching desire I have to be with him, to feel safe in his arms. I've only felt beautiful twice since the accident ripped so much away from me. The first time was when we kissed, and I know he saw my scars but kissed me anyway. The second was when he told me as much this morning. I won't dare ask what he thinks of me now.

Chapter 12

Brooklyn

I t's only Lily in our room when I enter. I'm relieved. Morgan and I haven't found our footing again since she not-so-subtly told me Cameron wasn't good enough. It's this common theme from those I love the most—first her, then my father. I won't ask for Lily's opinion. She'd be as wrong as they are.

As wrong as I was.

"The T smells when it rains. Did you know that?" Lily is stripping from her internship clothes into a giant T-shirt, and I envy her for not feeling she has to hide as she does.

"No, does it?" I set my bag on the chair by my desk and pull my boots from my feet. The bottoms are damp from tromping across the wet walkways, but I hug them anyhow.

"It does. I think it's because everyone is wearing so many layers, and then those layers are wet, and we're all packed in this metal box on rails. I still feel like I smell like it. I know this is weird but smell my hair." She marches over to me and holds a lock of her damp hair toward me. I hesitate but sniff for her because Lily is sweet, and she saved me.

"It smells like rain, maybe." My shoulders lift with my half-hearted response.

"Are you all right?" she asks, dropping her hair and taking my boots from my chest. I was starting to cradle them.

"I'm okay," I lie. While Lily sets my boots on the floor at the foot of my bed, I step into the closet and shut the door enough to hide me from her view. I slide my leggings off then run my hand over the length of my leg. My knee hurts. The doctors told me the winter would be hard. Metal screws and winter.

I tug my tunic over my head and lay it on top of my laundry basket then spin so I'm facing the back of the closet door. My hand flattens against the wood. What if I open the door more, walk across the room like my roommates do, in their undergarments? Last year I would have without a second thought. With my eyes closed, I push the door slowly, feeling the light seep in through my eyelids. A rapid knock on our door has me shutting myself in completely.

"Sorry, I meant to tell you Theo is coming over," Lily says on the other side of the door.

"It's fine." Another lie.

Lily and Theo are perfect together. Truly. But they are also newly in love, and even if they are in here together to study, they're also . . . not. This room could be crowded yet somehow those two would feel completely alone. Intimate, really.

I hurry into my sweatpants and my Bruins jersey, shoving my feet into my gym shoes before bursting out of the closet to be greeted by Theo.

"Hey, look who's here!" He feigns surprise, which is mildly amusing. I like Theo. I like him even more now that he's worked through some of his issues.

He nestles into the corner of Lily's bed, tossing his backpack to the floor, and I get the distinct impression that very little studying is on the agenda. Good thing I have an econ project to prepare for as a distraction. Of course, I'm not staying in this room to study. And I don't think Lily and Theo want that either.

"I'll be out of here in a minute. I just need to get my stuff together. I shovel books into my backpack, and when my roommate and her boyfriend aren't looking, I stuff in Cameron's sweatshirt too. If I'm going to hole up in the study lounge for three hours I may as well feel warm in a way only Cameron's things can make me feel.

"You don't have to go," Lily says half-heartedly. Theo nuzzles at her neck, whispering something that makes her giggle.

"Oh, I'm pretty sure I do," I tease—*not tease*. "It's fine. I have a lot of studying to do."

I adjust my backpack over my shoulder and do one final check of my desk to make sure I have everything.

"Hey, you know what?" Theo moves toward me, reaching into his pocket. He pulls out a key on a small ring with a leather pad then reaches for my hand.

"I'm not going to your place," I announce. My insistence makes both of them flinch a tick, but thankfully they don't pry.

"Good thing this is the library key, then." Theo arches a brow and takes my hand in his, opening it and pushing the key in my palm.

"So, this is the key to . . ."

"The lair. Yes, that's the key to the fucking lair. You guys are never going to let that go, are you?" He steps back until his legs hit Lily's bed and he flops down next to where she's sitting while she and I laugh at his expense.

Cameron labeled the lower-level archive space that Theo

discovered the Lair mostly to fuck with his friend. We've been meeting in there for underground parties for the past two months, but James and Theo are the only ones with keys. That makes this gesture rather special, in a super high-brow snobby way.

"Thanks," I say, squeezing the key, grateful to have a quiet place to hide for a while. Maybe I'll finally be able to think. I need to study, but I'll never be able to crack open my books and pay attention if I don't come to terms with my feelings for Cameron and what battles I'm willing to take on to embrace them.

I leave Lily and Theo behind, a little envious of the place they are at right now. The ease of it. I crave the kind of comfort they have. I feel that way when I'm with Cameron. *Easy.* Even through the noise that comes with being a Bennett, the world stops moving so fast when he and I are together. He's been grounding me for years now that I look back on it. All the way back to the damn fake pistachio ice cream.

The main lawn is empty as I trek along the pathway toward the library, a light mist lingering after the rains. The hail has turned to ice in many places, so I'm cautious where I step. The light is out near the indiscreet side door Theo discovered, so I have to feel for the lock under the dry vines and brush. Theo is adamant about recovering the door anytime we leave this place because he doesn't want to draw attention to the door. I'm pretty sure everyone important at Welles knows this door is here. They just never assumed young adults would find a rarely used storage area and archive room appealing. Turns out, this place is the perfect spot to hijack bottles of alumni whiskey and be young and free.

And somehow, without a key, Cameron Hass has

managed to get inside. I lean back against the door I just stepped through, pushing it closed so I can stare at him from across the room. I'm somehow not surprised to see him here, and I wonder if that's because I wished for it.

"Of course, he gave you a key," Cameron says.

He holds up a tumbler half-filled with amber liquid as a toast to me. The Jameson bottle sits open on the desk he's sitting on top of. His suspenders hang loose at his sides and his white shirt is unbuttoned despite the black tie still dangling from his neck. He holds the glass to his lips and winks once before tilting his head back and swallowing half of its contents.

"How did you get in here?" It's the last question on my mind, but the only one I'm brave enough to ask.

Cameron breathes out a quiet laugh then turns his head and nods toward a long, skinny horizontal window by the oversized document scanner in the back corner.

"It's been open for years. I like to let Theo think he's special, though." His gaze returns to me as he offers a short-lived crooked smile.

Sliding the whiskey bottle along the desk, he stops when it clanks against the side of an empty glass.

"Can I offer you a drink? Or would that be taboo? There could be hidden cameras in here filming us." He lifts a brow, and his expression teeters between hurt and cruelty. I feel the impact of both, my chest tightening as my pulse starts to race.

"Cameron—"

He holds up an open palm to stop me, letting go of the whiskey with his other hand so he can pinch his brow.

"Don't. That was harsh and I'm sorry."

He hooks his thumb in his necktie and tugs until it loosens enough for him to pull over his head and toss it on the desk next to him. He leans back on his palms, his eyes hazed from the buzz but his gaze able to hold on to mine. I take a step toward him, letting my backpack slide from my shoulder to my wrist so I can leave it on the floor.

"My dad met my mom at a party at the old barn."

I stop moving as he speaks, not wanting to do anything to threaten this glimpse he's allowing me.

"My mom went here, which maybe you knew. Maybe not. She was the Welles golden girl, with perfect grades and offers from every Ivy League out there. My dad—his name is Michael—dropped out of high school when he was sixteen. He went to Public, in the city, on the southside. His mom, my grandmother I guess, was a single parent. His dad left right after he was born. Longshoreman with a real love for women and drink."

Cameron's lip puffs out with a tiny laugh as he looks to his side and taps his fingers against the side of the whiskey bottle.

"You aren't the same," I say.

His eyes meet mine again, his mouth pulled in tight as he leans his head to one side in doubt.

"Maybe," he relents.

His gaze drifts lower, so I step closer, taking a seat in one of the leather chairs about a dozen feet away. I pull my legs in, hugging them to my body, and rest my chin on top, desperate for more of his story.

"What was your dad doing at the party?" I ask.

He smirks, nodding at the ground.

"Prowling for women, like his old man," he says through an oddly fond chuckle. "He had no idea what he was getting into with her, though. One of his friends had heard about these rich girls who liked to get wild and crazy in the woods. My mom was one of them. It's hard for me to imagine her that way because the woman I've always known seems to repel fun and joy. She's serious and driven."

"You're serious, too," I try to encourage.

He lifts his head with a laugh.

"Thanks, Brooky, but I'm not the apple from my mom's tree. And I'm fine with that," he says.

Brooky. My lungs expand with new life hearing him call me that. He's not angry. He is, however, hurt.

"My mom and dad somehow had this magic connection, as he tells it. They fell in love hard and fast, and my dad would ride his motorcycle out this way to see her every chance he got. And *shocker!* They had sex and conceived me." He flattens his palm on his bare chest, which draws my eyes to his toned muscles. My gaze lingers longer than it should, but I indulge as he continues to share.

"My mom's parents are rather conservative, and they were not too keen on her life veering off their perfect little roadmap. They forbade her from seeing him. You probably know as well as anyone how well that works." He lifts a brow, his eyes boring into mine, making his point. I tuck my chin tighter against my knees.

"They were going to run away. They just needed the means to survive, and my dad . . ." Cameron's head falls back and his eyes close as he quietly laughs. "Oh man, Dad. You're tough, but a real dumbass."

"What happened," I croak.

Cameron stares at the ceiling for several long seconds, his jaw working as he chews at the inside of his cheek. Shaking his head and righting his gaze to mine, he draws in a deep breath through his nose, his mouth a perfectly straight line.

"He offered to do one job with his buddies, the same ones who took him to that party at the barn. They were robbing this old bank in Quincy, and they swore to my dad they did their homework, cased it and all that shit."

He rolls his eyes and shakes his head.

"My dad's gun wasn't even loaded. He was there to stuff cash in a bag and run. The place was crawling with under-covers, though. And his so-called friend? He shot one of them."

He stares at me, and I force myself not to look away. I press my lips into my knees to keep myself from speaking. I'm broken for him.

"He's served eighteen years and has been a model pris-oner. He was up for parole a couple years ago. He's got another shot soon, maybe in a few months."

"That's why you're studying law," I piece together.

He nods slightly, blinking his gaze away from mine to look down at his lap. My fingers itch to touch him. His life story is nothing like I pictured. Most of the students here see this daredevil who has money to bail his ass out. And sure, maybe his mom and grandparents can and do give him that privilege. But that's not what he wants. He wants his dad.

"What's he like? Your dad." I shift in my chair, letting one leg fall but clinging to the other.

Cameron chuckles as his eyes scan the room, almost as if he's collecting stories to tell. His focus stops on my chest, and I look down when he nods at my Bruins jersey.

"Hockey fan?" I ask.

Cameron punches out a sharp laugh.

"*Huge* fan. He'd like you," he says. Our eyes connect briefly, and I feel this falling sensation, as though we've just crested the top of a rollercoaster.

"Have you told him about me?" I can't believe I'm brave enough to ask.

His mouth curves as he glances down, pulling his hands into his lap to fidget his fingers.

"He's heard a story or two," he says with a nod.

I fall more.

I'm unable to pull my gaze away from him, his expression morphing from amused to tortured in a span of seconds as I assume his searches through years of memories—memories that are probably nothing more than stories his father told him over the phone, in letters, or at visits. His hands move to the edge of the desk, and he grips the side, his forearms flexing as he leans forward before popping his head up to look me directly in the eyes.

"What are you still doing here, Brooky? What are *we* doing here?"

My breath pauses at his question. The falling sensation no longer pulls my body down; I've landed at the bottom. This is as far as I go. I've fallen completely, and no matter what Cameron Hass says, he falls, too.

"I don't think I could bear it, Cam. I'm so afraid of leaving this room, of listening to my father, and never feeling like this again. You make me feel like everything is okay. You make me feel beautiful. I'm not some prize to be gained, or some strategic relationship to foster for political gain. With you, I'm just . . . I'm just Brooky." A half-laugh-half-cry gurgles from my mouth. Cameron slides from the desktop to stand in front of me, his shirt open, waiting for my hands to slide around his sides. His warmth waiting to embrace me. His mouth there for the taking. His heart . . . his heart bared along with his soul. He told me things he's never told anyone.

"I don't care what my dad says, Cameron. I can't *not*. I need you. And I'm so fucking afraid of never feeling any of those things again."

"So, don't," he says.

I shake my head, not sure what he's offering.

"Don't listen to your dad. You don't have to give up any of it. Brooky, I have been in love with you since you showed up in knee-high socks and a rolling leather suitcase alongside so many nannies and staff it's as if you were born to have secret service detail." His laugh spills out nervously and I bite my lip, trying not to cry.

"It's really sweet that you think I'm the one who makes you feel beautiful, but I've got nothing to do with it."

He takes a slow step toward me, followed by another.

"You're just beautiful. All on your own. Simply existing. And while damn, Brooky, am I a lucky man able to admire you, that admiration has nothing to do with what makes you beautiful."

He continues to move toward me until we're inches apart, and he places a palm on the side of my face. I lean into his touch as his other hand brushes my hair behind my ear. My hands grab hold of his open shirt, holding on and urging him close enough for my chin to touch the center of his chest. His hands cup my cheeks and I'm completely shaded by him, peering up into his warm mahogany eyes.

Drawing my lips toward his, his eyes hold on to mine until the last possible second and we're too close to focus. His mouth covers mine, suckling my bottom lip until I feel the sharp graze of his teeth. A soft moan slips from deep inside me without my control, which seems to speak to Cameron's most basic needs and wants. His kiss grows hungrier, and I grow bolder, allowing my hands to explore every disciplined muscle along his stomach, sides, and back. I've admired this body so many times but getting to touch it is entirely different. What seems smooth and soft is so hard and warm. And knowing how easily he could lift me over his shoulder and run away with me brings an amused smile to my lips that he must feel.

"Do I kiss funny?" he whispers against my lips, a smile stretching his own.

I break away from him enough to see his face and shake my head.

"No." My voice is raspy, colored with want and a growing confidence that has been missing for months. Maybe for years.

With my hand on the center of his chest, I urge him backward, toward the desk he was sitting on when I came in. A devilish smile plays at his lips as he lets me have control, and my heart races, my pulse thrumming throughout my body with nervous courage.

When he backs into the desk, I step away again. His hands fall to the desktop on either side of him and his gaze warms even more.

"I want you to see me," I say, my voice wavering but not my commitment to do this.

The way he studies me, his lips displaying a faint curve only broken by a slow pass of his tongue, drives me forward. I pull the hockey jersey over my head, dropping it by my feet but never once breaking our connection. A white cotton tank top thinly veils my hard nipples that ache for relief, which sends searing heat to my core. Scared but determined, I hook my thumbs in the band of my sweatpants and slowly work them down my hips until they fall into a puddle around my feet. I step out of the fabric, one foot at a time, my lips quivering as Cameron's gaze slowly works its way down my body.

Vulnerable and cold, I drop my hands to my sides and flex my fingers as his heated stare glides from my breasts to my clenched stomach and the lace trim of my white panties. My eyes threaten to close, but I force them to remain open to take in every small flicker of his gaze. I want to remember each nuance of his smile, the tick of his jaw, and hungry breath. He has painted me with his eyes, taken in all of me, even the broken parts. And yet I still feel beautiful.

"You're wrong, Cam," I rasp.

His eyes flit to mine, squinting with suspicion.

"It is you who makes me beautiful. I feel the way I do because of the way you look at me." My hands curl into fists and I nervously pat my knuckles against my thighs while Cameron steps toward me with his soft, one-sided smile and a shake of his head.

"No, Brooky," he breathes, the back of his hand beginning at my jaw then trailing down my shoulder to the side of my body, his thumb lightly passing over my nipple and lighting me on fire. My eyes close automatically as I gasp, but open when his fingers trail back up to my shoulder, his other hand gliding up my other arm until both thumbs have swept the thin straps of my tank top over my shoulders. He leans in, his lips nipping at my ear, a faint, breathy laugh sending chills along my neck and spine.

"You are just fucking beautiful. But I can make you feel," he says.

My eyelids grow heavy with want as I grow wet between my legs.

"You already are," I whisper just before his mouth finds mine, leaving behind a soft kiss.

Cameron's eyes dip lower, to my aching breasts, the rosy, puckered tips begging to be touched through the thin cotton. His hands wrap around the shoulder straps, pulling them down my arms until my nipples are barely shielded by the stretch of the collar. His eyes widen with sinful pleasure before one hand moves to my back and he leans into me, urging me to arch into his hold. My head falls back as he tugs the material lower with his teeth, my nipple hardening in the crisp air for only second before his mouth covers it and his tongue flicks against the sensitive peak. I moan, crying out when he sucks hard and lets go with a snap. My nipple aches for more, and my body arches toward his mouth, begging for relief. Low laughter, almost a growl, emanates from his chest, though, before he blows gently on my aching skin.

Cameron lifts me to stand straight again before tugging my undershirt down to my hips. He wastes no time continuing to strip me naked, rolling the shirt over the band of my panties and sliding them together down my legs. He kneels in front of me, pressing a kiss to my scarred skin above my knee, caressing my calf and guiding my foot from the fabric around my ankles. He does the same for the other, but remains on his knees after, his eyes worshipping each curve from my calves to my thighs. His hands slowly roam my body, his touch tender where I've been hurt. Skin I haven't had sensation in for months feels alive with heat, and my core aches for me to clench, to relieve the swelling need growing between my legs.

Cameron's hands slide around my body, following the curve of my ass until without warning, he stands, lifting me with him, his lips pressed to my stomach as he carries me as if I'm the weight of a feather.

In a breath, my ass is on the empty desk, and Cameron tugs me forward so I'm teetering on the edge. I barely have time to utter the word *what* before his fingers rake down my thighs and he spreads my legs apart. I never get to the rest—*are you doing*—because my head instantly swims with ecstasy at the stroke of his tongue along my swollen middle.

"O-oh," I stammer, falling back on my elbows and eventually lying flat on the desk.

Cameron's palm travels up my leg to my stomach, his palm stretching wide and holding me still as his mouth caresses my hungry core. I pulse with every pass of his tongue as he pushes me closer and closer to the edge.

"Cam," I eek out in a pant. I bring my fist to my mouth, biting myself and praying to hold on, to make this last forever. But I'm no use against his touch. His mouth controls me completely from below, sucking in my pulsing center as wave after wave detonates. My legs curl up, every nerve in my body fighting to run from the barrage of his punishing tastes yet the deepest part of me wants more.

I quiver under his touch, my palms flattening on the desk as he drags his tongue over my swollen and raw center one final time before standing between my legs. He runs his sleeve over his chin, his hungry grin nearly rabid now as I lay unable to speak, every breath coming hard and fast as I lay before him.

I arch my back slightly, a silent plea for him to touch my aching breasts, and his eyes flicker at the invitation. He slips each arm from his shirt, tossing it to the floor, then brings both hands to cover my breasts completely before centering on my nipples and holding each hostage with sweet pressure between his finger and thumb.

Inching toward the desk's edge, I press my center against the hardness in his pants. He pushes into me at the contact, leaning over my body and dropping his head forward, his messy hair falling over his eyes. I dig my fingers into the soft waves, and he turns to kiss the inside of my wrist as I do.

"Cameron," I rasp.

He brings his gaze to mine, his eyes heavy with want, lids heavy, lips swollen from kissing my body.

"I want this," I hum. He holds my stare through several breaths. I nod. "I do. I want this. With you. All of it. I want you now, and I want *us.*"

His nostrils flare.

"You want us," he echoes my last words. I nod.

"Yes," I breathe.

Cameron pulls his wallet from his pocket and slips out a condom, holding the packet in his teeth and never once taking his eyes from mine. Unzipping his pants and pushing them down, he pulls himself free as he tears the packet open with his teeth. I lift up slightly as he rolls the condom onto his cock, my center pulsing in anticipation.

"Are you sure," he says, positioning himself at my entrance. I've had sex before. It was not great, and if I could go back and talk to my sixteen-year-old self I would beg me to wait. *Wait for this. Let this be the one. That first one who means something.*

I nod, letting my smile paint my lips. Cameron's mouth pushes into his right cheek, dimpling with sweetness and seduction. He bends down and kisses the center of my chest, soft bites inching their way up my body to my neck and ear until I feel him stretch me. He holds still, half inside me, letting me get used to his warmth and thickness. His eyes close with restraint.

"Fucking hell," he groans.

My hands grab at his shoulders, and I pull him into me, urging him to push in more. His movement is slow, and I roll my hips to make room for him deeper. A gasp parts my lips and I arch into him on instinct.

"More," I plead. Cameron stands and pulls out entirely, holding himself in his hand, teasing me with his tip before pushing inside again. His thrust is faster, harder, and my body moves along the wood of the desk with his force. My legs squeeze at his hips, holding him to me as he pumps in and out. I grab at his sides, pulling myself into him with every plunge. His skin moist with sweat, his breath sweet with whiskey, he kisses along my breasts, biting my nipples gently at first and harder as his climax grows. I pulse around him, whimpers of pleasure uncontrollably falling from my lips.

Seconds seem to drag into minutes as Cameron chases every wave of pleasure, his muscles tightening, jaw rigid as he pumps into me before finally sinking in and collapsing on my chest.

Our rapid breathing takes minutes to slow, and we spend the time tasting the salty sweat on one another's shoulders and necks. The soft glow of a single lamp highlights our naked bodies, and as much as I don't want to separate, I crave seeing him like this—naked, satiated, *mine*.

He stands and disposes of the condom, his dick still hard as he walks around the room without shame. I pull my knees to my body as I sit up, realizing that I haven't thought about my scars since he began touching me. I'm too struck by his beauty to be weighed down by my flaws.

"Are you staring at me, Brooky?" He steps up in front of me, pulling my legs free and wrapping them around his waist.

"I am," I say, my voice barely above a whisper, my cheeks warm as I tuck my face into the crook of his neck. He laughs lightly.

"Oh, don't you go hiding and being all shy on me now. It's too late, missy. I've seen it all," he teases, scooping me up and carrying me to the leather sofa that I was sitting on with Lily and Morgan a month ago during one of our parties. He sits down, holding me to straddle his lap, and I relish his hard warmth that still presses against my center.

"I'm going to laugh every time Morgan lies down on this couch," I say. Cameron's body shakes with amusement, his fingertips gliding around my shoulders and arms in tender circles.

"I can't wait to see Theo pour a drink over there," he says, nodding to the desk where he took me completely.

I bite at my lip, my face warming again. I tuck myself against him, and this time he lets me hide. We sit in silence, so many barriers torn down between us. There is nothing about Cameron that isn't good. At least nothing that isn't good for me. Fear, doubt, melancholy, loneliness—they've all been replaced by this new feeling, one of belonging and being adored. He said he loved me in the way boys do about their youthful crushes, but I think he meant it completely. I feel it in his touch and sense it in the way his eyes linger comfortably.

I feel it, too.

I feel it, too.

Chapter 13

Cameron

Brooklyn Bennett is my fucking girlfriend.

I can't stop grinning at that thought. I haven't stopped since I walked her to Hayden Hall and kissed her good night. I can still taste her this morning, hours later. I smell the lavender of her hair, the sweetness of her sex. I'm bathed in it.

I'm glad she showed up when she did before I got deep into my self-pity party and drowned out the noise with too much whiskey. I was just buzzed enough to forget the risks of it all, of falling for a girl too good for me and weighing her down with all my baggage.

It's not that I don't still worry about those things. Or that I no longer care. I do, deeply. I just want her more than I worry about the bullshit.

"What dumb shit thing were you out doing last night?" Theo picks up one of my T-shirts from his bed and flings it at my chest. I'm already dressed and ready for class and for once, he's the one running late. He loops his tie around his neck, and I can already tell he's going to blow this attempt—the long side is too short.

"I was out teaching necktie etiquette to a bunch of first forms. They're now all pros at the Windsor knot."

His eyes dart to meet mine in the mirror just as he slides his knot in place and feels his way down to the lopsided ends of his tie.

"Fuck you," he curses, scowling and undoing his tie for the ninth time.

"Come here, brotha. I got you," I say, sitting tall at the end of my bed and ushering him toward me. His arms slumped at his sides, he relents and leaves his mangled tie in my hands. I stand up square with him and go to work.

I can't keep my grin at bay this morning. But I can feel the frantic energy roaring off of Theo right now, so I try not to put it in his face.

"Everything all right, man?" I pry as I swing his tie around quickly and fashion a decent knot in seconds. I slide it up to the edge of his collar then back away for him to take over.

"Thanks," he sighs out. He runs his hands through his hair about a dozen times and continues to pace. "And yeah, I'm just nervous. It's the first big meeting about that scholarship fund Coach helped me start. I just don't want to look like an idiot, you know?"

Theo is a better man than he gives himself credit for. His twin sister was his best friend, and I envied how close they were. It was a rare showing of family love, or at least it was for me. In many ways, she was his raft. His family situation is pretty messy, and he endured some pretty serious abuse. When Anika died, he lost his way for a while, but then he found Lily. They kind of found each other.

I place my hands on my friend's shoulders and force him to look me in the eyes.

"Deep breath," I say.

He grimaces at first, but I insist, exaggerating the deep inhale and exhale. He rolls his head, stretching his neck, and finally gives in, breathing with me.

"You've got this. You're going to do amazing things for someone, and Anika . . . she would be proud."

He stares back at me, unblinking, for several seconds before bringing his hands to my shoulders, too.

"Thanks, Cam. I needed that." He nods and I slap my palms on his shoulders twice before letting go.

I follow him out the door, my eyes instantly scanning the campus for Brooklyn. I spot her back as she slips through the door on her way to econ. She was so stressed when I left her last night because she didn't study, so I made her promise to trust me today.

I pound knuckles with Theo and pull my bag up on my shoulder to make it easier to jog and catch up to Brooklyn. My damn phone buzzes in my pocket, so I reach in and feel for the ignore call button on the side. The pause lasts about six seconds, so I repeat my action but pull the phone out to see if my assumption is correct.

MOM. Two missed calls.

We talked days ago, and it's not like her to want to be on a regular loop with me. This isn't a weekly check-in because we simply don't do that shit. I stop when my phone rings a third time in my palm, and I answer.

"Hey, I'm almost in class," I say, my stomach tight. I spin in a slow circle, searching for my mom, half expecting her to pop out and surprise me and explain that's why she called. She's here. I dismiss that stupid fantasy almost as quickly as I have it, though. She loathes this place.

"I know. I was hoping to catch you. Cam, he has another hearing."

I stop breathing. There are few things my mother knows about my father before me, and his parole hearing being scheduled is one of them because, despite the complicated shit their relationship is, she promised that for his next hearing she would pay for his attorney. His attempts to win over the board didn't go so well on his own. And whether it's because she knows this means something to me, or because deep down, he still means something to her, my mom wants him out.

"When?" The bell rings around me as I spin, no longer sure what direction I'm heading.

"Two weeks. I forwarded you the email I got from the state. Hal is lined up. I just thought . . . I thought you'd want to know."

Hal is my father's new attorney. He wasn't picked at random, either. He actually took my mom on a few dates that she tried to not tell me about. That was fine with me because I really didn't want to know. But coincidences started to line up and there were some intimate things she seemed to know about him when she started telling me about his background and credentials. Somehow, she and Hal remained good friends. Probably because my mom isn't capable of loving, not in the way most humans crave it. But she's a damn good conversationalist and good to have as your plus-one at a business event. That's their existence now, Hal and my mom. Platonic plus-ones.

"Thanks. I'll see him this weekend." My body tingles with excited energy. I've waited for this moment, and I knew it was on the horizon. I didn't know it would be so soon, though.

My mom ends the call, cutting off her own goodbye mid-word. I grip my phone in my hand and continue my rushed pace to class. I can't sit on this news without celebrating with someone, but my dad isn't an easy phone call away. After I slip through my classroom door, I pull my phone into my lap and fire off a quick email to his prison address celebrating the news. Hal may be a great lawyer, but so is Karl Lowell. Maybe he can look over the filings with me when they're ready and offer any tips to help my dad out. If I could tell Brooklyn about my dad, I think I can tell Karl. I've watched him with enough clients now to know he doesn't judge people based on one action.

"Mr. Hass."

My hands fumble with my phone and it falls to the floor as Mr. Philips clears his throat, hovering above me. I have no desire to spend today helping out the front office instead of earning credit for the Black Tuesday project in class.

"Yes, I'm sorry. I had to message my internship. It's away now, though. It's . . ."

He holds out his palm then curls his fingers twice in request of my device. I set my phone in his hand and wince. *Damn.*

"You know the rule. You can have it back at the end of the day. I do hope you have time to catch me before practice." He can barely hide his smug grin, and I swear I hear my phone buzz from his jacket pocket as he walks away. I wonder who the message is from—from my mom? From Hall? A response from my dad?

My eyes drift left and catch Brooklyn's mischievous grin as she waggles her phone in her hand then winks.

"Oh—" I murmur, narrowing my gaze with a teasing glare.

She drops her phone in her bag, proud of herself that she can send me a message that I'm going to have to wait hours to read. Anything from her is worth the wait, though, so joke's on her.

She glances at me over her shoulder, her smirk still in place. But as Mr. Philips begins his lecture before our interactive test for the day, her expression morphs into anxious panic.

"Look to me," I mouth, doing the pointing thing from her eyes to mine. She nods once and slides lower in her seat, her head turtling into her shoulders as her confidence wanes.

There are only a few things I can help Brooklyn with but climbing cliffs and navigating the Great Depression might be the two categories in which I am most qualified. They are eclectic credentials for sure, but by the end of this class, Brooklyn is going to thank my younger, strange self who decided to refuse to play field hockey for his grandfather and instead load up his library haul with books about Black Tuesday, the roaring twenties, and the United States economy before World War II. I thought I was putting a foot down and disappointing my grandparents, who methodically ruined nearly every summer for me as they babysat me for weeks at a time. Upon reflection, though, I'm fairly certain some reverse psychology was deployed. At least I got a guaranteed A on this assignment out of it.

After twenty minutes of review that I barely listen to, Mr. Philips flips on the small speaker on his desk and syncs it to his phone so he can play some big band music to set the mood. It hardly transforms the rich mahogany walls of his room into a speakeasy, but I appreciate the aesthetic. This one project, which Mr. Philips hosts every year, has the power to literally pull a failing mark up to an A. On the flip side, someone sitting with a comfortable A, like say one Brooklyn Bennett, could find themselves flirting with a C if they don't play their cards right. And cheating somehow never occurs. On our first day of class, each of us sign honor pledges to not give answers or tips to underclassmen, at the risk of expulsion. It's a scare tactic because seriously, how is he going to know if I school someone a few years behind me on what stocks to buy and sell during the Black Tuesday project? It seems to work, though, because I've never seen the code broken. And I have absolutely no desire to help out some fifth year. They can earn their own damn stripes.

I can't let Brooklyn flail, though. Not when she knows the answers but is simply too afraid to take the risks.

For the next thirty minutes, Mr. Philips turns our class-room into a makeshift stock exchange, doling out play money for us all to spend on stocks. The purchases span the rainbow, some people deciding to ride DuPont until the last minute, others looking to the growth in vehicle manufacturing during the twenties.

Every time I went up to make a purchase, Brooky followed. She never bought exactly what I did, but the categories were always close. I made sure to make eye contact with her when I sold my highs, and sometimes she held on an extra day to ensure our numbers weren't exact matches. And as easily predicted, the entire class sold before our fictional October 28, 1929. But when nobody did any shopping on October 29th, I made a few strategic purchases. Brooklyn made some, too, and while her moves earned her a knowing smirk and nod in praise from Mr. Philips, mine were received with a skeptical brow and a request to stay in after class.

"I will have everyone's totals by Monday, but I think it's safe to say you can all breathe easily," he announces as most of us file out of class. I linger, and because he can't kick me out today, he tosses in one little jab to make sure I know where I stand before everyone's gone. "Except you, Mr. Hass. You should not breathe easily."

I roll my eyes, which he *so* appreciates, and shoot a smile and wink to Brooklyn as she stops at the door. She nods out toward the hall, indicating that she'll wait for me, and I decide that Mr. Philips can fail me and I'll still walk out of here happy.

"I'd like you to show me your search history on your phone, Mr. Hass," he says, laying my phone down on his desk and ushering me over with the curl of a finger.

I approach slowly, giving myself time to mentally recall what I've Googled over the last few days. There are some embarrassing pages for sure, like the one about 'how to avoid foot funguses' followed by the queries of 'what does foot fungus smell like?' Of course, from there I fell down the rabbit hole of various fungus forms, which brought me into jock itch, then a series of memes about jock straps, and finally one semi-questionable photo of Thor buying jock-itch cream. I'm still willing to bet that was real and not photoshopped, but Theo says I'm full of it.

My conscious clear, I open my settings and display my history for his review. I can tell he's disappointed, albeit disgusted, when his mouth sneers, and he pushes my phone back to me.

"Go on and take it. I don't want to have to see you at the end of my day," he says.

I laugh off his insult, pocketing my phone.

"Gee, thanks, sir." I turn to leave, assuming I'm dismissed, but before I leave the classroom, he clears his throat and throws out one last, "Mr. Hass."

I turn and lift my chin slightly.

"You know what you did today, don't you?"

He looks like he's going to be sick. Mr. Philips is so proud of this little experiment he created a decade ago. It's grown over the years, and for the last five, he has given an award to the person who would have the most wealth today based on their stock trading in October of 1929. It's a shiny bronze cup, not plastic, but legit metal, engraved and all. And he hands it to the recipient during the graduation ceremony held in front of parents and alumni. This year, that person is going to be me.

My smile spreads, which only makes the green tint in his cheeks grow sourer.

"I sure do, sir. Looking forward to it."

I leave his room and find Brooklyn waiting in an empty hallway, leaning against a wall and chewing at her nails.

"Relax, he doesn't know I helped you," I say.

"I wasn't worried," she answers, her words so practiced and oversold I can't help but laugh.

"What?" Her brow pulls in extra tight. I press my finger in the dent between her eyebrows and wiggle. She looks up with mildly crossed eyes.

"Yes, you were worried. And you are a terrible liar. But adorable." I drag my fingertip down the bridge of her nose then tap the tip as her lips purse, trying to hold back a smile.

I swing an arm around her and pull her in so I can kiss the top of her head then move toward the door.

"So, are you going to tell me what he talked to you about? Or just let me pretend I'm not still worried?" She grins up at me with wide eyes and clenched teeth, a lot of sarcasm nuanced in her expression as she passes through the door I hold open.

"It's hard to explain, but Mr. Philips and I have played a very long game of chess, and today, I kind of called checkmate." Simply mentally replaying the look on his face makes me giddy.

Brooklyn studies me for a few seconds as we walk then jars to a stop.

"You didn't?"

I smirk and nod.

"I did," I say.

"How? I mean, you said you read all those books when you were younger, which is still exceptionally nerdy by the way," she teases.

"Hey!" I step back as if I'm offended and Brooklyn shrugs before we begin to walk again.

"Call it as I see it. But hey, Cam . . . you're the one who will be hoisting that *prestigious* trophy over your head on graduation day, so what do I know?"

I scowl at her kiddingly.

"I sense sarcasm in the way you said prestigious just now. I don't think you fully appreciate the art of sticking it to the man, which is essentially what that trophy in my hands represents. But to get to your first question, one of the books I obsessed over during that ridiculous summer of my youth was a biography about J. Paul Getty. The man bought oil low, and of course watched it go high."

I blow on my fingertips then buff them on my tie to sell my arrogance, but Brooklyn rolls her eyes and calls me nerd.

The easy conversation stops, and we're only halfway through our walk across campus. I'm not sure how to navigate things with her out in public. I want to show every single person who looks our way that Brooklyn and I are together. But even though she says she's ready to confront the haters— *aka her dad*—I'm not sure she's ready to do it boldly and through the Welles gossip mill.

We're an hour and a half away from meeting up with our friends for lunch, and the thought of deciding where to sit and how to act has me completely baffled. I almost feel guilty for not holding her hand right now, which is why I've kept mine in my pockets for most of the walk. The best way to play this is to let Brooklyn set the rules, but there's also this stinging sensation in my gut that is so damn afraid she's going to want to hide us. I get her reasons if that's what she chooses. It will hurt anyway.

Steps away from where our sidewalk literally divides, sending us in opposite directions, I start to laugh quietly to myself.

"What's wrong?" She tilts her head as we slow our steps.

"I feel like a twelve-year-old. Do I kiss the girl? What if my breath smells? Should I hold her hand?" I lift my shoulders and shake my head at my own ridiculousness while Brooklyn's face puzzles at me.

"I don't want to make you uncomfortable, and I know you said you don't care what people think, but this place is full of opinions." I give it to her plainly, familiar faces wandering in our periphery, lots of outlets to start gossip.

"Cam," she says, reaching for my tie. She holds it in her hand then rolls it around her grip, dragging me toward her. Lifting up on her toes, she tilts her head and puckers her lips, and I softly press my smile against them.

"Your breath is fine," she says, unfurling her hold on my tie and walking backward for a few steps as she leaves.

Chapter 14

Brooklyn

I played cool with Cameron, but in reality, he's right. I'm not sure I'm ready for the barrage of opinions about us. I know I have to endure them, though, to get us to the other side. Today is the first test, and it will trigger so many more in the coming days. It won't take long for my father to call and explain his message to me. I'm actually shocked he hasn't called yet to talk about the fight between Cole and Cameron. Maybe Cole didn't run to daddy to tattle, but it's hard to believe he grew a soul in the span of a few afternoons. That call is coming too. I feel it.

I finished my computational thinking classwork early, thanks to a lifetime of Excel spreadsheet training due to my dad's work. I know my way around a budget and polling data, so crunching numbers on pet licenses and the most popular barrows from the Boston Public Library was a bit of a cake walk.

It left me with plenty of time to think, which I suppose is what I've wanted. *Time to think.*

There is no Excel formula for the best way to tell your

friends you're crazy about the guy they think is all wrong for you, so I decided at the end of class that I was going to go into lunch with the same confidence Morgan goes into everything —a brash sense of entitlement. She's the one I'm stressed about most, other than my father, so I may as well beat her with her own game.

I give myself a mini pep talk when I reach the end of the cafeteria checkout line. Dropping my Coach wallet into my tote bag, I then loop it on my arm and take my tray in both hands as I march defiantly toward the table where all of my friends—*and Cameron*—are already sitting. The only open seat at the table is next to him, which helps narrow down my first hurdle.

"Hey, what did I miss?" I say as I slide into the open space, setting my tray down and plopping onto the seat next to Cam.

"Cameron said he won the Black Tuesday trophy. That true?" Theo arches a brow at me then glances to his friend on my other side.

I pull my lips into a tight line and nod.

"It is," I confirm.

"Dude! Nice!" Theo says, holding up a hand to high five his friend. They slap hands in front of me. "Mr. Philips is going to hate that. I bet he calls in sick for the graduation ceremony."

"Good thing I know where he lives, then, so I can get *the* photo." Cameron takes a French fry from my plate and pops it into his mouth, snapping his teeth closed before grinning. I give him a sideways look for stealing my food and slap his hand when he does it again.

My eyes drift to Morgan beyond his shoulder, her glare purposefully emotionless but trained on me. She's taking mental notes; I've known her long enough to know her tells.

She's gathering her facts and forming her arguments to support her already made-up opinion. It's times like these that I truly miss Anika's voice amongst our group. She was the only one who seemed able to show Morgan her flaws without drawing out her claws.

Cameron and Theo are mid-conversation about tomorrow's game, and James is sitting across the cafeteria wearing the same expression Morgan is, only his focus is on her. I'm not sure what is up with those two, but I can't help but think that her own drama is spilling over into her opinion of mine.

Okay, Morgan. If you're looking for something to judge me for, I'll give it to you.

"Excuse me," I say, using Cameron's shoulder to step up from my seat. I let my hand linger on his arm for an extra second then drag my fingertips around his neck as I pass behind him and head toward the napkin dispenser. I can feel his eyes on me, charged and maybe a little happy that I broke the seal on our secret. I also feel Morgan's, though, and when I turn around with two napkins I don't need, my eyes meet hers and I swear they are swimming with disapproval.

Maybe it's petty of me, but I hold her stare as I parade back to our table, pounding my heels into the floor with extra oomph to make sure the Louboutins really pop. I shouldn't be wearing shoes like this, and I especially shouldn't be stomping in them, but I'm fired up and when I'm pissed like this, nothing on my body hurts.

"Napkin?" I say with the tilt of my head as I offer it to my judgmental friend.

"I'm good. Thank you." Her response is curt as she continues to stare.

"Suit *yourself.*" I put a little extra juice on the *yourself* part, insinuating that she should mind her own business.

My catwalk seems to have halted all other conversation, and because Lily has been spending her lunch hour putting in extra time for the swim team, she's not here to diffuse what has become a pretty hot environment. Lily does not like conflict, and while I'm a people pleaser, I'm also a Bennett. My dad might have a thing or two to say about me dating Cameron Hass, but he'd never want me to back down from a fight. And this friction growing between Morgan and me right now? It's gonna be a fight.

"I hope everything works out for you two," Morgan says, making the first move. She purses her candy red lips and shakes her head in quick, tiny movements before poking her coffee straw into her mouth.

"Huh?" Theo glances at her with a furrowed brow and a full mouth.

"We're talking about Cam and me. We're dating. And Morgan doesn't think we should." I lean forward, clasping my hands and resting my elbows on the table as I stare down my friend. *Friend. Pfft.*

Cameron rocks back in his seat, blowing out air with a groan.

"Right, well . . . I'm not about to be here for this, so . . ." He stands and looks to Theo, who is still chewing his massive bite and wearing a classic *WTF* expression. He points to me then circles his finger in frustration.

"She'll explain, I guess," Cameron says to his friend, his mouth a relaxed, straight line despite the stiffness in his shoulders and neck. His gaze slides to me, and I swallow down the guilt. I didn't mean to turn us into a showdown. I'm already in it, though. And Morgan is never going to get on board if I don't convince her this is a real thing and her disapproval hurts.

"I'll see you before the game," I say, grabbing his arm as

he walks away. He nods as he steps away, his arm slipping through my fingers.

"Seems like it's really starting off with a bang," Morgan interjects.

I huff and turn to face her across the table, flattening my palms on either side of my tray. I doubt I'll be able to eat a single bite of my lunch. I feel sick.

"That right there?" I point to Cameron walking away. "That was your fault."

"I'm pretty sure I can't make Cameron do anything. He wanted to leave, so he did." Her appetite seemingly unfazed, she bites an apple slice in half and chews it slowly while continuing to stare me down.

My stomach twists on itself. This is where I usually falter with people. I dislike conflict, and even more, I prefer to avoid debate. I much prefer to listen to the room and form my own opinions, then keep them to myself. But keeping Cameron to myself isn't how relationships work. So to speak.

"What is your problem with him?" I level her with my gaze, and even though every bit of me below the table is quivering, I maintain perfect control over the muscles she can see.

"You and Cam? You're together, then?" Theo is still catching up, so I turn to him and nod.

"Yes, Theo. Cameron and I like each other the same way you and Lily do." I dumb it down, and my tone is a little condescending, which I regret, but I'm so angry I could toss this entire table right now.

Theo drops the unfinished half of his sandwich onto his plate and leans back the same way Cameron did, his lips twisted into an irritated slant.

"And I see why Cam left. I'd say congratulations but I'm afraid you'll punch me for it," Theo says, snagging one of my fries for himself.

I sink in my seat. This is not going well at all. I don't have time to run after Theo, though, and honestly, of all of our friends, he'll likely be the best with the news. I mean, he already offered congratulations . . . *sort of.*

Morgan's slurping sound draws my attention back to her. Having drained her drink, she pops her mouth open with an *ahh.* Her smug smile is coming from someplace that has nothing to do with me. I know her well enough to recognize when she is deflecting, and based on the hot-and-cold pattern she seems to have going on with our new quarterback, I'm guessing this is a distraction from that.

Mostly.

There are still some harbored feelings about Cameron that I need her to work through. I need my friend in my corner. And I have to believe that if she only let herself see how good he is to me, she wouldn't be so negative about him.

"Morgan, I *really* like him. Hell, I think I'm in love with him."

She punches out a laugh then sits back, crossing her legs and staring off to the side with an amused tight-lipped smile.

"Don't do that," I sigh.

"Do what?" She keeps her head turned to the side. "If you want to dive head-first into a steaming pile of chaos— *after the spring we just survived*—you go right ahead."

My shoulders drop as I sigh heavily and look at my now cold slice of pizza and unappealing fries. I should have told Theo to take them all.

"That's not fair, Morgan. You're being . . ."

I stop myself before the word rolls off my tongue. *Selfish.* Her gaze swivels to mine in a snap as if I said it.

My eyes sting with the threat of tears, and it's not because I'm intimidated by her. It's because she's my friend, and I want to be happy, but her reaction makes me feel as if that's unacceptable. *Not allowed.*

"Morg—" I choke, unable to finish her name as I swipe away the single tear that falls. I sniffle and roll my shoulders to regain composure, wishing she could look as sad as me.

Her features are still hard.

"You're going to get hurt. Cameron isn't that guy—the *relationship* guy."

"You don't know that," I argue.

"And neither do you," she fires back.

I puff out a harsh laugh, leaving my eyes on her with my mouth agape.

"That's your argument? I'm taking a risk?" I shake my head, baffled by this logic. Something is going on with her, and I wish like hell I knew what.

"Yeah, Brooklyn. You're taking a risk. And you know your dad is not going to be okay with this. Cameron probably has a rap sheet."

I swallow hard at her out-of-the-blue attack. My brow drawing in hard, I bite back, "That is absolutely untrue and an awful thing to say. He has always been kind to you."

My eyes flicker up in time to see Cameron standing a few feet behind her. My stomach drops to its depths, knowing he heard that. My reaction must not register with Morgan, though, because she keeps on going.

"Christ, Brooklyn. He's a fucking pothead who cliff dives and lit his ass on fire once. He's coasting through this school at the bottom of our class, and that law firm internship? Honestly? As if he's really going to be a lawyer some day. Ha! He'd probably get all of his clients sent to prison."

I'm stone frozen. My gaze is locked on Cameron, but his is a laser into the back of Morgan's head. His jaw is rigid, so much so I swear I hear it crack. He takes a deep breath, making just enough noise to awaken Morgan's senses.

My vision drops to her face as her eyes flicker in realization and she jerks around in her seat. Cameron doesn't move. In fact, despite the ire very visible in his face, his body is completely relaxed. Hands in his pockets, feet a foot apart, he blinks slowly looking at his—*our*—supposed good friend.

"I said what I said," Morgan says, and my eyes flutter shut. She does this when she's trapped. She lashes out and makes things worse.

Cameron's soft laughter urges my eyes open again, and I take him in, the faint one-sided smile playing at his lips, the slope of his eyes and flex in his jaw as he chews at the inside of his mouth. When he walks closer to her, I straighten my spine and Morgan leans back against the table behind her. Not even paying attention to me, he rests a palm on the table next to her and towers over her as she stares up at him.

I hold my breath and wait for his words. I root for him to tell her the truth, to explain the things she doesn't know about his life—his motivations, his passions. Those words never come, though. Cameron simply stares into her, holding her eyes with his rock-solid glare for nearly a minute—a long, uncomfortable, *silent* minute.

Finally letting out a single laugh, Cameron stands tall again and nods at her, his tongue pushed into his cheek. His chin lifts and his eyes come to me. All I can think to do is mouth *I'm sorry*. It's not enough. But maybe that's the point, and the reason he didn't lay into her just now. No matter what Cameron Hass says or does, it's never enough. People made their minds up about him, and there's nothing he can do to change them.

Those people? They're missing out.

My head tilts slightly to the side as I gaze at him, loving

the way his mouth morphs just a fraction from contempt into affection. The change is subtle, nothing more than the faint impression of a dimple. But it's there, and it's there for me as he turns his back on Morgan and walks away.

My eyes cling to his back, to the way his head falls forward and he brings his hand to his neck to stretch away the stress. Morgan turns back to face me, and I drop my gaze to her.

"Maybe that's what he needed to hear," she says, wiggling in her seat to straighten her offended posture.

I laugh out, grab my tray, and stand.

"That was really mean. That's what that was."

Her eyes widen, only a hint but enough that I know my truth stung. I leave her alone at the table and follow in Cameron's steps. Not sure what to expect, I ready myself for him to be angry when I catch up to him.

"Cam!" I call, my heels clicking against the cold pavement. My leg hurts, and I'm not making much progress, so I pull my shoes from my feet and hold them by the straps as I sprint, *well sprint for me,* toward him. He finally hears me when he's near the science building door, and I stop short, leaving a dozen feet between us.

"I'm so sorry you heard that," I say.

His mouth opens as if to speak, but nothing comes out. Instead, his lips morph into a hurt smile and he shakes his head as he marches toward me. I drop my shoes to the ground just as his hands push into my hair and his lips cover mine. I cling to his wrists and stand on the tips of my toes to meet his kiss, and when we break, he leaves his head against mine.

"Thank you for not being ashamed of me," he says.

I cackle softly in disbelief.

"You shouldn't have to say that. Don't say that."

I close my eyes and lower from my toes to stand with my

feet flat on the ground. Cameron wraps his arms around me, holding my cheek against his chest as he sways back and forth. A soft rumble of laughter echoes from inside him.

"If you just kept those damn Lolobobo shoes on you wouldn't have to stand on your toes to kiss me," he teases.

I form a fist and play-punch at his pectoral.

"That's not even close to their name, but yeah . . . you're right."

It feels safe here in his arms, even though every single person who passes by is staring at us long and hard. Okay, maybe not *every* person, but the ones with big mouths are. I suppose this is one way to get it all over with at once.

McKenna Lowell walks right up to us. I see her coming from the side and step back, patting Cameron's chest to get his attention in case she decides to slap him for hugging a girl that isn't her after breaking up months ago.

"I hope you know he's a cheating dog," she says, her face mere inches from mine. I flinch and take a step back.

"Okay, well, that was a little hostile, and I appreciate your concern, but—"

"No, Brooklyn. You don't understand. He's a user. Cameron Hass is a user. He used me to get to my father and now he's using you to get to yours." She whips around, smacking my neck with her ponytail along the way, and pushes her finger in the center of Cameron's chest. "You think you're so charming, Cameron, but I see you. I see right through you. Wait until I tell Daddy about *this* one! You know her dad and my dad are friends, right? Just wait."

Her eyes squint as she mashes her teeth so hard I swear I hear a molar crunching under the pressure.

"I'm actually scared shitless of her dad, so you got that one wrong. And go ahead and talk to yours if you want. Let him know I finished that research pile he needed for Monday. I left a note on it but just in case."

Cameron gives her a cocky shrug that seems to set her off even more. She makes a shrill sound through gritted teeth and bounces on her toes as if she's boiling over. Flipping back to face me, she presses her palms against my cheeks, giving me fish lips. My eyes dart side to side in disbelief that she is touching me.

"Listen to me, Brooklyn. Run. Don't walk, *run*." Her hands fly away from my face, and she steps backward away from me, but not before eyeing Cameron one last time and letting out what I think is a low growl.

"Wow." My mouth hangs open with my reaction as I turn back to Cameron. His eyes are as big as I think mine are.

"I'm really sorry she mushed your face like that. I think it will bounce back," he jokes, placing his hands in the same spots and pretending to adjust the shape of my face.

"Ha ha, super funny. Seriously, though. Did you know that things with her were that level bad?"

My pulse is still racing from the spontaneous attack as Cameron moves his head side to side.

"I actually met her dad first, for what it's worth. Our dates were his idea," he says, wincing with a guilty face.

My face bunches, too.

"That's somehow even more awkward," I respond.

"Yeah. You know how guys are supposed to ask girls' fathers for permission for things?"

"I mean, I think that applies for a hand in marriage, but I get your point," I say.

"Yeah, well . . . I asked him for advice on how to break it off. He understood and honestly, I think the fact I came to him worried about making her upset made him somehow like me more. I'm actually kind of good, so maybe yours will like me, too."

I bite my tongue and hold his gaze with tight lips and a sparse smile.

"Maybe," I finally say, sliding my hands around his sides again and resting my ear against his heart. "Maybe," I utter softly.

When pigs fly . . . and run for federal office.

Chapter 15

Cameron

My dad emailed back while I was at practice yesterday and gave me a time slot for a phone call today. Brooklyn went to dinner with her mom last night, so I spent most of the night and all of this morning reading up on successful parole stories in search of someone with a case like my father's. It's only a matter of seven years at this point, which bodes well for him getting an early release. Seems cruel to let someone out only a year early after serving twenty-four, so I feel good about his chances this time.

His lack of a lawyer hurt him during the last hearing. I read the transcripts, and while he said all the right things to the panel, he left a lot of important stuff unsaid—mostly the studying and work he's done while serving time. While the only degree to his name is a GED, my dad has read more than his fair share of college-level texts. He's taken every unwanted job for prisoners just to beef up his resume, even spending a year on toilet-cleaning duty—which in a prison is about as low as the work gets.

Earning parole is about so much more than simply saying *yes sir* and *no ma'am* to the standard questions. It's a sales pitch for one's life.

I have to be in the locker room for our game against Lipson Prep in thirty minutes. As far as private school competition goes, Lipson's one of the better teams. It should be a decent game, and if we can hold them to a low score, or even better, pull off a win, we may have a shot at taking our division this year. I don't care so much for me, but for our quarterback, James, this season means everything. I guess he had a pretty rough experience at his last school, which is why his family transferred here and his dad took the coaching job.

I'm not saying I am a vital part of the Welles football team. I am one of a very few talented pieces, though. I'll even admit to using the word talented liberally. I know the basics of the game and I'm aggressive and fearless. That combination gives me a slight edge on this field. If I'm late, though, James will be down to two passing options, and Theo is going to take the brunt of the hits. He's not built for the abuse like I am. I welcome it.

My phone buzzes in my hand while I pace circles around the fieldhouse track, and I practically fumble it to answer.

"Yes, I accept," I say before the prison operator even has a chance to finish her speech about the call and charges.

"You got the news." My dad sounds upbeat, genuinely. He's always put on a good act for our phone calls, but the older I get, the more real he lets slip into our conversations.

"I did, yeah. This is good news, right? Earlier than we thought?" I'm a little fired up, so I keep walking while we talk. If I don't, I'm afraid I'll run right over my dad's answers with my next question.

"By a few months. I guess they want to get through a lot of business before the holidays, so I got pushed into this year." My dad's voice vibrates, and I picture him walking in circles near the phone. He and I are so similar. The strangeness of it all hits me sometimes—my dad didn't really raise me, but I have so much of his personality. It can't all be from monthly visits and phone calls.

"Hey, I heard from that lawyer guy. You know him? He legit?" My dad knows Mom set him up with Hal. My parents have the strangest form of communication. It's like a child's game of telephone—my mom sends a message to someone who gets it to someone else who eventually tells my dad. Rarely they email each other directly. I used to read the messages they passed back and forth, everything my mom sends overly formal, my dad's reading more like apologies.

"He's good. He tried to date Mom a long time ago."

My dad coughs out a laugh.

"Key word, *tried,*" he says.

There's still a lot of love on my dad's part, and I think there's a big part of him that's happy Mom never had someone else.

"Honestly, Dad. I think she stayed friends with him simply because of his legal reputation. It's like she knew he would be handy down the road."

There's a long pause on the line before my dad says, "Huh."

I don't want to fill him with any false hope, but there are things my mom says and does that make it hard not to believe she doesn't still love him, too. She's not outright about it, but her mask slips around me sometimes.

"What can I do to help?" I sit on one of the benches by the track and chew at my thumbnail, my knee bouncing a thousand pulses per minute. I wish I were older, in law school myself or graduated, so I could represent him myself.

Hal is good, sure, but I don't think anyone believes in him the way I do. I hate feeling useless.

"You can tell me about this game you've got in a few hours, that's what you can do. Are you getting your reps? Coach using you?"

I shoot to my feet and start walking again. I don't want to talk about football, but I guess that's all I've got. And it makes him happy.

"Yeah, I get used a lot actually. Mostly to block, and when it's a tough line, I'm usually able to bully my way through."

"Ahhh, that's my boy," he says. The genuine pride in his voice when I tell him about my games always makes me smile.

I switch our call to speaker phone so I can check the time. Our call is almost over. Even if I could stay on the line with him for an hour, the rules don't allow it. Fifteen minutes is a gift when I get it.

"Hey, so . . . about the girl," I say, rubbing my palm along my face.

"Oh, ho ho, do tell," he says, a bit of fatherly teasing in his tone.

"I maybe kissed her." I smile even though he can't see me. I don't need to share more than that with him. He's a man, though. He knows.

"Alright! Now we're talking. And?"

"And . . . worth the wait," I laugh out. I'm giddy talking about Brooklyn with him.

"Ah, Cam. That's . . . man, son. That's everything. What's the status? Are you official then? I don't know what they call it now, is it talking? Or dating?"

"I'd say we're pretty official, yeah."

My dad's crackly laugh fills the phone line.

"I can't wait for you to meet her," I say.

"Me, too, Cam. Me, too."

The line goes quiet again, and that strain fills the void. It took me a while to define what it was exactly, but I've decided it's longing. We long for each other. I can't even imagine having these conversations with him anytime I want, or sharing a beer on a porch somewhere, or sitting on the bleachers out at Fenway.

"She knows about you, too, by the way. I kind of told her the broken love story," I say, my voice soft, words cautious. I've never really asked my dad how he feels about me talking to people about our business. He's never been the one to lay down rules about who gets to know what, though, so I figure he's all right with it.

"It's a real tearjerker, isn't it?" he says.

"I wouldn't call it a comedy," I respond. He breathes out a short laugh before letting the line go quiet again.

I want to tell him that it didn't freak Brooklyn out hearing that my dad is in prison, but I won't lie. It's hard to explain the reasons why, and I'm afraid without the context, he'll get defensive. He can be protective of me, even if it's only with words.

"Your mom meet her yet?"

I shake my head as I answer, "No."

"Well, that'll be the test. I mean that and your grandparents. *Oooof!*"

I sit with his warning. My grandparents are an entirely different issue, and while they made life hell for him and my mom, they would probably make it twice as miserable for me. They're not reasonable, even though they have given me a lot in life. They don't like when family strays from the rules they laid out. My mom strayed by falling in love with my dad and look where that got them.

"Hey, they're saying I've got to wrap it up," he says.

I check the time on my phone.

"Yeah, I've gotta get my ass to the locker room."

"You put a hurt on those other guys, all right? Don't hold back," he says, that sad pep in his voice. I wish he could see me play just once.

"I'll do my best, Dad. And hey, I have a really good feeling about this one."

He's quiet for a few seconds, superstition getting the best of him at first. But eventually he comes around.

"Me, too, Cam. Me, too. See you next weekend."

Our call ends before I get to say more, but my chest feels settled knowing I got to celebrate with him a little. I shouldn't get my hopes up. There are still so many things that can go wrong with his hearing. It could also get delayed or put back to its original schedule in January or February. But something feels different this time. Maybe I'm happier and that's all it is. Whatever the wave, I'm going to ride it.

We're down by six with about four minutes to go. I want to win this game for James, but I'm getting my ass handed to me out on the field. The good news is the Lipson guys have given up a shitload of yards to us with penalties. It's half the reason we're in the game. The bad news, though—they don't seem to care. It's almost as if they've been given a green light to play as dirty as they can. I'm starting to think winning is secondary to breaking me in half.

Our team manager—a tough girl named Mai who honestly should probably put on a set of pads and help us out on the field—shoots a blast of water through my helmet. I lap it up like a golden retriever, wearing most of it on my face.

It's strange that it can be so cold outside yet humid as hell at the same time. And I keep getting nailed in the places that are still tender from my fight. If my rib wasn't broken before, it sure as hell is now.

Coach is pacing along the line, flipping through his playbook while our defense does their job. We manage to stop a third down and he spins around, scanning the line until his focus stops at me. I was really hoping he was searching for someone else.

He lunges toward me and places his hands on either side of my helmet, pushing his face into the mask part so I can hear him.

"Hass, I know you're tired, but I need you to get in there for a few more drives. We need your blocking, and you're the only one who can pound out those yards."

I chew at my mouthguard and nod.

"Yes, Coach," I spit out.

My face hurts from all of the fists that have somehow found a way through my mask. I have what looks like a tampon shoved in one nostril, and my wrist is wrapped so tight I can't feel my fingers.

"Go, go, go!" Coach waves our squad out with one hand while clutching the playbook in the other.

James runs backward, checking the play calls on his wrist against the set of numbers his dad holds up with his fingers. When we get into the huddle, he stares at me.

"You good?" His eyes plead with me. He wants this.

"Yeah, I'm good. Bring it on, baby." I clap a few times to psych myself up as James calls the play sequence I anticipated. Basically, I'm going to try to eat up the clock by running the ball four yards at a time. When the time is right, they'll be expecting him to throw it to Theo for the win. That's what worked for our last two touchdowns. It's literally the *only* thing that has worked. But the Lipson guys don't know I have an extra level of crazy. You don't do half the shit I've done without shedding a certain amount of fear of being hurt. And as long as my legs work, I'll keep moving forward.

"Break!"

We scatter to our positions, and I line up to the right of James, legs primed and ready to barrel through what's coming. At the snap, I rush five yards ahead, where Lipson anticipates the block, and before James has a chance to get me the ball, I'm hammered into the ground after illegal holding.

"You like that, Welles boy?" The lineman pushes my head into the ground as he uses my facemask for leverage to stand up. The whole thing earns him another penalty and us another fifteen yards. It also gives me my first glimpse into what the fuck is going on.

Welles boy.

I can't know for sure, but my gut tells me Lipson might be surfer-cowboy Cole's school. If not, I have a suspicion that's where most of his friends attend.

James sets up and calls the same play, only this time I'm ready for the dirty play coming our way. I manage to dodge the reach for my collar and slip past the guy gunning for me. James flips me the ball and I turn to pound my feet into the turf as hard and fast as I can. I make it seven yards before I'm brought down by at least five guys.

"That's what I'm talking about," I spit out, nodding at the guys on their line as I flip the ball to the ref. I usually get whistled for trash talk, but I think they're granting me a little extra leeway today on account of the massive abuse my body has endured.

We pile in for a quick huddle, but there's nothing to say. James looks to me and nods and we all yell, "Break!"

We're running it again. And when they figure it out, we'll run it reversed.

I manage to make it ten yards this time, which puts us within field goal range. Worst case scenario, we go for an onside kick and hope for a fumble.

"Hey, eighty-eight!"

My favorite lineman has been shouting at me all night. He loves my number.

"Yeah, you hear me. The hurt is coming, son. It's coming."

What he doesn't realize is how much power his shit talking gives me. I can actually see the blood red skin of his cheeks when he shouts. I bet his veins are bulging at his temples.

James touches my chest in the huddle.

"Hey, you want us to change it up? You need a break?" He's worried about the number of hits I'm taking. My head feels fine, though. As hard as I've been knocked down, somehow nothing has rung my bell. I'm pretty sure my nose is broken, but my head? It's on right.

"I'm good. I'm good. Hit me again," I say, pounding my chest.

Theo laughs at my right.

"You're a crazy motherfucker, you know that Cam?" he says.

My mouth stretches into a wide grin while I chew on my mouthguard and bounce on my feet with this strange excess energy. I've reached that second level, the one beyond exhaustion. I could go for hours now. I feel good.

"Woo! Eighty-eight is your favorite number, baby!" I shout to my friend, echoing the other team's line as a way to piss them off.

"Yeah, you're my favorite . . . favorite dead man lying on the ground," my opponent growls as he sets up on the line.

I shake my head to right my focus and huff out my breaths like a bull ready to attack. James gets me the ball even faster this time, and I manage to spin and break out for an eleven-yard gain. I'm almost to my feet again after the play when my antagonizer flies at me with a strong arm across the chest, drilling me into the fifteen-yard line.

The whistles blast as I yank my helmet off and scramble to my feet to go at him.

"That's some dirty shit, man. You want to try that again? What's your problem?" I smack the side of his helmet with my fist, my knuckles instantly throbbing from the impact. It was enough to knock him off balance, though, during his second lunge at me.

Within seconds, the field is overrun with players from both sides, all scrambling to get their hands on the two of us. Some guys are trying to tear us apart, but others are throwing jabs of their own. My lip splits open in the mix and the metallic taste fills my mouth.

Fists fly haphazardly, some landing on me, others missing wildly. My own fists make contact at least twice with my nemesis's face. The satisfying crunch of his nose folding under the impact of my knuckles makes the sting under my wrapped fingers worth it. The brawl feels like it lasts for hours, but within minutes, the refs and coaching staffs have managed to untangle us from one another and usher us to our respective sides.

I spit blood on the ground and Mia throws me a towel from the ice water. Part of me wonders if she ran out there and got some good shots in, too.

"Take a knee! Now!"

I've heard Coach Fuentes yell plenty of times. Wrangling

a bunch of teenage boys on a football field tries patience, and we can be real assholes. His butt-chewing is always well-deserved. His tone now, however? He's livid. I might even be a tad scared to hear what he has to say.

"That is not how we settle things, you hear me? Unacceptable!" He walks up to me and points a finger in my face. My helmet no longer around to protect me.

"You have to keep it in check, Cam! I know you're pissed. Hell, I know that asshole out there deserved it! But we were inches away after that. The penalties would have put us on the one-yard line. We take two knees then punch it in when the clock has mere seconds left. Now, it's a break even. You get the spot, and that's it. I'm glad we didn't somehow *lose* yards in that fiasco!"

He backs away from me but offers one last thought before he lets his staff take over.

"Selfish! Gah!" Coach tosses his book out onto the field and yanks his headset from his neck as he walks away.

It's clear I'm done for the day. I might be done for the rest of the season. And I understand. Coach managed to gut me with the one thing that I fear the most—becoming my mom and grandparents. If given the choice who I wanted to be most like in my family, I'd pick the convicted felon every single time. Today I acted like the single-minded status whores who fed, clothed, and educated me.

And now that the rush of it all is gone, I feel like shit.

* * *

There was no after-game speech. We pulled out the win thanks to the only play that scored for us all night—a short pass into the end zone from James to Theo.

All of the bruises and aches I feel were for nothing. My

friends can lie to me all they want, and they have, telling me that I carried us down that field and made our win possible. I know the truth, though. When it really mattered? I lost my cool. I let the bear come out and thrash wildly instead of using my head.

Just like my dad would have.

I showered in silence, the guys thankfully sensing I wanted to be in my own head for a while. I dressed slowly, letting everyone empty the locker room so I could hang out in the dim light while Eddie, our equipment manager, collected dirty jerseys for the wash.

"It was a good game, Cam. Don't be so hard on yourself," he said on his way out.

He's been gone for ten minutes now, but I have no intention of leaving this room. I can't even bear to look at my phone. I'm sure there are missed calls and texts from Brooklyn waiting for me. I told Theo to let her know I needed some time alone.

I hope she wasn't disappointed in the version of me she saw.

That's the thought that I keep looping back to. I can handle those looks from anyone but her. For her, I want to be better. I *was* better. My goddamn temper, though! There are so many things I can handle, so many triggers that I've learned to shut down. Something about the constant beating tonight, though, felt personal. And I let it in.

When the locker room door pops open behind me, I jump to my feet. It's late in the afternoon, and most everyone should be at Main Hall celebrating with pizza and loud music. My chest thumps with panic as I peer around the bank of lockers by the bench to see who's come to visit, my brain split in two—one half wishing for Brooklyn, the other praying it's anyone else.

My reality, though, is something I never would have predicted.

"Cameron, right? That's you? Cameron Hass?"

Mr. Bennett files down the hallway toward me, his long coat slung over one arm as he takes his sunglasses off with his other hand.

"Yes, sir. That's me. It's . . . nice to see you again." It isn't really, but that's what I think I'm supposed to say. I hold out my hand, and thankfully he shakes it. I half expect him to give it a short laugh and refuse.

"That was some game. You guys sure pulled out a tough one," he says, propping one foot up on the bench. I remain on my feet because I can't handle the idea of sitting and allowing him to talk down to me. He's intimidating enough eye-to-eye.

"Thank you, sir. And yes. It was a little rough." I touch my fingertips to my puffy cheek. The same spot Cole nailed me was hit about four more times.

"Lipson plays dirty. Always has. We have family friends who have a son who goes there. He doesn't play ball, though. He's more of a tennis-type kid." His lip raises briefly on one side as our eyes meet, like making fun of tennis players is some silent inside joke between the two of us. I can't tell if he's aware of the history I have with the kid I'm pretty sure he's talking about—*Cole*—or if it's all one big coincidence. He's that unreadable.

"You played for Welles, didn't you, sir?" I'm not sure how I mustered the courage to ask a question, but I feel a little steadier on my feet having done so.

Mr. Bennett straightens his spine and rocks his head back as he smiles.

"I did, yes. I was the quarterback all four years I played. We even have a state title in that trophy case that I was a part of."

I nod, mentally touring the football section of our awards case.

"That means you were responsible for half of our championships," I joke.

He drops his chin and manages another smile and short laugh. He points at me, shaking his finger, then folds his arms on top of the coat resting on his leg. The man looks like he belongs on an issue of *Esquire*.

"You're funny, Cameron. That's good. It's a good quality. Always keep that."

My chest actually flutters with butterflies at his compliment. I'm so desperate for this man's approval, my limbs feel numb simply from hearing something close to praise.

"I'll do my best," I answer.

He mashes his lips together as his eyes narrow in thought. The pulse I finally managed to lower jets back up the longer he studies me, and the more seconds that pass without him cluing me in, the more my stomach sinks.

"I'm going to be frank with you, Cameron. And I do hope you know that it's because I like you. Respect you, even," he says.

I swallow hard, steadying myself and wishing now that I was sitting for this.

"I know your situation. Not because I'm nosy, but because in my field, I have to vet out every contact my immediate family has."

"My situation?" I'm playing dumb to an extent, drawing things out. We both know what the elephant in the room is.

"Your dad. Michael Hass. It's a tricky story he has, and I get that. I empathize, even. Wrong place, wrong time, wrong friends. His circumstances are the byproduct of a string of wrong decisions."

My brow draws in at hearing his explanation. It's maybe

the most accurate synopsis of my father's sentencing that I've ever heard.

"Okay," I utter. I sense where this is going, but I want to hear him say it. Maybe I want to see if he has the guts.

"I'm running for Congress. Maybe you've seen my signs."

I've seen his signs everywhere. His signs are enormous.

I don't even bother nodding. The bear inside is growling, and if I make any sudden movement, he's going to convince me to say a whole lot of the wrong things.

"I can't really be fielding questions about my daughter and her choice for a boyfriend while I'm out at meet-and-greets or on debate stages. I'm sure you understand," he says.

"I do not," I respond quickly. My answer earns me an arched brow and a muted guffaw.

"There's that fire I saw on the field today." Through it all, he's still smiling. I feel sick.

He takes every advantage, somehow smelling my sudden weakness, and he leaves me hanging in silence.

"I don't want you seeing my daughter," he finally says bluntly.

I blink and raise my brows.

"Actually, you *won't* see my daughter," he restates.

Still speechless, I hang on his words, waiting for the joke part to break through. The longer he smiles at me quietly, though, the kind of smile I picture a gangster giving his next hit back in the twenties, the more I realize there is no punchline. This isn't a test or a drop-in to get to know his daughter's boyfriend a little better. Even that bullshit about football and tennis players was all foreplay for getting emotionally fucked.

He stands, straightening his coat over his arm once more before he gives me a quick nod, his silent nail in my coffin. He makes it about a dozen steps toward the exit before my bear breaks free.

"With all due respect, sir . . . that isn't your choice to make."

His shoes stick to the floor, and he leaves his back to me for about a second before looking to his side. He never quite peers behind him completely, but I swear to God that man is still smiling. He remains in the dim hallway for a few seconds, the harsh bulb above his head a spotlight on his profile. As if he needed one more thing to add to his mystique.

He finally leaves without a response, and I wait another twenty minutes before I gather my things and leave the room. I never once sit down, though. I stay on my feet through the whole damn thing.

Just like my dad did when someone told him he wasn't good enough for a girl.

Chapter 16

Brooklyn

CAM: *I'm sorry.*

That's all he texted, and it's been hours—an entire trip of the moon's rise and fall—since he sent it. I only mildly understand football, but I know things escalated on the field. And I know Cameron was being targeted. I didn't know why until it was too late.

I couldn't warn him that Cole went to Lipson; I didn't find out until I saw him pull into the Welles parking lot with his father . . . and mine. Cam was already stretching with the team on the field. I feel like girlfriends should be allowed to interrupt sporting events to give their boyfriends vital information.

Cole has never been interested in football. I distinctly remember him throwing a fit when we were ten years old because his dad wanted to play catch with him during a fundraising event at Boston College. He donated a thousand dollars to get to throw the ball on the field with his son. Cole locked himself in a bathroom and refused. My brother ended up throwing with him instead.

He must have looked Cameron up and found him on our football roster. One invite to his dad of course led to another for my dad, and disaster ensued. While Cole's buddies made Cam pay on the field, my dad was fishing for information from me and Cole about how close Cameron and I had become. I had to spend the game sitting next to them because, as my father said, "We need to project the picture-perfect family image in case anyone decides to post a photo." Social media has ruined a lot of things, but the fact it has weaseled its way into the lives of forty-year-old men is a new low.

The brawl near the end of the game was basically the rotten cherry on top of a truly awful day. Morgan and I have started a cold war, which has made being in the dorm room awkward for all three of us. I wouldn't have been able to sit with her and Lily even if my dad wasn't at the game. Now it's Saturday, I can't find Cameron anywhere, and Theo and Lily have decided to drive into the city for the weekend, which puts my dorm room completely off limits. I can't be in a room alone with Morgan right now; I'm not sure what either of us would do. I'm pretty much stranded with no place to go and nothing to do but wander campus aimlessly in search of clues.

I tried our hiking spot first, and I've circled the library a dozen times. Even if I could finagle my way through Cameron's secret window to the lair, I doubt he's in there. It's the middle of the day and if he's really trying to avoid me, he would expect that to be the place I checked first. He doesn't want to be found.

I send him one more text, on top of the five I've already sent telling him he has nothing to be sorry for and to call me.

ME: *I only want to know you're ok. Take as long as you need, but please let me know you're ok.*

I stare at the cursor on my screen for a few seconds,

desperately wanting to add more to my note—a heart, maybe? I should just say *I love you*. But I'm not sure if that would help or hurt him. No . . . that's a lie. I'm afraid to say it in case everything falls apart. If I don't say it, then it isn't real, and I can't be hurt.

When my phone buzzes with a reply, I jolt, instantly flipping on my screen. It's not a message from Cameron, though. It's a reminder from Caroline Powell to stop by for the annual report and trustee's board portfolios for my dad. He's an honorary board member, another gesture the Powells made to court his good name and ride its coattails. It's a two-way street with the board, though. My dad has used the cachet of being an elite school board member to earn his way onto a few higher profile academic boards in Boston, including MIT. He hasn't said as much, but the day will come when he drops serving on the Welles board, no longer needing it. Maybe the Powells sense that, and that's why they are pushing so hard for every name drop they can get before I graduate. My father no longer has a reason to lend his name.

I spin on my heels and head back in the direction I came from, passing the library for a thirteenth time on my way to the headmaster's home. The groundskeepers are out working today, probably prepping the home for the annual fall open house. The rich oranges and golds have really started to pop these last few weeks, which is always a good selling point to lure more students from out of state. Locals like me are almost guaranteed applications, but drawing people east from the Midwest, or better yet, California, is always the goal. Not because the school wants to be diverse, but because they want to spread their political power, sinking hooks into more big names and out-of-state representatives.

I climb the grand limestone steps to the large glass and

iron door, pressing the ornate doorbell that calls to Caroline's office.

"It's me," I say into the intercom when it crackles with a connection.

"Brooklyn, wonderful. You got my message. I'll have Ashley open up for you. Be right down."

The door clicks and a second later Caroline's assistant, Ashley, is pulling the door open to welcome me inside. She leads me to the infamous library with the grand piano, and my mind instantly goes to Cameron.

"Can I get you anything? Tea? Water?" Ashley offers.

The last thing I want to have to do is pee in this place and somehow end up on a tour.

"I'm fine. Thank you," I say, taking a seat on the curved sofa that faces two leather chairs, an ornately carved wooden coffee table sitting in the very middle. I lean back into the pillowy cushion, a baffled laugh slipping from my mouth.

"Where were these seats at the last party?" I whisper to myself, sinking into a relaxing heaven.

"Do you like them?" Caroline bursts my spa-like respite with her voice followed by the punctuated clicks of her pointy-toed heels on the floor. She's wearing a pant suit. She always seems to be working, but I suddenly feel underdressed wearing jeans and a Welles sweatshirt.

"Very much," I say, sitting up tall again. I lay my hand on the cushion next to me and press down to test the softness. Yep, just as soft one seat over.

"I just bought them. This room felt like it needed more conversation areas. You know, for when we hold events and things. So people have somewhere to sit."

I practically choke on my *uh huh*. She doesn't even remember my fall, and that was only days ago. I'm sure she was *super* concerned.

"I sent Ashely to the storage room to get one of the nice leather folders for the reports," she says.

"Oh, you didn't need to do that." She's no longer looking at me, and it wouldn't matter if I told her that this report is simply going to be passed on to my dad's press secretary, Belinda, and by the time she's done with it, it will only amount to a bullet point on a fact sheet.

Caroline grazes about the room while we wait, casually dragging her fingertips along tabletops and trinkets, as if drawing attention to the opulence of this space. She doesn't really own any of this. She doesn't even rent it. The Welles home is under her custodianship as long as her husband serves as headmaster. And yes, the Powells have a good amount of wealth on their own, but the legacy of Welles is only something they are borrowing.

"You know, it's so strange to have a room this full of books and absolutely no time to read them," she says, stopping on a copy of *Jane Eyre*. She flips through the crisp pages, the spine crackling as if the book is being opened for the first time ever.

"That's one of my favorites," I say. She shuts the cover and glances up at me.

"*Hmmm?* Oh, yes. Glorious story." *She's never read it.*

She pauses at the ladder for a moment, tilting her head as she looks at it quizzically. It's exactly where Cameron left it after taking it for a ride the night he helped me escape this place without Caroline calling in a surgical team and an ambulance.

"*Hmmm*," she says, dragging it back to the place where Cameron found it. The wheels creak along the way.

"It's a beautiful piano," I say, wanting to fill the dead air.

Caroline's smile spreads and she moves toward shining black lacquer, the glow of the canned lights twenty feet above us shining in the reflection of the waxed lid.

"Do you play?" she asks.

I shake my head with a light laugh.

"My family is not musically inclined. We can't even play the kazoo," I say. She doesn't laugh along with me. Instead, her brow grows heavy and draws in with pity, as if she feels bad that I missed out on being able to have recitals.

"I played for years. I even had a concert once with the symphony at the old Orpheum Theater." She takes a seat on the bench and runs her fingers along the lid covering the keys.

"Do you . . . still play?" I won't be shocked if she grows animated and forces me to endure an hour-long performance with the way this interaction is going. Thankfully, though, she only laments the days when she did.

"No, again . . . who has the time. And my hands aren't what they used to be. Arthritis is a cruel woman," she says with a short-lived smirk.

"Why does arthritis have to be a woman?"

"Oh!" She cuts off my question immediately, rising from the bench and moving toward the grand bookcase again. Her hand zeroes in on the copy of *Gulliver's Travels*, and I hold in my amusement that she's discovering all of the things Cameron probably messed up in this room. I wonder if he didn't push the spine in perfectly.

"Now, this book. Oh, Brooklyn. I adore this book. So does my husband," she says, pulling it out the same way she did with *Jane Eyre*. Unlike that book, though, she's careful with the pages, which are obviously well-worn.

"You know, it's so funny . . . when my grandson was younger and lived with us for a summer, we forced him to read this book. Oh, how he hated it. I would make him sit right there on the floor while I watched, quizzing him a few pages at a time to make sure he was really reading because if I didn't he would pretend."

My lips part, and I keep my mouth from hanging open in an obvious way.

Her head swivels and her gaze zooms to me.

"You know what he said about it?" she asks.

"He thought it was boring . . ." The words slip from my mouth as if a ghost said them.

Her forehead dents.

"Huh. Actually yes. That's exactly what he said." She snaps the book shut. "He *hated* this book. And I know he read it because we discussed it at length after every chapter."

It can't be. Yet it positively is.

"Did he take piano lessons? Your grandson?" I fish because I need more to solidify my near-certain suspicion.

"When we had him at the house, yes. He took to it quickly too, but you know boys." She slides *Gulliver's Travels* back into its spot. "He didn't want to practice or show up for lessons. He would fake these stomach aches. He was always more interested in climbing trees than learning the arts."

Climbing.

"Ah, Ashley. Thank you!" Caroline abandons the source of her memories, and I'm left puzzling over these stories I am fairly sure she is not supposed to share. She meets her assistant in the center of the room and passes the leather binder along to me.

"Much better," she says as I slip the reports into the folder in front of her. My dad will never see this, but it's fine.

"If you don't mind sending me an email when you give this to your father . . ."

"Of course," I say through a courtesy smile. I stand quickly and move toward the exit, anxious to show myself out. My mouth is dry, which is inconvenient because I need my voice to work for *all these damn questions I have!*

I beat Ashley to the door, opening it for myself, which

seems to fluster Caroline. I hope she doesn't scold Ashley for not sprinting to get there first. I offer a polite wave over my shoulder and practically skip down the steps toward the library for one final inspection.

I would need a ladder to reach the window Cameron uses to slip into the archive room, and I'm too embarrassed to shout his name from outside. I should have kept Theo's key, but I also didn't want any evidence pointing to me in case someone learned Cameron and I were in there. Doing . . . what we did.

Defeated, I decide the best thing to do is actually study, or at least pretend to. My laptop is in my tote bag, so I maybe I can knock out my computational homework. It takes me longer than a lot of other students in our class to work through the Excel formulas, so I guess I may as well hide from my roommate and get caught up.

Mid-terms are soon, so it's a little more crowded than I'm used to in here. Most students escape to the city on the weekends unless tests are coming up. I pass through the crowded tables and computer stations, pausing to visit the giant gold-fish that we all call Bert before slipping into the stacks. If the chairs in the back are all taken, I can always find a quiet row near the reference books to make myself comfortable on the floor.

The first chair I come to is my favorite, so I pull the leather binder from my tote bag and fling it into the open seat, not bothering to glance at the ones behind it. I don't even notice Cameron staring at me, in fact, until I sit down and prop my legs up on the small table covered in books others have left behind.

I freeze the moment our eyes meet, and the only word I seem to be able to muster is *oh*. Cameron doesn't speak at all. My chest hurts, and the conflicting noises in my head pummel me. I want to know everything all at once. *Why haven't you called me back? Texted? Where have you been? What happened yesterday? Are you okay? Are the Powells really your grandparents?*

I don't say any of it, though. Because tears are sliding down Cameron's cheeks. I get up from my seat and move to the space between his knees, resting my palms on his thighs as his head falls forward to rest against mine and his hands cup my cheeks. He exhales a stuttered breath, and my heart cracks into a million pieces. He's hurting, and none of that other stuff matters.

"Tell me," I say. And maybe that tiny command is enough to cover everything. For Cameron, it seems to be everything. His weight shifting forward, I sit on the ground as he falls into me, all arms and shaking chest, his mouth muffled by the crook of my neck as he cries so hard I worry maybe he won't be able to stop.

Chapter 17

Cameron

Four Hours Earlier

"Wow, you look like hell."

Sadly, this is not the first time Theo has said those exact words to me. Probably because this is not the first time I have woken up on the floor halfway through our door after passing out drunk. It's been a while, but still, not a first.

I roll onto my back and work to pry my lips apart. They fused together crooked on account of my face being mashed into the floor for the last . . . *wait, what time is it?*

I groan as Theo steps over me on his way into our room. I flatten my palms on the floor on either side and sit up, the world tilting with me. My hand grips the door jamb and I squeeze my eyes shut, waiting for the rotating to stop.

"What time is it?"

"It's seven. Still early, if you want to crawl your ass in here and sleep the rest of whatever that is off," he says, drawing an invisible circle with his finger around my body.

I rub my face, trying to make sense of what seven means.

"Are you coming in? Or going out?"

I don't remember making it to my dorm. I do remember an excessive number of shots with Conner and Wade from the team out of the back of Wade's pickup. And I vaguely remember Wade trying to talk us all into heading into the woods to go camping, despite the fact we had zero equipment. I'm not sure whether they ended up going or not, but I had enough sense to skip that last shot—*not that skipping number six after five is something to hang your hat on*—and hop out of the truck bed and come here. Or almost here.

"Lily and I are going into the city for the weekend. I just popped in to grab my shit. I'm guessing by the state of things you won't be inviting Brooklyn over to spend the night?" His lips twist with disappointment. I wince and let my forehead fall into my palms.

"Dude, I don't even know," I groan. "Things are kind of fucked up."

"Yeah, well . . . I told you," he says over his shoulder, empty duffle in his hands.

"Super helpful." I lean into the door jamb for balance as I stand, my temples pounding inward, ringing my head. "Asshole," I mutter.

Theo chortles as he stuffs jeans and a couple of shirts into his bag. I make it to my bed and fall onto my ass. Theo tosses a bottle of Tylenol at my chest, and I manage to catch it. It takes me longer than it should to get it open, and by the time I do, my friend is standing in front of me with a plastic tumbler full of water.

"Thanks," I say, tossing three pills on my tongue then gulping down half of the water.

"Did she dump you?" he asks with such authority, so sure he's right and has this whole thing figured out.

I roll my eyes and fall back on my stack of pillows and laundry.

"Apparently the ass kicking I got for forty-eight minutes yesterday was courtesy of this guy Brooklyn knows."

Theo lifts a brow.

"What guy?" he asks.

"Cole *I-Wear-Boots-With-Everything-burg*, or something like that."

"Masterson? Oh, ha! That fuck!" Theo claps a few times through hard laughter. "Yeah, I know him. I didn't know he went to Lipson. Wait . . . he doesn't play, does he? He's not really a football guy. I mean, I threw a frisbee to him once and it cut open his eyelid."

I laugh at the visual, but only for half a second before my head throbs. I plant my fists on both temples and push lightly to relieve the pressure.

"He doesn't play. Brooklyn and I ran into him when we were at this coffee shop downtown during our internships. I guess he had a thing for her, and I was standing in line next to her, so I became target number one or some shit."

"That's why you had the black eye and busted lip . . . I mean before these new ones," Theo says, amused by his stupid joke.

"Ha ha," I overexaggerate. "But yes, Cole and I had a little bit of a *talk*."

"He kicked your fucking ass, didn't he?" Theo's smug grin pisses me off, so I zing the bottle of Tylenol back at him. It bounces off one of his pecs.

"I got him pretty good, too," I defend. My friend responds with a poorly muffled laugh.

"I'm sure," he finally says. His face clearly indicates he's lying out his ass.

"Aren't you leaving or something?" I grumble.

Theo screws up his face and studies me for a beat before moving his bag to the side and sitting down across from me.

"Real time. What does Cole Masterson have to do with you and Brooklyn, and what is really going on? No judgement, I swear. But I can't give you good advice if I'm missing pieces of the story."

His serious glare wears me down after a few seconds. I blow out, vibrating my lips and layering my forearms over my eyes.

"It's always been Brooklyn. And don't pretend you don't know that. I know who I am, and I'm not that guarded about how I interact with people. I've been an idiot around her since the day we met."

"This is true," Theo agrees. I move my arm and peer at him with one eye, but his expression is sincere. He's not making fun of me.

"We started talking a lot, and things sort of just . . . happened. It's so easy with her, bro. Like we could talk for hours, and I feel like myself with her. Maybe that sounds dumb, but—"

"It's not dumb. I get it," he cuts me off.

I flop my arms to my side and lift my head to meet his eyes.

"Her dad came to see me."

His face falls, his eyes hazing as he leans back on his palms and drops his chin to his chest.

"Fuck. Really?"

I nod.

"He was at the game. Came into the locker room after you all left. Told me not to see his daughter."

"Shit, man. What did you say?"

A short laugh puffs my lips and Theo tilts his head to the side.

"Cam, no . . . you didn't."

"I was professional," I defend. "I told him it wasn't up to him."

Theo laughs out hard as his eyes widen.

"Well," he says, sitting forward and rubbing his hands together. "He won't think you're weak, so that's probably good."

"You think?" I quirk a brow.

"No." He laughs. "Nothing about maneuvering a relationship with a Bennett is good. But is it worth it?"

I hold his stare for a few seconds.

"Yeah, it's worth it."

"Then, there you go," he says, standing up and pulling his bag over his arm. "See? You didn't need me. You just need to sober up, and I'm not the man for that."

He stops his steps in the middle of our room and looks at me sideways.

"Thanks, man. Seriously," I say.

He nods with a tight-lipped grin then leaves our room and lets the door slam behind him just to remind me that I'm hungover.

At the sensation of a text coming in, I feel in my pocket for my phone and pull it out. It's from Brooklyn, wanting to know I'm okay. It's not her first message either, and it looks like she's called me. I need to find her. I know she said it wasn't my fault, but I need to be better than that. I let those guys push my buttons. I let them win. I embarrassed myself, and now that I know Brooklyn's dad was there, I probably embarrassed her, too.

I gather my things for a shower and make my way to the bathroom to get cleaned up. I'm not sure how long I stand under the steaming hot water, but long enough to feel semi-human. I slip into a pair of jeans and a long-sleeved black tee that smells nothing like bootlegged whatever-the-hell-that-was-I-drank-last-night.

I grab my wallet and phone then head out the door, poised to call Brooklyn and beg her to forgive me for going dark last night. I make it to the stairwell when my phone buzzes with a book's worth of paragraphs type of text. I don't recognize the number, so I scroll back to the top of the message and stop to read it from the start.

UNKNOWN: *Hello Cameron. This is Hal Burkhauser. Your mother gave me your number and said I could contact you. I tried calling yesterday afternoon. I would have left a voicemail, but it said your inbox was full.*

I purse my lips and silently scold myself for being lazy. I haven't emptied my voicemail in a year. It's probably full of useless messages from dumbasses who want to get high or drunk. Angry at myself, I stop at the bottom of the stairs and take a seat on the last two steps, first spending an entire eleven seconds on deleting the messages in my voicemail—*seriously, I'm a lazy fuck*—and then reading the rest of Hal's message.

I'm researching your father's last hearing and I noticed that someone wrote a letter in support of denying him parole. I did some digging and was able to get a copy of the full file with the letter. It was written by Walden Bennett. You may or may not recognize his name, but he is running for Senate and is currently serving in the President's cabinet. Your mother said he's a Welles alumnus. I made a few calls, and it seems his daughter actually attends Welles now. In the event that you know her, I thought maybe you could reach out to see if she would be willing to help your lawyer connect with her father for some research. I don't want to put you in an awkward situation, so I can handle the details. We would like to know why he requested a denial, but more importantly, it would be good to know if he plans to do so again. Please let me know when you receive this and if you are able to assist. I'm really hopeful we can help your dad this time. Kindly, HB

I'm not sure how long I have been sitting in this stairwell staring at his message, reading it over and over with foolish hope that one time it will read differently. It never does because that's a stupid fantasy. Reality is shit. Reality is cruel. Reality wants to crush my soul and still my heart and bury my worth all at once.

I'm too broken to scream, and my body has lost the will to be strong. I can't even seem to cry on the outside. Inside, I'm drowning. How? How is this my life?

A door a few floors up slams and the stairs begin to echo with clomping steps and laughter. I get to my feet and run my hand through my hair, pulling it forward to hide my face in case they catch up to me. I manage to make it out of the building just as a bunch of third years rush out behind me with a football. They literally toss it to one another over my head as I trudge along the main walkway toward the library. I bypass my trusty window because I don't think I have the strength to scale the wall and pull myself through. Plus, this place is the first place Brooklyn will look for me, and I need time to process everything. How do I even share this with her?

The trail is busy with students today. It's one of those rare crisp mornings with a bright sun and an ocean-blue sky. If I were any of these other people, I would be out here too, loving life and breathing this air. This air isn't for me, though. The place I'm at—the darkness in my head—needs to be buried.

Desperate to get away from people, I decide to slip into

the *actual* library, somewhere quiet where nobody would look for me. Somewhere people go to read books for a long time and study their weekends away.

I find myself in the far corner where old newspapers are bound and organized by year and where donated sets of encyclopedias are collecting dust because we have a fucking Internet now. It's the most useless nook on this campus, and there's a chair. I wish there weren't four of them, but it's solitary enough for now.

My body sinks into the worn leather and I slump down, propping my phone on my stomach and holding it at the top with the tip of my finger. I tap the screen to wake it up and stare at the worst part of Hal's message again.

Walden Bennett.

Somehow, Brooklyn's father hated me before he even knew who I was. A premonition, perhaps. This can't be on accident. This isn't happenstance. This is premeditated cruelty. And I don't know how to handle it.

Present

I love her.

I love her so fucking much.

I loved Brooklyn before we got together. I loved her fiercely a day a go. Right now, I love her more than all matters of life.

I have cried twice in my life, not counting childhood bruises and scrapes. The first time I cried was when my mom told me I needed to live with my grandparents because her graduate programs were too demanding. I was nine, and I hated my grandparents. *I still hate them.*

This is my second cry. And it burns deep.

The first time my dad was up for parole, I was prepared. I knew it wasn't common for prisoners to be granted early release on their first hearing. I had hope because it had been sixteen years, but when it wasn't granted, I didn't cry.

Now, I cry for then. I cry for my present. I cry for the days stolen from my father and me for reasons I can't possibly comprehend. *For a campaign slogan.* That's the fear that has been tearing at my heart for hours. What if this was all about a campaign? Just like his threat to keep me and Brooklyn apart.

The sunset outside the library windows spills warm golden rays across the room, the dust particles in the air sparkling around us. They'll be closing the library soon, and we'll have to move. I haven't been able to say the words yet; I need to, though. It's been hours of crying and hours of sick silence. Brooklyn deserves to know why she found me like this. She needs to know everything, from the very beginning of yesterday's football game to this moment right now.

She needs context.

"Theo's gone for the weekend, and I would really like it if you would come to my room with me. I want you there. With me. There's . . ." My chest burns with acid, anger, and the weight of my helpless situation, and it takes my voice away. I wrap my hand around my throat and breathe, feeling the tendons and muscles work under my palm.

"Tell me. I promise it will be okay," she says. It's the same vow she has made all afternoon. But she doesn't know what she's guaranteeing. There is no way this doesn't hurt her too.

"I love you. Before I show you this, I need you to know that hasn't changed, and when I said I have loved you for years, I meant it. I love you, and not like a boy with a crush. I love your smile and passion and drive. I love that you are the smartest person in this school, and that you still worry over every single test you take. I love that you call me a nice guy when you tell other people about me. Not a pothead or a daredevil or . . . a jerk."

She shakes her head in protest at my self admonishing. I take her hands in mine and hold them to my chest.

"I don't care what other people say about me, Brooky. I care about you. What you say and see. What you feel. And when you read this, I need you to remember that no matter what, none of it has anything to do with you."

Her eyes droop and pool with tears that beg to fall.

"No, don't cry. You can't cry yet." A pathetic, breathy laugh leaves my mouth as I wrap my arms around her and hold her to me.

"You said yet," she says against my chest. She twists her head enough to look up at me. I won't lie to her.

"You will probably cry. Just don't do it yet." My words send the ready tears down her cheeks, and I erase them quickly with a brush of my thumbs.

I wait until her eyes dip below mine and her shoulders drop with her breath.

"I'm ready," she whispers.

I pull my phone from my pocket, the message I've nearly memorized still pulled up when I wake my screen.

"So much has happened in the last two days, and I wanted to tell . . . you . . ." I begin. I stammer when her eyes flash to mine. I tilt my head slightly, waiting for her to fill me in, but she simply blinks away.

"Sorry, go on," she hums, eyes back at my chest.

"Well, most important right now is my dad's next hearing was set. It's in two weeks."

And her eyes are back, her mouth open.

"Cam!" she whisper-shouts. It crushes me that her lips are tinged with a smile. I try to remember the good and force one on my face, too.

"Yeah, it's pretty amazing," I say, struggling not to choke on my words.

"You don't sound amazed." The glossiness returns to her eyes, and my heart hurts.

I'm not able to keep up with the pretend smile. It was pitiful to begin with.

"My mom has a friend who's like this really good lawyer. She doesn't talk to my dad, and their relationship—if you can even call it a relationship—is pretty fucked up. I know she still loves him. She'll never say it out loud, but it's there."

"A lawyer sounds like a good thing." Her voice has a tinge of hope. This will crush her.

"I thought so, too. Thing is, he's been doing some research. And honestly?" My head falls back and I squeeze my eyes tight, steeling myself for the next minute of my life. "Gah! It's better for you to read his words. I got this text this morning."

I hand her my phone, and she cradles it in her palms, her eyes lifting to meet mine before she reads. My mouth a tight line, I nod once. I have to let go, and honestly, I need her to know everything I know. I am so tired of being at the bottom alone.

Her gaze drops and I hold my breath as her eyes scan left to right. It's when they stop moving that I know her heart just broke.

"Remember what I said. None of this is you. Nothing changes about how I feel about *you*."

Her head nods softly, but her eyes remain on my phone screen. It's hard to wait through the silence, but I must. This isn't the kind of thing that can be rushed, no matter how badly I want to race through to the end, to find something happy there. Anything happy.

It takes her minutes to finally release my phone from her grasp. I tuck it into my pocket and nudge her chin up until our eyes meet. Her light is gone, and I'm so sorry I was the one who turned it off.

"Your dad came to see me yesterday, after the game."

Her eyes tilt and her brow grows heavier.

"He told me not—"

"Don't." She presses her palm on my chest, stopping me before I relay her father's warning to me.

She shakes her head as her eyes blink rapidly before her gaze snaps to mine.

"What he said doesn't matter. Nothing he says . . . matters." Her jaw flexes at the end of her words. I recognize this mixture of heartbreak and anger.

I lean my head to the side.

"Come home with me?" I need her. She needs me.

She blinks away tears that are not coming. She's too angry to cry. Too disappointed to cry.

"Home," she says, pulling that single thread out and letting it settle the static in the air.

"Home," I echo. I guess yes, this place, my tiny half of a room, is home—the most home I've ever had, really. My six years as a student here have given me a place to build an identity, and it's the only place in my entire life that I've been able to.

Brooklyn hooks her fingers through mine then leads me away from the chairs, picking up her bag from the floor and some leather folder that she shoves inside. Like zombies, we amble through the shelves and the silent library lobby, across the main lawn, and into my dorm. Without a single word exchanged, I slip out of my shoes and shove the clothes from my bed before lying down against the wall so I can pull Brooklyn into my arms to rest against me. Back to chest, we take long, deep breaths. Sleep won't come for me, and I doubt it will for her, but this quiet room with nothing but the two of us is the only medicine I need. This is therapy. It's real love.

"I wish you told me about your grandparents."

Her soft voice still cuts sharp. My chest tightens, but only for a minute. I've gotten so used to not talking about my relationship to Welles, to the headmaster—at their request—that deception was never my intent. I've spent years hating them and their rules, resenting the times I was forced to stay with them for months at a time. When I turned fifteen and was able to stand up for myself, to refuse, I was liberated. Lying about who they were quit being a lie. They became an occasional obligation. I needed this school. Mom needed their money. And that was it.

"I wish they weren't my grandparents," I finally say. It's all there is to say. It's the truth.

After a few seconds, Brooklyn pulls my hand to her lips and kisses the back of it before pressing my palm against her cheek.

"Okay," she breathes. "Okay."

For hours we lie in silence. I stroke her arm with a gentle touch and visualize that I'm actually burying all of the garbage that's been heaped upon us in the last twenty-four hours.

Fingertips roam to her wrist—*I push the shovel into the dirt.*

A slow line drawn up to her shoulder—*I throw the dirt over my shoulder.*

Once the hole is deep enough, I push everything in. My mom's resentment and fear. My grandparents' harsh rules and greed. Every single day I missed my dad. It all goes in the hole, and I bury it with every breath Brooklyn takes in my arms.

Chapter 18

Brooklyn

A t 4 a.m., Cameron finally found sleep. His body and mind agreed he had enough, that he needed a break. I turned in his arms and watched him for hours. Every twitch of the eyelid and part of his lips made me wonder and hope if he was in a dream. His mouth rested in the softest smile, the hint of it so small that if I weren't looking this closely, I would miss it.

But it's there. The smile is still there. Even now as the sun threatens to break through his window and light up this room.

I slip out of his bed, careful not to make any sudden sounds or wake him with jolting movements. My eyes feel bruised with emotion. I can't seem to cry no matter how badly I need to. My face feels swollen with exhaustion.

My tote bag sits on the chair by his desk, my phone turned off in the bottom. My instincts told me to shut things down. My father's call is coming. Or an email or a text, more likely. That's his preferred method of difficult conversations with me. Always at a distance.

On my hands and knees, I inch my way along the floor and slowly pull my bag to my lap. I tear a sheet of paper from the report Caroline gave me. It's nothing but a decorative pattern, an unnecessary expense added to a book filled with names. That's all this report is. It's not even a *thank you*. It's a make good. For ten thousand dollars, the names in this book get to exist.

I sift through the bottom of my bag for a pen and write a short note to Cameron, letting him know that I had to go back to my room but will be back before noon. I sign it the way he deserves.

I love you.

I leave the note on his pillow, and despite my craving to crawl back into his arms and kiss him, I let him sleep. I have no idea when he will have this opportunity again. That, and I can't have the painful conversation I need to with my father if Cameron's eyes are on me. Nothing about what I need to say makes me proud, and I don't want to share that shame with anyone. Not even him.

The hallway is clear when I peek out his door, so I tiptoe into the hall and latch his door with a nearly silent click. I pull my phone out to check the time once I make it to the stairwell. It's a little after seven, which probably means Morgan is asleep in her bed in our room. I pause before I step out onto the campus lawn, faced with another decision point. I would love to change my clothes. A shower would be a dream. I'm not sure which conversation I'm looking forward to least, the one with my father or the one with Morgan. I wish I could sit them both on a sofa and hash it out all at once.

Deciding my father's conversation is the one that matters most to Cameron, I step outside and head toward the river instead of my dorm. I wait until I'm by the water to dial my father's number, anticipating I'll need to call him more than once to spur him to actually answer. Instead, he picks up on the second ring.

"Good morning." His voice is cheery. He's probably been up for an hour.

"We need to talk." My voice wavers, and I hate myself for it.

"I assumed this call was coming," he says.

A door snaps closed through the phone. He must be stepping outside onto my parents' patio. My mom has a small garden in the back of their brownstone. Over the summer, when I couldn't do much else, I sat in one of the loungers and watched her and Eva, my mother's assistant, plant a variety of herbs and spices. Once campaign season picked up, though, she let the plants go. That patch of ground is nothing more than dead twigs now. Last time I was home, she was talking to Eva about ripping everything out and covering it with brick for an outdoor fireplace. That won't get any use either.

"Mom home?" I don't know why that matters, but this conversation will be easier for me to have if my mom's ears aren't listening in to his half.

"She's with the society ladies at the club. They're hosting a brunch later for the campaign," he says.

It's good that he can't see my face. Normally, I am invested in these things, asking to help. But this world has lost its luster. Looking back on the last year, I think it's been a gilded cage for a while.

"Good," I say.

"I've already talked to your mother about this, Brooklyn. And she agrees with me." My feet tumble to a stop on the gravel trail, and I drop my tote to the ground.

"You and mom discussed . . . what exactly?" I know what they discussed, and I know how that conversation went. My father said it would be a bad look for me to date Cameron Hass, and my mother agreed because that's what she does with everything. Like when I was in the hospital recovering after a horrible accident that took away my best friend, and my father didn't bother to come because he was "tied up in Washington." He told her she could handle it. So, she did.

"Brooklyn, I don't know why you're making such a big deal out of this. You don't have the time to be dating boys and having boyfriends anyhow. We have more important things on our plate."

My mouth hangs open, and after a second, the single laugh that was caught in my throat flies from my mouth.

"It's not *my* plate, Dad. It's yours. And you have no idea what I do and do not have time for. I'm shocked you know how old I am. In fact, *do you* know how old I am, Dad?"

His sigh is heavy enough to vibrate the phone.

"You're eighteen. We took you to your favorite restaurant on your birthday." He remembers because it was *his* favorite restaurant, and he's wrong about the date.

"Yeah, it was a week after my birthday, but I guess you were close. You couldn't fit me in on the actual day." I snag my tote bag handles with one finger and march to a large bank of rocks by the water so I have a place to sit, not that I'll be able to quit pacing anytime soon.

"Brooklyn, what's this all about? You're being dramatic. There will be other boys."

I stomp my foot like a child and cup my mouth to keep myself from screaming. It takes a few seconds to put the fire out in my head. I sit on one of the large flat rocks and rest my forehead in my palm, my elbows propped on my knees.

"There will be other boys," I echo through low, irritated laughter. "Dad, I need you to be honest with me."

"I always am," he answers quickly, wearing those three

words like a badge of honor. Let's time test this pledge to always tell me the truth.

"Why don't you want me seeing Cameron Hass?"

I expect silence. Fumbling through words. False starts. But true to his word, Walden Bennett is direct and to the point.

"His father is a convicted felon and being connected to him in any way would be a stain on the campaign."

My eyebrows shoot up.

"Wow," I say. I'm not necessarily surprised that he said it. I'm only shocked that he didn't spin it more. There was zero sugar-coating to his response. But he did leave out one important detail.

"Is it because of Michael Hass's crime? Or because you wrote the parole board to request denial of his parole?" This question proves a bit trickier, and I don't get such a rapid-fire response.

"Yeah, I've learned a few things, Dad. And maybe you're aware of this, maybe not, but he has another parole hearing in two weeks. Your letter showed up in his lawyer's research."

The line is still silent, and that fuels me. I much prefer the fast truths. The silent plotting is the kind of thing he should reserve for opponents, not his own daughter.

"Dad, please say you aren't—"

"I am. I already did," he says.

I shoot to my feet and scan my surroundings before cupping the phone.

"You already *what* exactly?" I seethe.

"Wrote another letter supporting denial. Brooklyn, he's a convicted felon."

I laugh out at his logic.

"Says the candidate running on prison reform! What happened to your strong belief in our justice system and reforming those in it to become meaningful, contributing members of society once again?" Bullshit. It's all bullshit! It always is, but I was blinded by my admiration for him. I thought my dad was different. I thought he stood for more than simply getting the gig that leads to the next gig. I'm sick.

"It's not so black and white, Brooklyn. You don't understand the details," he says.

"Well, good thing I'm getting an expensive prep school education that has armed me with a fairly good understanding of the law, history, and the Massachusetts judicial system. Michael Hass's weapon wasn't loaded. He wasn't the one who pulled the trigger, and he cooperated fully with police. Dad, he's literally the poster child for the point you're trying to make. Cameron says his dad has completed more educational hours than any other prisoner in the past two decades."

"Brooklyn—" He cuts me off, which I hate. He's done it since I was a child. When I'm on a roll and making a point, he simply uses an authoritative tone and brings my ideas to a halt. My train of thought is already gone.

"What?" I shout. I'm out here alone, but anyone walking within a hundred-yard radius probably heard that.

"Do you know the Powells?"

I shake my head and part my lips as my brow draws in so tight it folds.

"Yes, I know the Powells. They're Cameron's grandparents. Headmaster Powell. I go to this school, so yeah . . . I know who they are." I'm flustered and pissed, and I can't stop pressing my palm into my forehead.

"I wrote both letters at their request."

And . . . *fuck.*

My hand falls to my side.

"They asked you?"

"To request a denial. Yes, they did," he finishes for me.

I spin slowly, my mind pivoting back to Cameron, his peaceful dream, and the faint smile on his lips when I left him minutes ago.

"Why?"

"They have their reasons," he says.

"That's dodging my question," I bite back.

"*Hmm*," he mutters into the phone.

The line goes quiet again. I glance down at the leather folder in my tote bag, staring at it while I wait for audible clues of what my father is thinking, what he's doing, and where this conversation is going.

"I owed them this, Brooklyn. They have done a lot to support me through the alumni network, and I have promised to help them when I can. Not every part of politics feels good. But I wouldn't make decisions I didn't believe in on some level. It's the right thing to do now, like it was then." I can tell by his tone that he believes it.

I let his argument simmer in my chest. I try to find the places where it fits with what I know. I would give anything to be able to match the man I thought my father was with this act and everything I know about Cameron and Michael Hass. And in the end, I simply can't.

"Then I'm ashamed of you, Dad."

I end our call and drop my phone into my bag. My throat closes briefly, my chest feeling the weight of a lifetime of worship crumbling down on it. That stupid leather folder teases me, and that is at least one thing I can do something about. Without pause, I bend down and pull it from my bag then fling it into the freezing stream of water. It snags on a few rocks as it floats to the lower portion of the river, where the bottom is deeper and the current less gentle. With any luck, in minutes it will be waterlogged and buried under algae and sand a mile away.

* * *

I'm self-aware enough to avoid going directly from the river trail to my dorm. Things are so jacked between me and Morgan, the last thing our relationship needs is the complicated noise of my father.

Instead of bringing that baggage upstairs with me, I decide to return to Cameron's room and watch him sleep a little longer. His rhythm is peaceful. When I'm lying next to him, I can't help but breathe with the counts of his heart. Maybe if I lie there long enough, I'll fall asleep too.

Still early on a Sunday morning, it takes nearly thirty minutes for one of the third years to exit the side door. I compliment the young freshman on his choice of shirt—a classic Prince T-shirt—and it brings a smile to his face and maybe spawns a tiny crush on his part. It's enough to get him to hold the door open for me and let me sneak inside.

I take the stairs slowly, my body exhausted and my leg in need of rest. By the time I reach Cameron's floor, I'm winded, which is a bad sign of the shape I'm in. I'm going to need to do more climbing with Cameron. And since I won't be spending time volunteering for my dad's campaign anymore, I'll be able to work out with him more often.

Once my pulse stops drumming in my head, I run my sleeve across my damp forehead and reach into my bag for a pencil to stick in and hold a makeshift knot of hair on top of my head. I'm quite literally a hot mess when I slip into the hallway and roll my feet in near-silent steps toward Cam's door.

"I don't know what's wrong with me."

Morgan's voice spills out Cameron's ajar door. I stop hard and swallow, holding my breath to make sure I hear clearly.

"There is nothing wrong with you. That word . . . wrong. It's, well. That word is *wrong*," Cameron says. Morgan's raspy laughter follows.

I lean into the wall to let this moment play out for them. If I were a better person, I would back away and give them privacy. But I'm too invested in the budding friendship to abandon my spy position.

Morgan sniffles, and my mind races back to the last time I remember the sound of her crying. It was at my bedside after my first surgery. She also spent more time in that room with me than my father.

"You're funny sometimes, Hass. You know that?" she says.

"I do."

I cover my mouth to hold in my laugh. He's so fucking charming. She better not fall for him. She can accept him, but that's the line.

"I'm sorry about what I said at lunch the other day. I didn't mean it," she says. My mouth tightens into a hard line and my forehead dents. She was cruel.

"You meant it a little bit, but it's okay," he says. My rigid expression eases with a dose of pride at his response. I love how honest he is.

"It's not okay. And Brooklyn was right. It was unfair, and I don't know you like she does."

If he responds to her, it's inaudible. I wait anyhow, hoping for more. After several seconds, Morgan breaks the quiet.

"I think she might be in love with you," she says. Without seeing her face, it's hard to tell if those words were meant to be thoughtful or repulsed.

"I love her, too," he says without pause. A timid smile tugs at my lips. I press my fingertips against my mouth to hold it at bay.

"If you hurt her, I'll fucking claw your eyes out."

My eyes bulge from my head at her instant defense of me, and I nearly laugh and give myself away. Thankfully, Cameron laughs loudly enough to hide any sound I make.

"Point taken, Bentley. Point taken."

"Then, let's shake on it, Hass. A gentlewoman's agreement," Morgan says. I picture her spitting in her palm and holding it out for him like she's always done. For someone branded as the hottest girl in school, she can mix it up with the grit of a very manly union boss when she wants to. And heaven help the poor sap who thinks he can beat her in a game of pool.

The thud of footsteps moving closer to the door injects me with a hit of adrenaline, and my ears ring from the rush of blood. Not being able to hear definitely works against the entire spying plan, so I draw in a deep breath and force myself to step into the room. I nearly run nose first into the center of Cameron's chest when I do.

"Oh! Sorry," I say, grabbing a fistful of his shirt instead of face planting.

I look up into his crooked smile and he bends down to kiss me. His lips linger on mine for an extra beat, probably to show off our affection for Morgan and prove his point—he loves me. I bring my palm to his cheek to prove hers—I love him back.

Knowing Morgan is in the room, I pull off a fake startled expression when I see her sitting on the edge of Theo's bed. She's wearing her break-up pajamas—blue plaid flannel pants that she stole from the college guy she was dating last year and the Bruins sweatshirt she stole from my closet two years ago. When love goes wrong, Morgan dresses for the occasion.

"Uh . . . why are you here?" I stammer. It's only half-pretend because while I listened in on their conversation, I don't have much context for it.

My friend stares at me with red, heavy-lidded eyes. In a matter of seconds, her bottom lip puffs out and she jets to her feet, rushing me with open arms. I glance to Cameron for help, but he shakes his head quickly and slowly blinks to indicate my friend needs me, and however angry I am, I need to accept this embrace.

Our bodies collide and I hug her tight, instant tears and snot pouring onto my shoulder. My face sours and I peer to the side, meeting Cameron's gaze. He laughs soundlessly, but waves his hand in small circles, encouraging me to give her more. I rub my hand on her back, and she takes long breaths until her sobs finally stop.

"I'm so sorry, Brook. I was a total bitch. And you and . . ." She lets go of me and spins to face Cameron. "You too. You are both good people and you deserve each other. You might be the only good people left in this stupid ugly place."

Her acidic tone cuts deep and melts most of the ice I've been forming as a wall between us. She turns back to me and her eyes pool with the weight of a broken heart. I'm not sure what is happening in her life, but this breakdown is proof enough that our petty beef wasn't the cause.

"She came here looking for you," Cameron says over her shoulder.

I glance from him back to my friend. She tries to pull her lips into an apologetic smile, but it falls flat. My head tilts to one side and I reach up and tuck her tear-and-snot clumped hair behind her ear.

"I was about to come back to our room. How about we get you in the shower and then maybe we talk?"

Her nod comes fast, and it relieves the last vestiges of pain in my chest.

"Cam can come too. I mean, not in the shower, but—"

"Damn," Cameron interjects, his typical boy-humor urging Morgan's smile to grow even more.

"Maybe the three of us can hang out for a while and catch up," she suggests.

My eyes flit to Cameron, and his soft expression says he's in.

"That would be nice," I say.

Walden Bennett may have broken my heart a little this morning. But Morgan Bentley? She just shot up in the polls.

Chapter 19

Cameron

Girls have a very different way of bonding and cheering each other up over relationship trouble than dudes do. When we got to Morgan and Brooklyn's room, I set up Brooklyn's laptop to stream the first season of *The Office*. It's a go-to when you need to laugh at absurdity. It works for any situation. Theo and I have our favorite episodes timestamped. The birthday episode. When Michael declares bankruptcy. Dwight . . . period.

Apparently, though, I know nothing. Within minutes, *The Office* turned into the Matthew Macfadyen version of *Pride and Prejudice* because, and I quote, "It is the superior P and P," according to Brooklyn.

It has initials. P and P.

I will admit I liked it better than the book, but probably because I rolled my eyes about a thousand times when I had to read the book in third form. If I had to woo Brooklyn with fancy balls and agreeable walks along the water, I'd be a hermit.

I must be doing something right, though, because ever

since Morgan fell asleep, she has been calling me Darcy. He seems like a good dude, so I accept it.

"Thank you for being here for Morgan. I'm not sure what's going on between her and James exactly, but it meant a lot to her that we spent the day with her." Her voice is quiet so we don't disturb Morgan.

I don't say it, but I would have spent the day in this room with just about anyone to get to lay here next to Brooklyn and run my hand through her hair while she nestles into my chest. It was pretty much my perfect day, minus the really crappy truth about my dad and Brooklyn's dad that hovers on the periphery of our happy bubble.

"Young love is hard," I say, peering down at her as she shifts against my chest to meet my gaze. Her mouth tugs up into a brief, one-sided smile.

"I guess we would know, huh?" she says.

I match her tired smile with my own, and we spend a few seconds looking hard into each other's eyes. I'm not sure what she's searching for, but I'm looking for the doubt and hurt. The last few days have been a whirlwind. After years of secretly loving my friend, the universe wove us together with circumstances both accidental and cruel. I worry about how she's weathering it all.

"I talked to my dad," she whispers.

Both of our strained smiles straighten into emotionless lines.

"You didn't have to do that," I say, tucking her hair behind her ear.

"I did," she responds.

I get it. It's her father's actions, and she deserves to be the one to question him about them. I never would have asked her to. I planned to approach him myself, which probably would have not gone well at all.

Brooklyn sits up and glances toward Morgan's bed, probably checking to make sure she's deep asleep. Her bottom lip is trapped by her teeth when she peers back to me, so much uncertainty weighing down her eyes.

"I don't care if Morgan hears about my life. My grandparents are the ones who prefer to keep things quiet, and since I don't really think of them as family, I try hard not to think of them at all. When it comes to my dad, I simply don't like having to defend him over and over, so I keep him to myself."

Her lips tug into a soft smile bit it quickly fades as her eyes dip from mine to my chest.

"Your grandparents are the ones who asked my father to write the letter requesting denial," she says. The instant her words leave her lips, the puzzle is complete. It all falls in place.

I sit up and pinch the bridge of my nose, eyes shut tight as I take in the full picture.

"And Cam," Brooklyn hums.

I pull my hand away and look her in the eyes, expecting the words that quickly come.

"They asked him to write it again."

The floor falls from under me, my entire being diving deep into a place that strips my stomach from my body and leaves me with nothing but sickness. There's only one option for me to take, and it's honestly the last thing on earth I want to do. Just in case, I spend a solid two minutes staring at Brooklyn's ceiling, her room quickly losing light with the setting sun.

This can't be a phone call. This ask has to happen in person, which won't be convenient or comfortable for either of us. But the difference is seven years of my father's life being spent right where he is or maybe, just maybe, somewhere on the other side of the wall where he and I can go to that damn bakery together, catch a Sox game, and talk about my graduation.

My eyes shift to meet Brooklyn's, her forehead lined with worry and lips pulled in with anxious expectations.

"Would you drive me into the city?" It's the last place I want to go. But I need to. And I need the flexibility of being able to move around Boston.

"Now?" Brooklyn asks.

I nod, my lips pursed with guilt.

"You want to meet my mom?" I ask, figuring since Brooklyn will be with me, I may as well show her all of my baggage.

"I'd love to," she says. Her eyes don't light up in excitement, though, and her smile stays cautiously the same. It's good that she gets it. Meeting my mom isn't like meeting your average boyfriend's parent. Our relationship is strained, a constant ten-foot pole between us keeping her from showing up to big things in my life and keeping me from calling her to tell her about my girlfriend. My mother and I are a business relationship. A pleasant one, but it's never been full of affection. It's barely been marked by a handshake.

"We should go soon," I say.

She nods, shifting in the bed to gather her things. I get to my feet and pull a sheet of paper from the printer on Brooklyn's desk. I hand it to her with a Sharpie and she quirks a brow.

"You write nice notes," I say with a wink. I still have the one she left for me this morning in my pocket.

Brooklyn draws a heart and writes the word HUG above it then scribbles a quick note inside her drawing, letting Morgan know we had to run an errand. I decide I like that label for what we're about to do. An errand. It's so much better than calling it what it is—playing a game of family-drama Jenga and pulling out the last piece from the bottom.

Sunday night traffic is light, so we get into the city in under forty minutes. It's been a while since I've been to my mother's building, so I guide Brooklyn on a screwy route before I spot the building trimmed with green iron and the park with the world's smallest fishing pond across the way. It's close to my mom's campus, and a lot of the professors live here. It's one of the reasons she moved in here during grad school. She's always been big on visualizing and actualizing goals. A family simply isn't one of those goals, hence I'm not in the picture much.

"Should we call her and let her know we're here?" Brooklyn asks.

I chuckle because what a sweet and perfectly normal question.

Shaking my head, I say, "Nah." It's better if my mom doesn't know we're coming. I don't want to get into the ugliness of the truth right now, but the odds are fairly good that my mom would take the advance warning to instantly be anywhere else. It would be *due to an emergency*, of course. It's only been within the last couple years that I realized the inordinate number of emergencies my mom tends to have right before I arrive.

Brooklyn locks her Mercedes with her fob and we scurry across the street to my mother's building. Thankfully, she hasn't changed any of the codes, so we don't need help from security when we get inside. We take the elevator up to the eighth floor and seconds later, I'm standing in front of her apartment—number 8F.

F. So appropriate. *F all of this.*

I breathe in deep and knead my hands together.

"Do you want me to stay? I understand if you've changed

your mind. I don't mind going. I can wait in the car." Brooklyn's hand covers my fidgeting fingers and I freeze then swivel my head to look her in the eyes.

"I'm pretty sure if you wait in the car I'm going to chicken out," I say, gritting my teeth and forming a strained but honest smile.

Brooklyn's shoulders shake with a silent laugh.

"Well, I was pretty much chickening out, which is why I suggested it," she says.

The option of leaving is stripped away in an instant when my mother's door swings open and the three of us are standing face-to-face-to-face. It helps that my mom's expression is about as panicked as I feel. Her workout bag slung over her shoulder, she's dressed in yoga pants and an oversized sweatshirt that hangs off of one shoulder. I bet she checks that peephole every time she leaves this place from now on lest I surprise her like this again.

"Cam!" Her smile never fully realizes, probably because her mouth is still wide open in shock.

"We were in the neighborhood," I joke. Brooklyn elbows my side.

"Oh, well . . . I was heading out." She looks over my shoulder, probably wishing she had a friend she could say was waiting on her. I step into her line of sight, my lungs tight with embarrassment at how pathetic my relationship with my mother is. She's actively looking for an escape, and Brooklyn is seeing it.

"It's really nice to meet you, Mrs. . . . . *Hass?*" Brooklyn stumbles on that part, and I realize I probably should have schooled her a little on our way here.

"Powell," I fill in. "My mom's last name is Powell."

This insight, of course, isn't much better. My mom's eyes widen with a warning to me that I'm sharing too much.

"It's fine, Mom. She knows about my grandparents. Brooklyn is my girlfriend." I'm shoveling the information at her now, burying her in it. Her expression morphs from that typical motherly excitement of a girlfriend to fear of letting someone see behind our big-ass curtain of deception.

"Mind if we come in?" I invite us knowing that my mother won't. It's weird because I sort of have a bedroom here. I hardly every sleep in it. Even over the summer, I never spend time in this place with my mom. Sometimes I kick it for a few weeks with Theo or one of the other guys from Welles. Last summer, I went to work at a camp. Eight weeks with ten-year-olds in the pines was a cake walk compared to spending the summer here.

"I'd offer you a drink, but I really only have water and soda," my mom says as I lead Brooklyn by her through the doorway.

"It's fine," I say, showing Brooklyn to the living area. She takes a seat in one of the chairs and I sit on the arm of the large leather couch. "We'll only be a minute or two."

It's hard to hide my ire. It colors my tone to the point that even I hear how ticked off I am. My mom shuts the door behind her by leaning back into it. She leaves her bag and keys by the table just to the right and shuffles forward, stopping just short of being in the same room as us. Always on the border, one foot out and ready to go.

"Are you in trouble?" My mom's eyes hover between me and Brooklyn, and Brooklyn must get the gist of what my mom is insinuating about the same time I do.

"Oh, no! No, nothing like that. Nope. We are all good and definitely not . . ." Brooklyn's entire neck and face are bright pink.

"No, ma. I didn't knock her up," I step in. Brooklyn's head falls forward and she catches her mortified face in her palms. I shrug because that kind of talk is easy for me. My mom has not exactly been shy over the years about lecturing me on safe sex. Wouldn't want me to have to grow up fast like she did. Hard not to take her lectures with a bit of a resentful sentiment.

My mom's color comes back to her cheeks, so clearly she's relieved by my answer. She still nervously picks at the collar of her sweatshirt, though, as if she's waiting for me to wheel out a dozen grandbabies that I've kept hidden from her.

"If you're worried about my face, don't," I say, knocking off the next logical leap I can think of her making. I still look a bit roughed up. My lips are almost back to normal, but the bruises under my eyes have turned into faint blue lines. It looks like I drew them there with a smudge from a Crayola marker.

"I assume that is from one of your stunts?" My mom doesn't get up to inspect my day-old injuries any closer. I don't think she has as much as given me a bandage once in my life. My big set of stitches, the scars now buried in my eyebrow, were courtesy of Grandma Caroline and a trip to the ER. She caught me trying to fuse my wounded brow together with packing tape after a bike fall. It was my first attempt to jump from the smaller cliff by the water onto the trail. I can make that jump in my sleep now, for what it's worth.

"It was a tough game yesterday. We won, though. Don't worry . . . you didn't miss anything." My snarky tone earns me a slight scowl from my mother. She's never seen me play. I doubt she'll show up for senior day at the end of the season.

Rather than prolong this guessing game where my mom wonders why I'm here, I decide to get to the point. I'm mostly full of doubt that my mom will do anything with the intel I have, but at least the burden will be on her too. Somehow, that makes it better.

"Brooklyn's dad is Walden Bennett. I'm sure you're familiar?" Of course, my mom is familiar. She had a conversation with Hal about him a day or two earlier. She leans into the wall as the realization that I've come here with a clue settles in. What she doesn't know is that it's more than clues I bring. I have answers that beg harder questions. No better time than the present to rip off those uncomfortable Band-Aids.

"Yeah, Hal texted me. Thanks for giving him my number, by the way. You two probably talked about this, but to make sure you're up to speed, he thought I might be able to talk to Walden's daughter since we were in the same class. The irony that she happens to be my girlfriend!" I punch out a laugh, part heartsick but mostly pissed.

"Cam, I didn't know," my mom starts. She glances to Brooklyn, probably wishing she could have met her under different circumstances. My mom, while not close to my grandparents, is a lot like them when it comes to wanting to garner friendships with important people. Walden Bennett is quite the shiny bauble.

"Yeah, I guess we don't really talk and share things about our lives, do we?" Brooklyn clears her throat at my side, so I stop myself from traveling around the bitter road with my mom in front of her.

"Brooklyn talked to her father. And like Hal wanted, she found out some details for us that might help with Dad's case. There's just one little hiccup." My mouth forms a tight straight line and I wait for my mom's eyes to drift from the floor to mine. "Seems Grandma and Grampa asked Walden to write that letter in support of Dad staying in the slammer.

Oh, and this is good intel . . . he penned another one for this hearing!"

Sarcasm oozes from my tone, and I'm not proud of slinging it around. It's just so hard to be rational and calm when everything is falling to shit around me. Especially when it's all kind of shit to begin with.

My mom moves to the other end of the sofa. Taking a seat on the edge, she palms her knees and stares out into the empty hallway. Her lips barely part as her eyes seem to haze at the blank space.

"Yeah, this seemed like it was above my pay grade," I bite out.

The room fills with unbearable quiet, and eventually, after nearly a minute, Brooklyn shifts in her seat, her legs sticking to the leather. It draws both my mother's and my attention.

"Sorry," Brooklyn says. "About . . . I guess, just . . . sorry."

Her eyes flutter down to her lap as she pulls her feet in and folds herself up in the chair.

"No." My mom's voice slices through the harsh quiet, instantly driving my pulse to a thousand beats per second. She lifts her chin and snaps her gaze to me, repeating herself —"No."

I raise my shoulders.

"No to what? I mean, I wish that was a solution. I've tried saying no to things and shit still comes back to get me." I've seen this side of my mom before. It's aggressive and confident, a small slice of her character, and one she uses rarely.

"No, you don't say sorry, Brooklyn," my mom says, her eyes still on mine. Brooklyn utters a whispered *okay* at my side.

"And no, he doesn't need to write another letter. My parents have asked enough of him. They've asked enough of all of us." While she continues to stare into my eyes, her focus seems to drift, her thoughts somewhere else besides me. I believe she is here for the words, for her commands, but I think she's also maybe deploying a chess strategy, one that has her thinking four or five moves into the future.

Brooklyn and I glance to one another, silently exchanging thoughts and clearly both unsure of what my mom means for us to do now, other than *no*, which I guess means *nothing*.

"I'm sorry you came all this way, and I know this is a strange way to meet, Brooklyn, but I need to ask you both to leave." My mom's gaze finally drifts to Brooklyn, and it's to kick us out.

"You're serious right now? That's it? I come to my mom with this massive problem and your response is *I'm sorry but you gotta go?*" I get to my feet and step closer to my mom, pulling her focus from Brooklyn and back to me.

"I need to think." That's all I get from her. It's always the bare minimum with this woman.

"You know, for a minute there, you seemed genuinely angry at something you should be livid about. I thought maybe you were going to *feel* something for once, something that wasn't about you or your degrees or what status you might get at the university, or . . ."

Brooklyn's hand runs down my arm and I jerk. My anger cools when I flinch and twist to meet her eyes, though. Her head to one side, her eyes are dewy with sympathy.

"Give her time," she whispers.

My face feels pained, just like my heart. The wrinkle is deep in my brow and my head hurts from this entire situation. But Brooklyn's calm voice wraps around me somehow and I step back, dropping my forehead into my hand to rub away the stress that is putting my head into a vice grip.

"You're right," I say, nodding mostly to myself.

"I need time to think. That's all," my mom repeats.

I lift my head and meet her gaze, her focus still hazy and less present than I would like. It's hard to have faith in someone who has a habit of avoiding responsibility for anyone other than themself. Rather than raising me, my mom left me with the wolves, the same animals who are doing everything in their power to keep me and my dad apart a little while longer. Excuse me if I don't believe that anything is going to change by giving my mom some "time to think." But staying here and pushing her won't work either, and I know that from experience.

"It was nice to meet you," Brooklyn says, standing from the chair and moving to stand square with my mom. She holds out a hand and my mom blinks her stare down at it, pausing as if she's never taken anyone's hand before in her life. When she finally does shake, it's slow and awkward, the entire time her eyelids moving with the energy of her constant thoughts.

"I look forward to seeing you again," Brooklyn says, her mouth stretched into a hopeful smile that practically begs my mom to react.

"Yes. Cam?" My mom's hand falls from Brooklyn's and her ghost-like voice calls for me.

"Yeah, ma," I say, doing a piss-poor job of hiding my irritation.

"I'll call you. Soon. I will think and I will call you," my mom says.

For a moment, the look in her eyes is clear and serious, and I actually believe her. That confidence and will fades quickly, though, and by the time she's walking us out her door, she's back to the diluted version of herself.

I keep it together until we make it to Brooklyn's car. Even when we get in and I'm buckled in my seat, I am calm. It's not until I let my mind fast-forward to an hour from now, a day from now, and finally, two weeks from now, that my pulse jacks up and my head pounds in frustration.

"Fuck," I grit. My hands form fists that pound down on my thighs. "Fuck! Fuck! Fuck!" I repeat, hitting myself with each shout.

"Feel better?" Brooklyn asks, and somehow her sarcastic tone breaks through my wall of anger enough that I relax my muscles and flatten my palms on my knees. I roll my head to the left and meet her worried eyes.

"I don't. And usually, a good tantrum or two does the trick," I say, forcing my mouth to lift on one side.

Brooklyn leans across the console and holds her palm to my cheek. I cover her hand with mine and hold on to her stare for a few breaths.

"I don't know what to do," I finally admit. That's the crux of it all. I feel stuck, and more so than normal. If I don't want to sleep somewhere, I call a friend and stay at their place. If I need to be alone for a while, I go for a long hike and climb some boulders. When my insides feel claustrophobic, I borrow one of my buddy's cars and get in a drag race. I could jump from cliffs and race trains at railroad crossings all day, though, and I would still have to face the fact my father is screwed. And what's worse, it's my own damn family doing the screwing.

Chapter 20

Brooklyn

Cameron didn't talk much when we got back. Morgan noticed, but somehow I think she sensed not to ask him what was wrong. I made a deal with Lily to swap rooms for the night, not that she and Theo aren't almost always in each other's beds anyhow. The sixth form prefects aren't really enforcers at Welles, so room checks never truly happen. By the time we're all eighteen, we're not so hip on tattling on one another for getting all coed in a dorm. I'm pretty sure the staff realizes that, too, but the job duty and the little checklist that gets submitted every night makes certain parents happy, so we all go through with the pointless ritual of saying "no boys are on the floor." *Check.*

Morgan and I settled in for another replay of P and P, which Cameron could not fathom how we could watch again so soon, but part of my impetus was boring him enough to get some rest. Somewhere, around the time of the carriage ride, when Darcy takes Elizabeth's hand, Morgan and I checked out.

It seems among the three of us, nobody heard my mom

knocking at the door. I didn't notice she was in the room until twelve seconds ago when she stood at the side of my bed, arms folded, and cleared her throat in that way only she can. It's the kind of sound that says *your ass is mine so tread lightly, my dear.*

Cameron is already sitting at the foot of my bed, his feet on the floor and his disheveled T-shirt physical proof that he slept here. Thank God, Morgan is in the room, otherwise this visit would take a high-and-mighty lecture route, as if she didn't sneak into my dad's room when they were students here.

"Mom, wha— Why are you here?" I rub my eyes and pull my phone from my dresser top to check the time. It's just after five in the morning. This is early, even for her.

"Well, I thought it was to have a meaningful chat with my daughter, but apparently I need to write a check to Welles to add sex ed to their curriculum." She holds her mouth in a tight line, a slight hint of sarcasm in her tone. That amusement does not make it to her face, however.

"We were watching a movie and all fell asleep. I swear," I say, glad that it's honestly the truth. Now, the other times? Not so much. For this one time I can get away with this excuse without breaking the Bennett code of not lying.

My mom tilts my computer screen back from where it sits on the other end of my bed, the end title screen for Pride and Prejudice paused on the screen. She glances to Cameron and taps the top of my computer.

"You enjoy the classics?" she asks him specifically.

"I find it to be a perfectly agreeable film, ma'am," he responds. I suck in my lips to hold in the laugh, but Morgan fails, letting hers out.

My mom pushes the computer screen shut and glances to

Cameron again, then to Morgan. Would you two mind if I had a minute with my daughter?

"I was just about to get to my room for class," Cameron says, hovering after he stands, unsure whether he should kiss me goodbye or not. I'm willing to put on a show for my mom, but I think maybe he's had his fill of judgement for the week, so he simply nods his head and slips out of our room.

"I have a hot shower calling my name. Take your time," Morgan says, bundling pieces of her school uniform inside a gray Welles sweatshirt to carry away.

When she disappears from the room, my mom takes a seat across from me on Lily's empty bed. No comment on the fact my third roommate is not in her bed at five in the morning. I guess Lily is not my mom's problem.

"Do you mind telling me why your father said you are off the campaign and will not be attending any of the stump events with us?" My mom has devoted her life to helping my dad rise to this very place. Our falling out is as much of a jolt to her as it is to him.

"Probably because I told him I was ashamed of him," I say.

I'm holding my own, but I do swallow hard when she shifts her weight and tips her head to look at me over the rims of her gold-trimmed glasses.

"You're . . . I'm sorry, did you say *ashamed of him?*" My mom fingers the turtle pendant that hangs from the chain around her neck.

"I did. I am," I reply.

"I see," my mom hums. She drops the pendant against her breast plate and her gaze drifts off to one side.

"You know, Shelby and I were in the room next door when we went to Welles." My mom loved her time at Welles.

It's where she met my father. He was a year ahead of her, though they're only five months apart in age.

"I'm not sure how a trip down memory lane with you is going to get me to suddenly not be angry with Dad." I get up from the bed to gather my things for the day. I don't like arguing with my parents. It's rare, and I think the last time was over a summer curfew when I was still seventeen. This is a different kind of disagreement. And she knows it.

"It's funny how much of this place is the same, yet so much is different," she continues. I do my best to pretend she's not really here, that she's merely radio noise while I get ready for class.

I'll skip showering today, despite how badly I want to stand under a stream of hot water and drown out life for a little while. I slip out of my clothes, not realizing that I'm standing in the middle of our room rather than hiding in my closet. I don't notice until my mom's breath catches as my tights are halfway up my legs. I freeze and look at the scarring on my leg then glance to her, a soft but pained smile on her lips.

"You're not hiding it," she says.

I chew at the inside of my mouth as my gaze falls back down to where my hands have gathered the top of my tights.

"I'm trying to be better with it. Accepting," I say in a hushed tone.

I stretch the thick black material up over my hips.

"You're beautiful," she utters, and rather than it floating by me without notice, I take her words in. She has to say those things. It's in the mom playbook. But hearing her say them now makes me think of Cameron saying them to me.

"When your dad and I first started dating, my friends, Shelby especially, all told me I was crazy to trust a man going into the military who looked like him," she says. It's story time. Some lesson from my parents' past that she will no doubt attempt to string into a meaningful reason why I need to believe in him again.

"I guess it worked out," I say as offhanded as possible.

"Not at first. No, it definitely did not," she says.

I pause with my arms halfway through my Welles sweater and peer at her over my shoulder to test her expression. She's not looking at me, but instead at the wall that is shared with her old room.

"I thought you and Dad had the perfect fairytale. He went into the military, you graduated and went off to Sarah Lawrence, and eventually you followed him around the world."

My mom's chest quakes with silent laughter, and she shakes her head.

"That's the short version, I suppose. There's a lot of fast-forwarding involved, including how my roommate Shelby hooked up with him after I broke it off on her advice."

My mouth hangs open at the revelation and my mom's gaze moves to me, catching my reaction.

"That's right. The same Shelby you call *Auntie* Shelby. There's a lot of water under bridges, believe me." A single, sharp laugh leaves her chest.

"How are you so close with her now? She was in your wedding!" I snag my shoes and move back to my bed to put them on. If anything, this walk through the past is more interesting than others.

"Ah, you mean how did I forgive them? I didn't at first. And I had one hell of a romance myself my first year at Sarah Lawrence. That's a story for another day, but *ooof!*" My mom fans herself and my only option is to let my eyes bulge so wide they're about to fall out of my head. She laughs hard when she looks my way.

"We were young, Brooklyn. And then we got a little older, and your dad came to visit me on one of his leaves, and I got to know the man he was becoming. I won't pretend there isn't a lot of narcissism there. I saw it then, built into his drive and this picture he painted of his future. But I think it takes a stroke of that type of egotism to get some things done in this world. It's an evolutionary trait maybe, one some people are given to help our species survive our worst actions. It takes someone like him, who yes, maybe isn't present when we need him to make us feel better, but it's because he's busy focusing on the big picture. And he loves us, in his way. He loves us enough to tolerate dislikeable people who can help him take steps forward, toward his goals—*our* goals."

"People like the Powells?" I quirk a brow, gathering where she's going with this.

"People like them, sure." Her mouth rests in a straight line and I mimic her expression while we stare at one another in silence.

"I don't know," I finally say, pulling my gaze away. Maybe I don't have the stomach to follow in my father's footsteps. Perhaps that's the grand lesson to learn here, that my young ambition has been misguided. This path isn't for me, because I don't think I can endure relationships with people I don't trust or who reveal themselves to be unworthy. People who hurt other people.

"Brooklyn, honey . . ." My mom moves to sit right next to me, stopping short of putting her arm around me. As tough as I'm trying to be, I think if she did that, I would break down in tears right now. All of this feels so awful.

She leans into me, and I lean back. It's enough to break me open briefly. I let one sob out before chastising myself for doing so and pinching my brow. I draw in a stuttered breath, fighting to keep it together.

"Nobody gets it right all of the time," she says.

I nod.

"Nobody gets it right all of the time," she repeats her words, reaching for my chin and forcing me to look at her when she speaks. Our eyes meet, and the full circle of her story comes together. That's why they're together, why she loves him and supports him. Even after he dated her friend, probably to get back at her for breaking up with him in the first place.

"Your dad said to give you this." She pulls a sealed envelope from her purse and hands it to me. Nothing is written on the outside. I'm almost afraid to open it. "And he said if you would rather not attend the gala, he understands."

I let out a short laugh-cry. The stupid gala. I have a gown hanging in my mom's closet at home that we spent weeks picking out.

"Is it poor taste to want to go only to wear that dress?" I half-joke.

My mom levels me with a serious gaze.

"There is nothing in poor taste when it comes to a Roberto Cavalli," she says. Her mouth ticks up on both corners, breaking character.

We both stand and hug, and I walk her to my door just in time for Lily to open it. The shock hits my roommate a lot like it struck Morgan, Cameron, and me when my mom showed up, only Lily is actually wearing nothing but a long T-shirt and sockless shoes. If she tries to say she was just out for a run, I'm going to lose it.

"Mrs. Bennett. Nice to see you," Lily stammers, her eyes flitting to me for help. I shrug because I've got nothing.

"Lily," my mom utters her name in that special way that is both a greeting and a scolding. She glances down to Lily's bare thighs and shakes once with a laugh before looking back to me. "Some Welles traditions never change." She smirks and lifts a brow then leans in to kiss my cheek before heading down our hallway.

"I'm mortified," Lily croaks as soon as our door is closed.

I cover my face with my palm.

"Yeah, well, I'm pretty sure my mom just admitted to having sex with my dad when she went to Welles, so I'm pretty horrified, too." My response prompts Lily to screw up her face in confusion. "It's a really long story. We're gonna need a girls' night."

"Okay," she says skeptically.

Morgan rushes into our room seconds later and does her best to fill Lily in on at least half the story, the part about my mom showing up and Cameron being here. I then have to backtrack to get her up to speed on the fact Cameron and I are dating. Neither of them is in the loop on Cameron's dad and the situation with my father and parole letters and the Powells. I decide to save that for another time because it's not fully mine to share.

My roommates rush out the door to make it to class, but I linger behind, wanting some privacy for whatever happens to be in this envelope. It's sealed, which for some reason gives me even more pause. I feel like breaking it open is an irreversible decision, and maybe that's my father's point with all of this. Or maybe it's my mother's doing. *Trust the deliveryman and have some faith.*

I hold it up to the light to see if I am able to extract anything without fully committing, but the paper is too thick. With a heavy sigh, I slip my fingernail under the edge and work my way inside the envelope, tearing it open along the top and pulling out the folded, type-written document.

The formal address sinks me immediately.

Massachusetts State Parole Board.

I take a seat and buckle up for the read, starting and stopping several times to reread and make sure I understand.

As a result of new information, and my own personal conversation with Mr. Hass, I would like to reverse my previous recommendation in favor of the granting of parole. I feel Mr. Hass may be an example of the work our system does, of the success that is possible when justice is served humanely and with the full intent of creating positive outcomes. It is my full belief that Mr. Hass is ready to be a contributing member of our society.

I hold the letter on my lap and let those words marinate in my mind. He spoke with Cameron's dad. This must have been yesterday, after we spoke. The letter is dated today, and it's stamped as a copy at the top, which makes me believe he already submitted the original. He changed his position because of me . . . *for* me.

That's what my mom was trying to tell me. People mess up. My dad isn't perfect, and he's messed up plenty. It's not about the times people get it wrong, though. It's about when they get it right.

Chapter 21

Cameron

Spending time with my mom on a non-holiday is rare. Seeing her twice in the same week is near anomaly status. The fact she's at Welles right now, waiting for me at the front office? That's a sign of the apocalypse.

I half expect to see a roomful of people I'm only close to through my bloodline waiting for me as I step into the Welles welcome lobby. This is how interventions start. I know because I watch them on TV all the time.

The lobby is quiet, though, and my mom is standing by the opposite door when I step inside. I glance to my left to check the headmaster's office, and the door is closed. The conference room doors are closed too, which probably means there are discipline meetings going on.

I look back to my mom and she nudges her head toward the door.

"I signed the form on Karen's desk. You're covered," she says, a mischievous smile playing at her lips.

My face pulled tight with caution, I adjust my bag over my shoulder and loosen my tie as I follow my mom out to the parking lot to her car. I toss my bag in the back seat and get into the passenger side before leaning over to check her mileage. She's still under a thousand.

"You never drive. What's this about?" I ask as she pulls her blazer off while standing just outside the door. She folds it and hands it to me to put in the back seat then gets in and cranks the engine. With both hands on the wheel, she locks her arms straight and draws in a full breath before letting it out slowly, as if she's breathing through a straw.

She twists to face me.

"I'd like to see your dad," she says.

I blink a few times, part of me waiting for the prank to reveal itself. When it doesn't, I lean back and fully take her in. She's dressed for an interview. White blouse under a bright blue blazer, black pants, and pointy-toed shoes that look like they belong in Brooklyn's collection.

"Shit, you're serious," I say.

"I am. It's been too long," she says. Her eyes are steady, zero sign of tears or worry. She seems resolved, and it's a strange shift from the woman who refused to talk to him with me when I was younger. Hell, she refused a month ago.

"All right, then. So, why am I here?" I tilt my head as her lips grow tight and her gaze dips with thought. Her eyes flick back up to mine with a shrug.

"You're here so I don't chicken out."

I stare a moment longer to make sure this isn't one of those wild ideas she doesn't plan to follow through with. After a few full breaths, I decide there are worse ways to spend my Monday, so I buckle up and let her drive.

I shoot Brooklyn a quick text to let her know I won't be in class and not to worry. Of course, her immediate response is to ask me what's wrong.

ME: *Nothing wrong. I don't think, at least. My mom*

pulled me out of school to see my dad. So it's weird. I'll let you know.

Her response doesn't come right away. In fact, for most of the trip to the prison I stare at the three dots that indicate she's typing and deleting and overthinking what to say. I laugh quietly when her text finally comes through as we pull through the prison visitor gates.

BROOKLYN: *Ok.*

I follow my mom into the visitor center, the process giving me flashbacks to the hundreds of times she did this so I could visit dad while she looked on. It's a hard habit to break, and part of me feels as if that's how this is going to go down. I'll sit with dad while mom watches.

But it's different this time. We're led down the same hallway I've traversed so many times I'm surprised I don't have a floor tile engraved in my honor. The guard shows us to the large room and rather than leaving me at the table by myself, my mom sits eagerly on the edge of the bench next to me. My eyes zero in on her nervous hands, her pale pink nails used as tools to pick at the sides of her fingers to stave off her impending panic attack. I reach over and cover her hands with one of mine and the touch stops her breath. Her eyes dart to mine, and they're overwhelmed with fear. Rather than say something meaningless, I model a deep breath, urging her to take my lead. I'm able to put some of the pink back into her cheeks by the time the guard returns with my father. When my parents' eyes meet, everything is quickly undone, but none of that matters.

"Hey, Dad," I say, standing and closing the distance between us. We hug, but I can tell through the entire embrace that his eyes are on Mom.

"Michael," my mom says, her voice a mixture of longing and apology. I've only ever seen hints of it, like when she asks me how he looked after one of my visits. There's so much endearment in this room right now, and I can't fathom why she's fought against it so hard.

"Laney."

I don't know that I've ever heard my mother's name said quite so softly. I also always thought she preferred Elena. I guess this is their version of Brooky.

After a few awkward gestures and failed attempts to embrace, they settle on taking each other's hand. It's not a handshake, really, but more of a testing of waters. My father's fingers gently play at hers, his thumb caressing the knuckle of her index finger before they let go of their brief hold and take seats on opposite sides of the table.

"It's a week full of surprise visits, it seems," my dad says.

"Oh?" My mom's head tilts, her eyes still memorizing his features, taking in the way he's aged, his sharp angles and well-formed wrinkles. My dad's a handsome man, even with his hardness. I have always liked that I have his eyes.

"Did Hal come to see you?" my mother asks.

My father nods and reaches for her across the table again. She hesitates for a beat but eventually gives him her hand, her breath hitching when he covers it with both of his.

"He did, and Laney . . . thank you for getting me help. It means—"

"I know," my mom cuts in.

My parents don't break eye contact for several seconds, not even a blink. My dad is the first to glance down, his mouth in a bashful smile like a junior high boy asking for his first dance. He chuckles as his hands hang on to hers, bold enough to return to playful touching, his thumbs drawing what I swear are hearts on her skin.

"Some fancy bigwig came to see me, too. He's running for Congress I guess. Said he read my case and wanted to get to know me on his own. Might write me a letter of support, so that's . . . that's something."

My mouth goes dry hearing his news and I itch for my phone to call Brooklyn. Instead, I settle for quick eye contact with my mom. My lips part, ready to spill my guts, but she gives me a slight shake of her head, and something about it triggers caution in my chest.

"Something wrong?" My dad can't miss the instant static in the room at his news, but my mom is quick to explain it.

"That just sounds exciting. Cam . . . he really wants this to happen," she says, her soft pink lips widening into an earnest smile.

"And how about you?" my dad asks, his eyes moving from their tethered hands, now frozen still on top of a metal table, to my mom's face.

She licks her lips and shifts with a thoughtful breath before answering.

"I really want this to happen, too."

The long quiet that follows her response feels different. In fact, everything that comes after that exchange feels shifted somehow.

I decide to give them space to talk on their own, so I say goodbye to my dad and check in with the guard to leave them alone in the meeting room. Instead, I spend some quality time with the complementary water cups, near-empty cooler, and a poorly stocked vending machine. I insert my credit card and decide on corn nuts that get stuck and require a decent hip check to knock them into the tray. I hold them up as proof when the guard on duty eyes me.

"My nuts," I say, amusing myself. He's less inclined to find me entertaining, so I pace to the other side of the waiting room and eat my stale nuts one at a time.

My mom comes in to get me about twenty minutes later,

and I sense that we should hold our conversation for the car. I toss my trash on our way out and do my best to stay in step with my mom on our way to the parking lot. By the time we reach her car, she's visibly trembling. She finally gets inside and manages to close the door and toss her purse into the back seat, and she falls to pieces.

After a few seconds of heavy sobs into her steering wheel, my mom does the unthinkable, and I let her. She leans over the console and hugs me. It's a bit messed up in that the dynamics are pretty reversed from the norm, the child comforting the parent. But still, it feels nice. In this heartbreaking moment, this connection feels more real than anything ever has with her.

The drive back to campus has a completely different feel. For the first time since I was a little kid, my body teams with hopeful energy. I truly believe my dad may get out, and it scares the shit out of me that I've fallen so far into the positive thinking. But this day, man. This day has been a miracle.

Even in the face—or should I say *faces*—staring at us as my mom pulls right up into the spot marked HEAD-MASTER in the Welles parking lot, something feels different.

"Gramps is gonna be pissed you took his spot," I say.

"Good." My mom shifts into park with the flick of her wrist as her eyes haze with her glare at the double doors flanked by Grandma Caroline and a few of the Welles board members.

I'm not sure whether I should get out of the car or stay here and help her stew. Part of me wants to stand behind her and slap her shoulders a few times like a hype man sending in his fighter. Something tells me she's been practicing for this moment for a long time, though.

"Wanna see something utterly fantastic?" My mom's eyes are locked straight ahead still, and I'm buzzing a little with the unpredictable energy drifting from her.

"Sure. I mean, who doesn't like utterly fantastic things?" I laugh lightly, but she doesn't. I pull my phone out to send a text to Brooklyn just as my mom presses the volume button built into her steering wheel. Within seconds, her car is literally throbbing with Joan Jett's "Bad Reputation," an iconic classic that in a million years I would never predict was on any playlist she owned.

ME: *Do you hear that?*

I'm guessing every person on the Welles campus hears us, but maybe I'm simply at the epicenter.

BROOKY: *What do you mean?*

ME: *My mom is having a mid-life crisis ala Joan Jett in the school parking lot.*

BROOKY: *???*

My laughter makes my head fall back on the head rest. I'm not sure what her question is for—the fact that this is fucking nuts or that she has no idea who Joan Jett is. Either way, she needs to see this.

ME: *Just get a pass. You'll hear it as soon as you leave the building.*

The hard knock against my passenger window makes me jump. I'm startled to see my grandmother standing right outside my window, her teeth clenched so hard I half expect to see them crack. I'm not even sure if those are real or veneers.

"I think she wants you to roll down the window," I say to my mom, doing my best to interpret the narrowed eyes and pointing gestures toward the locking mechanism.

"I'm sure she does." My mom pushes the volume higher. My lip curls a little with pride.

I shrug through the window and point with my thumb at my mom, as if there's nothing more I can do. Really, there isn't. This is her battle to wage. But fuck if I'm not thrilled to be in the front row seat.

My grandmother marches back to the two men in suits and three women with long coats and leather gloves who look fairly horrified at what's playing out in their school's parking lot. I glance to the far right, where the iron gates wrap around the main welcome center. A small crowd has gathered. Theo is standing in the back and he lifts his phone so I check my texts.

THEO: *Why is your mom rocking out to oldies?*

I laugh out loud, and my mom isn't even fazed. Her eyes are still straight ahead where my grandmother is now pacing while talking on her cell. The way her tongue is pushed between her molars and into her cheek reminds me of myself. She's been so scripted, almost unemotional, for my entire life. I should probably be nervous at this massive emotional break-down, but I seem to find myself wanting to root her on.

ME: *There's a lot I need to tell you, dude. Let's just say my mom is finally showing up.*

He sends back a thumbs up, and when I look back to find him in the crowd I see that Brooklyn is standing at his side, pushing up on his shoulder to get a better view. I'm about to send her another text when my mom abruptly kills the engine and cuts the music. If her car stereo were a record player, this is where the screeching scratch from the needle would happen.

Her eyes are hard on the rearview mirror, her mouth closed tight as her nostrils flare with her quickening breath. I sit up and look over my shoulder through the back window and see my grandfather's Lincoln SUV parked directly behind her. He steps out, tossing his gloves into the seat before slamming the door and taking long deliberate strides toward my mom's side of the car.

"Oh, shit." I don't have time to react any more than that before my mom flings her door open and steps out of her car.

It's like watching a strange game of chicken as she marches toward him and he barrels toward her. The moment they connect, my mom flattens her hands on either side of his chest and shoves, sending him staggering several steps backward.

"I hate you so much! I hate you!" My mom's rage jets to red hot, and before my grandfather can gather his balance she's shoving him again. My grandmother comes rushing to him as he stumbles into the front of his SUV.

"You're being insane, Elena. Stop it! Stop it right now!" My grandmother's effort to enact peace through discipline only seems to fuel my mother more, and it draws her anger toward both of them.

"You've ruined my life! Ruined it! I let you, and I hate myself for it. I hate myself every day, but now . . . I hate myself even more. How could you? He was going to get out!" Her voice is hoarse from screaming, but it doesn't deter her from leveling more *hate you's* at her parents.

My phone buzzes in my lap.

BROOKY: *Are you ok?*

I stare at her message for a few long breaths while I'm serenaded by the sound of my mom standing up for herself. God, I wish she had this break years ago, before I had to spend countless summers and holidays with those two. But she's having it now, and beggars can't be choosers.

ME: *I think maybe I'm great.*

I laugh at that thought, a bit like a lunatic, then twist to rest my arm on the seatback and prop my chin on my fore-arm. There's a lot of pointing and screaming, and at least twice my grandmother pretends she's overwhelmed with emotion and needs to sit down. The bell rings somewhere in the midst of the epic smackdown, and soon the entire campus population is clustered around the main building to get a glimpse of my dysfunctional family meltdown.

My mom shouts something about a tattoo, which sends my grandfather over the edge, and he storms toward his office. My head swivels to follow his path as he passes my window before standing in the main doorway, his back holding open one of the heavy glass doors. The board members, who were probably here for a regular, boring old meeting, all back away and eventually head to their own vehicles. I step out as my mom stomps toward my grandfather, still shouting about how it's *his turn to listen for once* while my grandmother rushes behind her.

I shut the door and debate whether or not I should follow them inside, but when I spot Brooklyn lingering off to the side, one of the few students who still has not gone to class, I decide my mom has this handled. It's her war to wage anyhow.

To save myself from getting sucked in, I toss my bag over the fence then lift myself over to join Brooklyn. She slips her hands under my arms and around my sides, pressing her chin to my chest to look up at me. I kiss her nose.

"I'm not even going to begin to understand what that was," she says.

I glance to my left toward the building. I swear, if I hold my breath I can hear my mom's voice booming from inside.

"I think that was the culmination of living a lie," I say. My mind recalls the way my parents looked at one another less than an hour ago. Those longing looks were kept so distant for my entire life. I saw them in fragments, whenever my mom would slip, or my dad would open up. They love each other. They always have.

"I have news," Brooklyn says.

I return my attention to her, brushing her hair to the side and cupping her face. A faint smile paints her lips, and I brace myself.

"My dad sent a new letter. I have a copy for you. He's supporting your dad's parole."

My chest warms with her news. Somehow this day got even better. I hold her eyes for several seconds, diving into the deep brown orbs and golden-touched lashes. I let my forehead rest on hers and give in to the massive wave of hope sweeping me toward the bright side.

Chapter 22

Brooklyn

The Welles rumor mill is a well-oiled machine. By lunch the next day, everyone knows who Cameron's grandparents are and that his father is in prison. The Welles Daily even tries to get comments from Cam, me, and the headmaster on the controversy that played out in the school parking lot.

None of us say a word, though. Well, except Cameron. His big epiphany quote flanks the top of the school paper.

"Some people really suck. Others, not so much."

That mantra is quick to catch on. Morgan really likes it, her obsession to the point that she's currently forcing Cameron to look at T-shirt designs on her phone app.

"I like it in orange. And that font really pops," she says.

Cameron runs his palm over his cheek and smiles through his teeth.

"I'm probably not the one to ask about popping fonts and all that," he says.

My phone buzzes for the fifth time with a call from the same unknown number. I send it to voicemail, like I've done every time, and wait to see if the caller leaves me a message. A minute passes with no notification. I have my suspicions on who is trying to get in touch with me, but I don't want to assume the worst.

"Everything all right?" Cameron squeezes me at his side, and I shake off the funk and smile at him.

"Yeah, just some spam. Has Morgan gotten your permission for merch yet?" I try to lighten my mood, but while Cameron laughs softly at my joke, his eyes penetrate mine in search of what's really bothering me.

"Yeah, I agreed to give her ten percent. What spam?" He's not going to let that go, probably because he's the most perceptive man I know. I breathe in deeply and pull my phone out to show him the string of missed calls. I underestimated, there are eleven.

"You call it back?" He arches a brow.

"Oh, God, no!" The thought of calling back an unknown sends my anxiety roaring like a five-alarm fire. The only thing that could make that thought worse is actually following through with it. Which, of course, now that Cameron's stolen my phone, is happening . . . right . . . now.

"Cam! Stop!" I whisper and grab at my phone. He holds me away with a stiff arm and presses the phone to his ear. He holds up a finger when I assume someone on the other end has answered.

"Yes, hi. I'm Brooklyn Bennett's assistant. She's busy right now, but can I tell her what this is regarding?" His professional voice is deep, and it would be dreamy if it were any other situation, and if his forehead wasn't creasing deeper with every second that passes.

"I see. Yes, I will let her know you called and what you're looking for."

He nods at her response.

"Yeah, you too."

He hands me my phone back then leans forward, resting his elbows on the lunch table as he knots his hands together into one big fist.

"It was the press, wasn't it?"

Cameron nods.

That's what I was afraid of. It's happened before, after my dad was appointed to the Energy Department. There are a few reporters who seem able to outmaneuver anyone. They get to the root of stories faster and catch people off-guard, getting them to spill details that aren't meant for public debate. Private things that aren't meant for public sharing. Embarrassing things that should remain buried.

"Holly Knight. Examiner," he says.

I let my eyes fall shut. I actually gave her my number because she was the only one who wrote a fair story after my father's appointment. It was a rash decision, one made with emotion. I figured if the time ever came that I needed someone to be fair to him, I'd reach out and see if Holly could help. And in return, I let her have unprecedented access.

"Did she say what she wanted?" My gut tightens with my hunch.

Cameron nods. I lean in close, and he turns to press his lips to mine briefly then rest our heads together side-by-side.

"She wants comment on her story about how your dad did a favor for his daughter's boyfriend's father. She has a copy of his letter, and I guess someone saw him visit my dad."

My eyes close. I remain at Cameron's side, my head resting on his, the faint smile I'm forcing on my lips tingling with the want to protest. Two steps forward, eight steps back. I'm sure one of the guards mentioned it to someone who dropped a call to the press. To Holly. My dad has a lot of supporters, but there are a lot of people out there rooting for the other guy. It doesn't take much to spawn a firestorm in local media during an election season.

I expect I'll be hearing from my mom again before the day is done.

* * *

When my mother called later that afternoon, I readied myself for the lay-low advice. That's my family's typical response to bad press, not that granting a man parole who has done the work and earned it should be bad press, but it's all about the spin. And my dad's opponents are good at flipping things completely sideways.

Surprisingly, though, renewed warnings to stay away from Cameron didn't come. Instead, she wanted to let me know she booked my dress fitting for the gala. The party of course is no longer hosted by Welles Academy, part of the cold war my dad now has with the Powells. The Women's Club will be the official host on the program, and since it was always to be at the Ocean Club, it's not strange to change the host.

"Remind me again why you have to try on a dress you've already tried on to make sure it *really* fits?" Cameron holds the heavy door open for me as I cradle my gown like a baby and carry it into the tailor's business.

"Because Cavalli deserves to fit like a glove," I say, blowing a kiss in the air.

"Ah, of all of that, I understood the word glove," he jokes.

My mother and I have been using this tailor for years. Alice is in her seventies and still the best at making a woman feel like a supermodel with just a little nip and tuck of fabric. She learned to sew from her grandmother when she was a little girl and despite living in Boston for most of her life, still holds on to her thick French accent.

She greets me with open arms when we walk in. Not to hug me, though; she wants the gown.

"Ah, let me see," she muses, taking the bag and laying it down on the large ottoman in the center of her room. She unzips the bag and unfurls the Champagne-colored satin and netting.

"Okay, that seriously looks like a cake," Cameron says, earning him a glare from every woman in the room. "I mean that in a good way. Like, the woman in that dress could sit on top of a cake. You know, like wedding gown pretty? Ha . . . ha."

His pained eyes zip to mine with panic, and all I can do is laugh. "Maybe you should sit over there and look through the magazines for a little while."

I point to the opposite wall, where Alice's husband usually sits when he joins her at work. Cameron practically sprints to the safe harbor. Alice mutters something in French, and I get a few key words that I've learned over the years, most notably "idiot men."

Alice ushers me into the dressing room and I strip from my jeans and T-shirt to slip into the gown. It feels like an expensive hug as I slip it up my body, poking my arms through and letting the weight of the fabric hold me to the earth. There are places where I feel it's loose, and Alice spots them as soon as I step out of the dressing room.

"Ah, yes. There. Don't move," she says, pulling pins from her mouth.

I spin slowly with my arms straight out, and when I rotate so I'm facing the chairs where I sent Cameron, I'm hit with his look of wonder. I blush instantly, my skin reddening enough that Alice notices it creeps down my neck. She glances over her shoulder to see Cameron standing, hands in his pockets as he stares at me with adoring eyes and the kind of smile reserved for admiring art.

"He likes it," she says, smiling at me and winking. "You like this idiot who thinks this dress is a cake?"

I giggle then nod.

"I do. I like this idiot very much," I say.

Alice gives me a puckered smile before nudging me to turn more. I try to maintain eye contact, but eventually I have to give in and look ahead while she pins spots on the back of the gown where it swoops down to the curve of my spine. This was my favorite thing about this dress. It's what sold my mother on it, too.

"Okay, I think I have it. Wait here and let me get the tape for a few places." She pats my shoulder gently and slips off to her back room where the magic happens. I turn, lifting the heavy fabric gathered around my ankles. Cameron steps up to the platform I'm on the moment I face him, quickly erasing the inches between us so he can lift my chin with his finger-tips and kiss me softly.

"I didn't get it before. The dress. I get it now, though. I'm pretty sure it's the woman," he whispers, his mouth brushing against mine. A devilish chuckle slips out as he nips at my lips one more time before sliding one hand around my waist until it's flat against my bare skin. His touch sends shivers down my body, and I tremble in his arms. He holds me closer when I do, taking advantage of the situation I fully put out there to be taken advantage of.

"I can't wait to see what we look like together—you in a tux, me in this dress," I say.

Cameron's eyes hold mine, the smile on his mouth frozen in place as his focus drifts from one eye to the other. We only talked briefly about the gala. I knew he had to work as part of his punishment for the whole boxer short incident, but now that Welles wasn't officially serving as a named host, I thought maybe he would be free to be mine for the entire night.

"You don't have to work still, right? That's done. I mean nobody from Welles will be there, except our friends and the people my dad knows. Your grandparents aren't—"

"I promised your dad I would stay home," he says.

My hands drop from his arms, and I step back. But I step too far and slip from the platform and stumble onto the sofa covered in discarded dresses from the resale business attached to Alice's shop.

"*Mon Dieu!*" Alice sets the tape down on a nearby table and rushes to help me back to my feet without tearing the gown.

"Brooky, I had to." His head falls to one side as his teeth clamp down in the back. It's a guilty expression. I've seen my dad make this same one before.

"No, you didn't have to. You let him bully you," I protest.

"I offered. Brooklyn, it was my idea. When you got that call from the press yesterday, I knew that showing up at a fundraising event in the city with me around would only feed the frenzy. There would be pictures on social media and things would escalate and get used in attack ads. You probably know the ins and outs of this better than I do."

I breathe hard, my hand clutching my chest as I stand with flat feet a foot lower on the floor. Alice works to spread my dress out around me, checking to make sure the pins are still in place and nothing is torn. But I no longer feel safe in this dress. I don't feel beautiful. I feel used, like a piece on a crowded chess board. An expendable pawn given up to save the king.

"And what about the rest of us? What about now? There

could be someone sitting across the street waiting to snap a photo of us. The story will always be there, but my dad knows how to handle things like this. He has people for this."

Cameron peers through the window at my suggestion, his brow drawn tight. He's actually worried about that. His eyes flit back to mine, and I feel him leave, though physically he's still here.

"Brooky, I'm just being careful. And only until the election. I owe him this after what he did for my dad. I owe him."

"This is how it starts," I mutter. Alice is working at my hem, and I can tell she's listening intently to our conversation but I don't care.

"How what starts?" he asks.

"Letting them make decisions for you. I bet your mom thought she was taking good advice and doing what was best when she cut ties with your father." And I know the minute I compare us to them I've crossed a line. Cameron's expression falls, his eyes touched with a hint of resentment.

"We aren't my parents, Brooklyn."

He called me Brooklyn.

"I hope we aren't. Cameron, I want to be with you," I plead.

Alice gets to her feet and leaves us alone.

"And we're together. I only said we'd keep it on the back burner until the election," he says.

I laugh out, "Back burner."

"You know what I mean," he stammers. The saddest part is I do know. He sounds just like the rest of them—like me before I considered life without a campaign attached to it.

"You'll see, Brooklyn. A month from now with the polls closed—"

"My dad will be a Senator, and the scrutiny will only get harsher," I cut in. "There will never be a convenient time for his daughter to date the boy whose dad he helped earn parole. That story will exist forever, and we either walk right through it or let it set the rules."

That's the part he doesn't see. I've seen it far too often, though. I watched my brother deal with it during his own military service, the constant comparisons to our father, especially when he didn't measure up. My mom is graded on every charity she supports, each event she hosts—hell, on the color she wears for an interview. Everything in my circle is subjected to criticism, and most of it isn't kind.

"I have to get changed," I say, hauling the folds of my gown into the dressing room with me.

I'm struggling to get a full breath as I step out of the gown, and I accidentally cut myself on the sharp point of one of the pins in my side. I dab the small trail of blood up with the tip of my finger and suck it away, the sting of my frustration threatening to spill down my cheeks. I hurry into my jeans and rush my shirt over my head, putting it on backward and inside out. My urgency is pointless, and deep down I knew it would be. The second I step out of the dressing room, Cameron is gone. My purse and keys sit alone in the red velvet chair he should be in.

"It's a beautiful dress," Alice says behind me in a reverent tone.

"It is," I say, my focus on the door and the empty sidewalk outside it. "It really is."

Chapter 23

Brooklyn

My eyes still have not adjusted from the hot glare of the lights and the flashes that hit my pupils every six seconds on my way into the ball. Every person I greet is covered by a scorched blob in the middle of my vision.

"It's a gorgeous dress," one woman says. My mom gave me a tip for most of the people here, and I'm pretty sure this is the wife of the big development group looking to revitalize one of the old squares in the southside of the city.

I curtsy.

"Thank you so much. I love yours," I respond.

My mom coughs at my side, and I don't understand why until the woman moves away from us and I see she's wearing a black suit with very little fanfare. She could step in and join the wait staff and look underdressed.

"I'm sorry. I still can't see," I say through my plastered-on smile.

"I know. Me too," she mutters next to me under the same expression.

We never know when someone is going to take a photo, so at events like this, it's imperative to constantly be on. The moment you aren't, that's when they pounce and that's the one that goes to the tabloids.

I brought Morgan and Lily to the ball with me for a girls' date night. It was fun dressing Lily up, though she would probably argue that it was more fun for us than her. The boys had their big rival game today. I couldn't go because I had to help my mom with a few last-minute details for the gala, but Lily and Morgan went. Apparently, Cameron was the MVP of the game. I wish I could have seen it. I wonder if he would have walked off the field to keep a promise to my dad.

It isn't fair for me to put the blame on him completely. He's trying to be respectful, and he's grateful for my father's support for his dad. But I feel because my dad did the right thing, it doesn't mean he deserves an award for it. It was the right thing to do, whether Cameron does him a favor in return or not. More and more, I realize I'm not made out for politics. I love policy, and I love doing good, but the glad-handing and side deals make my stomach hurt.

"We should get inside," my mom says, looping her arm with mine.

We wave to the press and meet up with my father, and I let the two of them walk in together for a few photos by my dad's staff. I linger on my own until Lily and Morgan sneak around the rows of tables inside the Ocean Club to stand by my side.

"I have never been to anything like this," Lily gushes. She spins in the blue satin dress Morgan and I forced her into, and the skirt swings out as she does. She's gleeful, and I'm jealous yet happy for her.

"I have to admit, this party is pretty fire, Brook. And I have been to *a lot* of these things," Morgan says.

I smile, taking some of the credit for the last-minute touches I helped my mom complete. Rather than spending money on decorations that would only get thrown away, I convinced my mom to work with a florist friend of Alice's who builds living sculptures out of greens and petals and the most vivid flower arrangements. Everything is locally sourced, and I spent the morning making placards to post around the displays that detail what each plant or flower is and where it can be found in Massachusetts.

I follow my friends down the lit corridor to the grand ballroom where a band is playing to an empty dance floor. Morgan takes the initiative, along with both Lily and my hands, and drags us out there to get things moving. It's a cover of a Taylor Swift song, so most everyone who enters the room instantly recognizes it and a few find their way to the floor to join us. After one song, there's a steady flow of people moving on the floor, and the rest are power guests making connections throughout the room.

"I have to take my shoes off. Just for a minute. My feet want to die," I say to my girlfriends, ditching them for the comfort of a chair. After a little whining, they disappear into the growing crowd dancing to a mash-up of top hits.

I slip my feet from the Louboutins and turn my heel out under my chair so I can run my palm down my calf and onto the small blister forming along my tendon.

"If you didn't wear Looloobobos you wouldn't have this problem." My hand halts at the sound of Cameron's voice, and I both want to smile and shove him on his ass at the same time. After a breath, I continue to massage my calf.

"Yeah, well, I don't have a date, so I had to make up for it with really amazing shoes." My leg aches from spending hours on it helping my mom today, so I work the knee and thigh with both of my hands while trying not to look up and into the eyes that will slay me. I want to stay mad at him, even if he's here, like I wished for him to be.

Irrational much?

My plan is foiled when he kneels in front of me and takes my foot in his palms and begins to rub. I stop short of actually saying *ahh* as he eases my tense muscles with his touch. His hands move up the sides of my leg but stop short of my knee. He's aware of everyone around us. So am I. Everyone looking at us right now is aware that they are participating in a group activity. This is exactly the scene I thought he promised my dad he would avoid.

He stands up straight and my eyes follow his movement, betraying me and taking him in. Every last delicious inch of him.

"Dance with me."

I glance around us and shake my head.

"Everyone is watching."

Cam bends down and holds out his palm. His hair is damp from a hurried shower, his tie crooked and cuffs undone. He smells like whiskey and cinnamon.

"I know. But dance with me anyway."

And then comes his crooked smile.

I'm on my feet before I realize it, swept up in his arms as my bare feet graze across the wood floor as everyone—my parents included—look on. I give in more, wrapping my arms around his neck and shoulders and stepping up so my feet are on his. His mouth dips into the crook of my neck as he laughs then presses a soft kiss against my hot skin.

"You showed," I say.

"I did." His lips graze my body as he speaks, causing my eyes to flutter closed.

"I thought you were worried about the press, and owing my father favors," I say. I carefully note every set of eyes on us in the room. Lily and Morgan are dancing like a couple and grinning at me like fools. My mom, who I expect to look disgusted, considering she walked in on us sharing a bed, actually has a rather affectionate expression. Her eyes are soft, and she smiles as she talks to one of my father's donors at her side. And my father, who has the most to lose, keeps pointing to us, almost as if he's bragging.

He is bragging.

"Did he call you to come as a favor?" My insides twist, ready to rebel.

"Uh uh," Cameron says in my ear. He briefly guides me away, spinning me on my toes under his arm then bringing me back in and lifting me to stand atop his shoes again. He keeps his hands on my back for support so I can see his eyes.

"This really politically savvy girl I knows told me that everyone is spinning stories all the time, and it got me thinking. Maybe I could spin something in my favor for once and be here with my girl."

He lifts me and spins me around once, holding me up a little and drawing more attention our way. I scan the room, my cheeks burning from the attention. I smack at his arms and will him to bring me down.

"And how did you manage that?" My tummy is full of butterflies, the good kind, and they're taking over my entire body. I'm tingling from head to toe, and I'm scared to give in so quickly.

Cameron stops our swaying and brings his hands up my sides to my shoulders, neck, jaw, until he's cradling my face. His eyes penetrate mine, his full lips parting with a breath.

"I pointed out how my story is exactly the kind he's running for. My dad's story is his campaign promise. Building a state where everyone can live to their full potential."

My mouth falls open then slowly spreads into a massively

proud grin. I play shove at his chest then grab the lapel of his jacket along with his loose tie. "Damn, Cam. That's really good."

"I know," he brags, his eyes drifting to one side for a beat.

The band kicks into a fast song just as he's about to kiss me and I laugh. He does, too, only with less fervor and no intention of stopping us from taking it slow.

"I think they're about to launch into the Prince medley," I say.

Cameron glances up for a few seconds, seeming to focus on the beat and melody. Once he recognizes it, he mouths, "Let's go crazy," in my face then tilts my head just enough to give his lips room to take over mine completely. I remain on his feet, floating somewhere above Earth for at least six of Prince's greatest hits. Nobody is ever going to get away with saying Cameron Hass is bad for me again. And if I have to get a black belt to defend his honor, I guess I will.

Epilogue

Cameron

I thought my life had peaked when my dad was able to stand with me on the field for senior day. But that was nothing in comparison to this moment.

"I don't quite understand why this particular award is such a big deal," my dad says. My mom laughs because even though Mr. Philips arrived after her Welles days, she's heard the stories. The man has built up his Black Tuesday Award into something of local legend or lore.

"It's important to your son, so that's what makes it a big deal," my mom says, pursing her lips into a tight I-told-you-so raspberry. My dad chuckles and rolls his eyes but reaches out a hand for hers. They hold on to each other with a brief show of affection.

Moments like this are happening more often between them. I try not to insert myself into their private business, though I guess I have some right, being their son. They have a lot of baggage and hurdles to clear. My grandparents never liked my dad for their own obvious reasons. He was, and is, the opposite of everything they believe. He's rock-n-roll to their ultra-conservative way of life. And when my mom came to them in tears when she found out she was pregnant, they did what every other couple in their circle in the same circumstances did—they tried to send my mom away.

That's how indiscretions are handled in their society. They're hidden. My dad's side of the family tree, however, likes to hang the laundry out for everyone's inspection. And if people have problems with something, they take it to the alley or drink it out over a beer. My dad wanted to make fast money to take my mom away from it all—and by extension, from my grandparents. When he got caught, they chalked it up to a blessing, and they indoctrinated my mom to feel shame for ever loving him.

But she did love. She still does. Though she still hasn't said it for any of us to hear. I wonder if she has to him, though. Verbally, I mean. She says it in the way she looks at him every single time they're together.

My dad got a job at a high-end foreign car repair shop. One of the areas he studied most in prison was mechanics, reading every book he could get his hands on and watching YouTube videos during his rec hours. His dream was always to open his own garage, and I think he might realize it one day.

My grandparents won't be helping, though. That cold war is still going strong between them and my mother. She let them have it that day in my grandfather's office and hasn't spoken a word to them since. It's only weird on days like today when we're all in the same place.

Of course, nothing is weird for me today. Because I'm the winner of the Black Tuesday Award, and I am going to relish every freaking moment.

"Sorry I'm late," Brooklyn says, slipping me the bag I asked her to grab from her car. We did some last-minute shopping for the graduation ceremony, and it's a surprise only she and I know about. I think she'd prefer to not be in this loop, but everyone warned her that dating me comes with hazards.

"I'm going to go change," I say, kissing her cheek so I don't mess up her soft pink lips. I've learned how to navigate that woman's makeup before photos. It's an art.

I pass her father in the auditorium lobby on my way to the restroom. I try my best to sneak by without getting caught but he hooks my arm before I can get away. I turn and act surprised to see him, shaking his hand. His shake is still firm —still the shake of a father who is also a senator and has the backing of the federal government to throw me in jail if I break his daughter's heart. *He's literally said this to me. Multiple times.*

"Congratulations, Cameron. I'm really proud of you."

"Thank you, sir," I respond.

Thing is, I believe him. When I pitched him the angle of me being the kind of kid he wants to help out, it wasn't total bullshit. It was selfish, yeah, but honest. And he saw that. I wouldn't say we're close, and maybe we'll never be, again with me dating his daughter and him having the backing of the government to make me disappear. But I truly feel his support professionally. He wrote a recommendation for me to Georgetown, and I think it's half the reason I got in. I say half because I'm not sure how thrilled he is that I'll be living with his daughter in Arlington since she's going to Marymount.

"I have my camera ready," he says, pulling the corner of his cell phone from his suit pocket.

"Very well," I answer with a wink.

Even the most prestigious of Welles alumni are stoked to watch me accept my award. Maybe it's the years of torture for the assignment, or the way Mr. Philips taunts some of the smartest students who don't end up earning the honor. There have been years when nobody was a recipient, and I think those are the years Mr. Philips is happiest. He's smug that way. An expert in his tiny little world. Only I'm an expert, too. So much so that I decided to double major in economics and justice studies, and only slightly to spite him.

I slip into my surprise outfit in the bathroom and leave my pants in the stall before rushing out to take my place in line. I slip in just as the music begins and we all filter down the aisles to the front few rows. I'm between Theo and Brooklyn, and a row away from Morgan, Brooklyn, and Lily. I've spread the word to start the rumor mill, so I know I'll get the cheers when I need them.

If it weren't Brooklyn being called to the stage, I don't know that I would pay attention. But it is her, and she's worked so hard to be our valedictorian. She's practiced this speech a thousand times, but her hands still tremble as she holds the note cards I don't think she needs.

Throughout her speech, I travel back to this year, to the years before it. Her theme is the journey we've all been on, and while maybe it sounds hokey on the surface, it's really got a lot of depth. Our school was changed forever last year when Brooklyn, Lily, Morgan, and Anika drove off the bridge into the river. Losing Anika was something that affected every single person who knew her. I didn't realize just how much it changed me until later. I'm not sure Brooklyn and I would have found one another the way we have were it not for Anika looking over us. I'm not very spiritual, but Brooklyn swears Anika nudged her my way, knowing she would need someone to care for her. Not *take* care of her. Nobody needs to do that. But we all need love. Brooklyn did, and so did I. And we love each other fiercely.

As her fellow students look on with genuine awe as she speaks, I wonder how many of them are trying to measure up to her. She's graduating with eight college credits already under her belt. She has a standing job offer with the Boston Mayor's Office and an invitation to work with six of the largest public policy research groups in the country after college. She hasn't told anyone but me yet, but she's actually been thinking of going into social work. I can't think of a better heart to give to those who need it.

Brooklyn leaves the stage, and the moment she's next to me again our hands fuse.

"Good job," I whisper in her ear. She merely squeezes my hand harder, the nerves of public speaking still coursing through her body.

My grandfather reads the same words he does every year, the Welles mission statement, and the promise for a lifetime of brother and sisterhood. I suppose that is a promise I've found here. It's no thanks to my grandparents, though. They managed to retain their contract to stay on with the school even though Brooklyn's father disassociated himself with them directly. There's always someone in the wings willing to kiss ass to be kissed back, I guess.

My leg starts to bounce when Mr. Philips stands from his seat on the stage. His eyes meet mine instantly, his frown taking over most of his face while the shit-eating grin spreads like an infection on mine.

"This is it," I say, readying myself to take to the stage. I unzip my gown enough to make it easy to slip out of while Mr. Philips recants the story of how this one student whom he never in a million years thought could win his award pulled off the impossible. He wasn't shy about what a pain in the ass I have been for him, and it's clear everyone at Welles —and apparently their parents—is fully aware of our history.

"Wish me luck," I whisper to my side. Both Brooklyn and Theo wish it for me as I stand, and Mr. Philips calls my name. I pass Brooklyn, glancing down to catch her bright red cheeks just before she covers her face and hides her laugh with her hands.

I'm doing this.

I make it to the center aisle and hold my fists over my head in celebration, taking the steps up to get my award much like that famous scene in Rocky.

Mr. Philips holds the cup out for me to take one side and I turn to stand next to him as everyone readies themselves to take pictures.

"You're a real asshole, you know that, right?" Mr. Philips mutters out of the side of his mouth, his half-ass smile intact.

I laugh out hard because this could not be more perfect.

"Yeah, I do know," I say, letting my gown fall to my ankles just as the cameras go off. I knew what I wanted to do the second I spotted the light-up flamingo boxers at the mall during a trip with Brooklyn. She tried in vain to talk me out of it, but I convinced her this was twenty-nine bucks well spent.

Mr. Philips groans next to me as the entire audience gets to their feet with applause. Cameras flash and I'm sure I'm trending on social by now. He endures the embarrassment for about five seconds before leaving me with the cup and exiting the stage. I milk every second, holding the bronzed cup up and kissing it as if I've won Wimbledon.

Eventually, my grandfather clears his throat into the microphone, the noise crackling and squealing through the speakers. I wave at him and mouth, "All right," and then leave my gown on the stage at his feet. He can have it. He can have Welles too, for all I care. Instead of taking my seat, I weave through my classmates and take Brooklyn's hand to pull her in for a full-mouthed, I'm-showing-off kiss then lift her up over my shoulder. There's no reason to stick around now. I've got what's important. Family. A great love. And the fucking Black Tuesday Cup.

THE END

Preorder Habit Now!

The Boys of Welles continues with Habit, book 3 in the series.

Habit

James and Morgan's story

The Boys of Welles Book 3

Free in Kindle Unlimited

Preorder here:

My Book

If you enjoyed this series, you might also like:

The Varsity Series

A New Adult Sports Romance Trilogy

Free in Kindle Unlimited

Begin Your Binge with Varsity Heartbreaker

Lucas Fuller is a lot of things.

He's the boy next door.

He's the first crush I ever had.

He was my first kiss.

He's also the only person who has ever broken my heart.

For two years, I've wondered what happened to the us I used to know.

We were best friends, and then suddenly...we weren't.

I tried to run away from it. I even changed schools just to make the hurt disappear.

But no matter how hard I tried to not think about Lucas, I just couldn't stay away from the high school quarterback with perfect blue eyes and so many secrets.

I'm back. We're seniors now. We've grown—all of us. And Lucas Fuller might be different, but I'm different too.

This is my time to take risks, to experience life and to fall in love for real.

I want Lucas Fuller to be a part of my story, but I know for that to happen, I need to know the truth about our past.

BUY NOW ON AMAZON

Acknowledgments

Thank you so very much for spending time on my words. I know I say that constantly, but it's because I mean it. It is the most rewarding thing to know that I've earned a piece of your time. It's precious, and I am forever grateful. And I hope I have entertained you and made you feel.

In case you couldn't tell, I'm a little bit #TeamCameron. Yes, he's a smart-ass stoner, but it's the stuff when you scratch beneath his surface that I love. At his core, he is good. And while it is fun to write those bad, twisty, messed-up boys, it's also nice to write the sexy goofball who means well. That's Cam.

I have so many people to thank for helping me get this book out. I was wrapping this baby up just as we were driving our son across the country for college, so talk about the feels! LOL. Enormous love to my husband and son for always understanding my odd writing habits, which this time maybe included proofing in the back seat of a car across Texas and Oklahoma (and parts of Missouri). Brenda Letendre, you are my favorite Marvel Superhero. You are the most amazing editor and friend, and I am so grateful for you. Mom, your eyes on my words and support for what I do is everything to me. You make me better in so many ways. And Autumn. *Oh Autumn.* My spine, my heart, my air, my energy, my calm and peace. Don't you ever leave me. I will find you!

Readers - you are the reason I get to live my dream. I love

hearing your reactions, reading your reviews, seeing your graphics and posts. It's all I need. If you enjoyed this book, please feel free to drop a review or do any of those bookish things we all enjoy so much. It's good publicity, yes. But also, it makes my ever-loving day. I said this with the last book and yes, I am saying it again. Your reviews and shares give me fuel to do this again and again.

So now I'm off to tell the story of the mega-rich influencer who feels invisible and the super hot QB1. Can't wait to get more Welles in your hands.

About the Author

Ginger Scott is a *USA Today, Wall Street Journal* and Amazon-bestselling author from Peoria, Arizona. She has also been nominated for the Goodreads Choice and RWA Rita Awards. She is the author of several young and new adult romances, including bestsellers Cry Baby, The Hard Count, A Boy Like You, This Is Falling and Wild Reckless.

A sucker for a good romance, Ginger's other passion is sports, and she often blends the two in her stories. When she's not writing, the odds are high that she's somewhere near a baseball diamond, either watching her son swing for the fences or cheering on her favorite baseball team, the Arizona Diamondbacks. Ginger lives in Arizona and is married to her college sweetheart whom she met at ASU (fork 'em, Devils).

FIND GINGER ONLINE: www.littlemisswrite.com

facebook.com/GingerScottAuthor
twitter.com/TheGingerScott
instagram.com/authorgingerscott

The Falling Series

This Is Falling

You And Everything After

The Girl I Was Before

In Your Dreams

The Harper Boys

Wild Reckless

Wicked Restless

Standalone Reads

Candy Colored Sky

Cowboy Villain Damsel Duel

Drummer Girl

BRED

Cry Baby

The Hard Count

Memphis

Hold My Breath

Blindness

How We Deal With Gravity

Also By Ginger Scott

The Boys of Welles

Loner

Rebel

Habit (fall 2022)

The Fuel Series

Shift

Wreck

Burn

The Varsity Series

Varsity Heartbreaker

Varsity Tiebreaker

Varsity Rule breaker

Varsity Captain

The Waiting Series

Waiting on the Sidelines

Going Long

The Hail Mary

Like Us Duet

A Boy Like You

A Girl Like Me